SINGING
IN SILENCE

STEPHANIE BAILEY

FURZE PUBLISHING

This is a fictional novel based on the author's life experiences. Any resemblance to actual persons, living or dead, events or localities is entirely coincidental.

Published by:
Furze Publishing
The Old Brewery
8 High Street, Uffculme
Cullompton, Devon
EX15 3AB, UK
Tel: +44(0)1884 841770
E-mail: furzepublishing.uk@gmail.com
Website: www.furzepublishing.co.uk

Copyright © Stephanie Bailey.

The moral right of Stephanie Bailey to be identified as the author of this work has been asserted in accordance with the Copyright, Designs and Patents Act 1988.

All rights reserved; no part of this publication may be reproduced, stored in a retrieval system, or transmitted in any form or by any means, electronic, mechanical, photocopying, recording or otherwise without the prior permission of the Publishers or a license permitting copying in the UK issued by the Copyright Licensing Agency Ltd, Saffron House, 6–10 Kirby Street, London EC1N 8TS.

First published 2016

ISBN 978-0-9934607-0-8 paperback

British Library Cataloguing-in-Publication Data
A catalogue record for this book is available from the British Library

Typeset by Streamline Photography & Design, Uffculme, Devon
Printed and bound by TJ International Ltd, Padstow, Cornwall

Front cover image: © Shutterstock
Back cover image: © Shutterstock

I am dedicating this book to Doris and Trevor Bailey, my Mum and Dad who sadly are no longer with us. Mum was a dressmaker and Dad was an engineer and motorbike racer in his younger days and, later, an avid collector of motorcycles until the day he died.

Without their consent to take a chance in life this book would not have been possible, as they personally encouraged and supported my decision to go and work in the Middle East.

I was born in Nottingham and from the age of eight years old grew up in a Derbyshire village. I was twenty-eight when I moved to Yorkshire where I settled for the next twenty-one years, married, working and bringing up a family.

I have five adult children: Lori, Ross, Alexis, Tom and William who, individually, I am incredibly proud of. A Mother's love is unconditional.

After a short spell of four years living in the Middle East, I now reside in beautiful Devon. I awake at 6am each morning to write, gathering my inspiration from the far-reaching, ever-changing farmland views, whilst glancing at all the peculiarities of local village life.

A special thought for Michael and to say, thank you.

PROLOGUE

Life is not what it seems in the Arab world, but I am taking this in my stride. No one can prepare you for the cultural shock of living in the Middle East. My experiences here have led me to be insightful to the 'unspoken' Arabic culture.

The year is 2001. I met him by chance — or so I thought.

On this particular day, I had no conception that my life was going to change so dramatically — a full one hundred and eighty degree turnaround. My mother, God bless her, would have turned in her grave, what with me always being the wilful daughter.

I am Janey Green, a *middle* class, *middle*-aged woman who has always just been in the bloody *middle* somewhere!

Not a high-flyer, not illiterate, attractive but not stunningly beautiful. Just balancing nicely in the middle in what you might call a safe place.

Having just released myself from a twenty-year marriage I am now as free as a bird to do what I like. Who said I am naïve? Sorry, but I thought I heard a comment from someone!

This story is nearly true. Well, some of it has to be fiction, or my father would have turned in his grave and I could not cope with both parents looking down, frowning on my life.

I am not green around the gills! Although, I was not prepared in my middle life to find true old-fashioned romance or erotic encounters of the third kind. Well, you might ask, what is 'the third kind?' Another pleasure that I did not know existed!

Most importantly — and this is the big one — I was not prepared for a dangerous liaison that brought unimaginable wealth into my life. An addictive liaison that I had to protect and eventually defend from the militant organisation, Hezbollah.

CHAPTER ONE

The Sailing Club

On this particular day I am not looking my best. I step out of the warm sea and slip on a light beach dress, wearing little make-up with my hair damp and unkempt. I walk through the bar area of my local sailing club, The Royal Jubai, to order food. This club has become a little private hub where my friends and I spend most of our time at the weekends.

The club decor is from a past era, Cuban in style though a little shabby around the edges. There is a huge fan in the middle of the ceiling. Behind the bar are highly polished mirrors that sit in a labyrinth of exotic coloured cocktail and spirit bottles. It resembles a scene from a 1950s film set.

The club has a small private beach and mooring for up to thirty yachts. It is not a glamorous place, but The Royal Jubai, as its name suggests, is for members to pose and to learn the art of sailing whilst gathering solace at the end of a busy working week. It is the place for expats, a community of mainly Europeans. The local Arabs would not spend time here, as it serves alcohol which, of course, is forbidden if you are a Muslim.

It is Friday today and the start of the weekend here in Jubai and for me the week has been particularly challenging, sorting property deals in the office and motivating my sales team.

I have at last reached a good place in my life, feeling happy and relaxed for the first time in a long while. I have made a handful of good friends, mainly South Africans. I'm grateful to them for bringing fun, laughter and adventure back into my life.

I have been living in this desert city for several months. It's the driest, dustiest heat one can imagine and sweat pours down your face after just a few minutes of venturing outside.

The streets are empty this morning as I make my way across town towards the beach road to the sailing club. I turn into the club car park and stop the car abruptly to show my membership card to Abbas, the security man. Over the past six months he has become my friend, practising his English on me at every opportunity. He bends forward as I lower my car window, his long white Arabic dress flapping hard against my car as we make conversation.

'Very windy today ma'am.'

'It's a good day for sailing Abbas.'

He looks over my car and smiles showing a set of sparkling white teeth. 'You have new car. Hellwa! Hey, like you ma'am.' Hellwa means beautiful in Arabic. 'Beautiful new car for a beautiful woman,' he adds at the top of his voice.

Abbas is a young good-looking local man who often feels the need to give me a compliment. Maybe it's because he knows I am a single woman! I have never encouraged him though as I'm old enough to be … well … I won't go down the age route this morning. Today the surprised look on his face makes me giggle.

I thank him for the compliment and drive into a space. I am not a materialistic person, but today I feel a sense of achievement as, after six months of working hard and keeping my head down, I am finally earning a decent salary.

I remove my beach bag, lock my car, stand back and admire the fact that I have worked very hard and deserve this BMW.

Abbas inquisitively arrives by my side. 'You must have very good job ma'am buying a new BMW?'

We chat for a few minutes about my job in real estate until another car arrives at the security gate.

Simone and David, my South African friends, are due to arrive around 9am with their daughters. I ensure that I arrive before them in order to secure an outside shady table for the day. I order a coffee and settle down to read the weekend paper, *The Gulf News*.

The kitchen staff are busy setting up an outside breakfast buffet table and my taste buds are fizzing in anticipation as the aroma of smoky bacon floats in the air. Yes, bacon! I mustn't get carried away. I remind myself, I am in a Muslim country and it's turkey bacon. Pigs are considered dirty animals here. All week I have been longing for today just so I can switch off from the office environment and enjoy a full English breakfast.

The wind is blustery, perfect for sailing and, as the club members begin to arrive, there is a sense of excitement. This is due to the weather forecasters predicting strong winds early this afternoon. Sailors love the wind and there is nothing more exhilarating as you hoist up your sails to attain a speed of eight knots. Anything beyond is sailing heaven!

Simone, David and their girls arrive. I share hugs and kisses with them and, after chatting for a while, we all sit down to breakfast. My friends are from Johannesburg in South Africa. They fled during the political unrest and, after a short spell in London, moved to Jubai for work.

My life would not be the same without them. David is a good friend to me and Simone, well, she has been my lifeline! Most weekends we all meet up. They live in a large apartment not far from me and, during the week, we entertain together in each other's homes and invite our other friends to join us. We usually end up around the pool as the sun sets, following a few bottles of wine.

After breakfast David takes the girls for their usual sailing lesson. As they are both under twelve years old they learn on small Laser sailing boats. Simone and I head down to the club's beach for a swim in the sea. Even though it is quite blustery the water is still as hot as a bath. The next few hours are bliss. One of those perfect days in life where you feel you are in a hazy warm space lying on a lounger drifting in and out of sleep, the hours passing very quickly.

The wind is now whipping up, blowing fine particles of sand everywhere, smarting our eyes and stinging our skin. So we quickly exit the beach and head back to the club to join everyone. It is a hive of activity with nearly all the members sailing today in the perfect conditions.

I organise the food order for us all, slip on a light beach dress over my bikini and walk into the bar area of the club to order drinks and lunches for everyone. It's busy and noisy as I wait my turn in the queue.

I chat to a few people who are also waiting to order. Then one of the men tells me a really amusing story, something that happened to him at work this week. I laugh uncontrollably and take a while to compose myself. I then recount my Russian mafia deal story to him and how I had a narrow escape in the office. As the service is slow today these funny stories help to pass the time.

I catch a glimpse of myself in the mirrors that line the bar area. Oh dear, not my best look as my hair is a little wild from the wind! I stand looking around. Eventually the room becomes less crowded and it's my turn.

Abdul the bar manager takes my order. He first prepares the usual mojito cocktails for Simone and I, spending more time than usual in deep conversation with me. We speak about real estate prices, his wife, children and general chat on what's happening in the sailing world. As he chops and crushes the fresh mint he asks me about my new car. Abbas must have told him on the gate. News travels fast!

Suddenly, a strange sensation comes over me. You know that feeling when, for a few seconds, your life stands still and all the noise fades into the background. Well, I am having one of these moments right now. I know what you are thinking, but no, it's not a hot flush!

I look up again and stare into the mirrors that reflect the exotic coloured cocktail bottles around the bar. In the background a local Arab man is looking over, his eyes totally fixed on me.

Singing in Silence

I pretend not to notice him. I hold my head high whilst carrying on my conversation with Abdul. The minutes go by and his eyes are still fixed on me. Abdul, who has also clearly noticed the situation, blushes almost on my behalf as he completes the drinks order. He asks which outside table we're seated at before he delivers the food order to the kitchen. I do not turnaround to look at the Arab gentleman but it's clear his eyes are looking directly at me.

The bar area clears and I can see a few people's reflections from where I am standing. It's interesting, thinking about him, the Arab I mean. I'm fairly sure our eyes have met before in here but I know that I've never been introduced to him. He's the only local Arab I have ever seen in the club and that, in itself, does seem rather strange!

Thinking about it, I have seen him chatting to groups of members before, usually the more dedicated sailors.

I am standing in a trance like state and completely intrigued by the present situation. I feel I am being mentally stalked!

I sign my bill, feeling his eyes piercing my spine. Finally Abdul arranges a waiter to bring the drinks to our table.

Abdul looks at me. 'Janey are you all right?'

'Fine, of course, thank you.'

As I walk away my spine tingles as though I am on fire. What is this? I have no sensory recollection of anything like this before. I put my credit card back into my purse and turn around to walk to the rest room before rejoining the others. His eyes follow me until I pass his table and then, out of the blue, he stands up. We are now face to face.

He speaks in a fine public school English accent: 'Hello, so sorry to startle you, I see you are with your friends today.'

'Excuse me?' I reply nervously.

Just as I am about to carry on walking past him he says, 'Would you and your friends like to join me? My name is Mojat.'

He makes a move to shake my hand and, as I reciprocate, he

lifts my hand to his lips and proceeds to kiss it. 'And you are?'

Dazed and still a little shocked the words only just stumble out of my mouth. 'Janey ... Janey Green.'

'Janey, we have never been formally introduced, even though I have noticed you many times.'

The words roll off my tongue without hesitation. 'Thank you, that's very kind of you, I will ask my friends.'

For a brief moment, the logical side to my brain says, what the hell are you doing Janey? I have always been inquisitive and interested in people. Quite boldly I say, 'Your English accent is perfect. It took me quite by surprise, almost a BBC voice.'

He is amused and smiles, revealing a perfect row of white teeth that almost illuminate against his light olive skin. 'I studied at a university in the UK. That was many years ago now.'

'How interesting, which university?'

'Cambridge, I read Politics.'

I remain inquisitive — he is very attractive for an older man.

I know this sounds old-fashioned but Jubai is still lost in time and holds very traditional values regarding introductions between men and women. For all its futuristic tall glass buildings the old way of life remains in the Arab culture.

I walk back outside to my friends and see that the drinks have already been delivered to our table.

'Janey we thought you'd got lost. Where have you been?' asks Simone.

'You know, the usual queue at lunchtime.' I look at David. 'David, I have been talking to a local gentleman in the club and he has asked if we'd all like to join him for drinks?'

David and Simone look at me, and then they look at each other. David, who always feels like my chaperone when we are out, looks really surprised! 'Janey, which local man?'

Simone impatiently pipes up, 'David, there is only one local man!'

They look at each other in amazement.

'Janey love, it must be Mojat, he owns this club,' says David. 'Remember the other day you were asking me who owns the super yacht?' He points to the huge yacht sitting in pole position in the moored area. 'You know the one that hardly ever moves out of the marina?'

I think about it for a few seconds. 'Yes, I do remember.'

'Well, it's his!'

After initially feeling hesitant, my friends who have been members of this cosy elite club for at least 2 years before I arrived in this country, are giving me all the signs that Mojat is a man worth getting to know. They assure me that he is a real gentleman.

David walks back into the club with me and shakes Mojat's hand, at the same time apologising that he and Simone have to decline his invitation to join us, as their children are about to have another sailing lesson.

CHAPTER TWO

The Chance Meeting

David and Mojat connect on a man level, discussing sailing and David's yacht. Mojat mentions a future club sailing event that is taking place soon. As I watch and listen to them both, I feel a powerful energy around me.

Mojat is dressed in the traditional white dishdasha and keffiyeh, the local long white dress and head garment worn by the local Emirati. He is the only local I have ever seen in the club, which is not so strange now I know he owns it!

He is a tall, slim, elegant man with a pronounced Roman nose. His face is lined and characterful, having past his prime in life.

Previously, on a few occasions in the club, I have watched him chat and laugh with the other members and, like most Arabs I have met here, they communicate with their hands. I could not help but notice that his flow in a graceful melodic way, as though he is leading a symphony orchestra. He speaks eloquently and in perfect Queen's English.

Mojat then takes me by surprise by standing and pulling a chair out from his table. 'Janey my dear, please sit down.'

David begins to walk away. He turns to me and gives me a sign, as if to say, you will be fine.

There is a softness and warmth in his vocal cords that is different from other local Arabs I have met through work. We begin our first conversation, talking generally like one does when you're not familiar or sure of a person.

I now sit opposite him feeling embarrassed regarding the state of my dress and my wild damp unkempt hair. I am relieved to see my mojito arrive and a pint of Carlsberg for him. I look at his glass and smile, thinking to myself, that's an interesting one! An Arab drinking a pint of lager? I'm curious! He is obviously not a religious man!

Mojat's traditional headdress is secured in place with a bright red and yellow cord. I put my beach bag down on the floor and look down at his feet under the table. He is wearing a full moccasin shoe on bare skin, not the usual heavy style. They look Italian and beautifully made of the softest kid leather.

We chat about his university life in the UK and he asks me about my work and what brought me to Jubai. The next hour seems to pass very quickly. I get the impression that he is a humble man who is intelligent and interesting. He makes me laugh a few times which is refreshing, as not many men have managed to do this.

He catches me looking down at myself as I try to smooth out my flimsy almost see-through beach dress, hoping for at least an extra two inches. His eyes follow my hands down over my hips.

He reassures me. 'You look beautiful — don't worry. There is no need to feel embarrassed.'

I feel flattered, considering I have never thought myself to be beautiful. 'Well, Mojat, you are so covered up in your long white dress that it makes me feel positively naked.'

He laughs a little and tilts his head on one side, as though no one has ever said this to him before. His direct approach and charm is not what I am prepared for. Next, he lifts his glass and takes a drink, carefully lowering it on to the tabletop. He then clears his throat. 'Janey, when you first walked into the club several months ago my life stood still for a few moments and, every day that has passed since, you have been at the centre of my thoughts. I find you enchanting my dear.'

I am aghast and astonished by his words but also stunned by his forthrightness. I have never met anyone before who is so in your face direct.

I look into his eyes and a rush of blood runs into my neck and face. I acknowledge his compliment and inquisitively I ask, 'When did you first see me?'

'I suppose back in November when you joined the club.'

'November! That was months ago, you flatter me.' I glance at his manicured hands before our eyes meet again. 'You surprise me, for all these months I have been on your mind?'

'Janey, you probably know that I own the club.'

'Well I didn't know actually, until today.'

Our conversation changes to his business and life here in Jubai. Then I break off, making my excuses to visit the ladies room.

I stand in front of the mirror with butterflies and a churning stomach, talking to myself. 'Why is he having this effect on me?' I splash my face with cold water and stare into the mirror. 'Jesus, I look like shit!' In fact I have never looked so dishevelled and weather-beaten!

I wander back into the club and the room is now full of crew; sailors from the competitive racing yachts which are now moored up outside. There has been a long race today and they have all returned full of joviality.

For a few seconds I cannot see him as he is out of sight and not at his seat. He then spots me and beckons me to come over. He is chatting to a French crew, which he then introduces me to. I am amazed as he speaks in fluent French with them.

After a few minutes they soon realise I do not understand a word, so they very kindly begin to speak English. This very sociable crowd have just won a race battling against a gale-force wind and, like most sailors, they have stories to tell and a thirst for alcohol. They are full of laughter, banter and excitement. Mojat was clearly enjoying the French interaction, until I arrived.

We return to our table. The sandwich I ordered earlier finally arrives and I begin to tuck in enjoying every mouthful. He comments on how busy the club is today and apologises to me for the slow service.

Singing in Silence

Whilst I eat he seizes the opportunity to tell me interesting stories about his university years at Cambridge and his time as a student in the mid 1960s; the 'Summer of Love.'

'Janey, I used to drive around in a Mini Cooper. I had long black hair in those days and a moustache. Many people mistook me for Omar Sharif which, of course, I took as a compliment.'

'Omar Sharif!' I say with surprise. 'You were obviously a very handsome man?' I wanted to add that you still are, but decide against it.

'I used to wear flower power shirts and hipster bell-bottoms.'

My mind has conjured up a picture of the swinging sixties: miniskirts, pirate radio stations, the psychedelic era and the 'Summer of Love.' Of course, I was too young to remember everything, but I used to listen to Radio Luxembourg at night and recall The Yardbirds, Jefferson Airplane, The Doors and the various DJs commenting on the Woodstock music festival.

I listen attentively to him whilst I eat, watching his facial expressions and hand gestures. It fascinates me that most Arabs talk with their hands and can be quite loud vocally when they speak. They're not showing off or trying to attract attention to themselves, but just love to express every detail.

I find him fascinating, intelligent, funny and already I feel there is a strong attraction between us.

'Janey, it's so good to finally meet you, I've enjoyed watching you and your friends over the last few months.'

'You have stalked me Mojat?'

'No, just a fascination with you.'

'Fascination? More like creepy!'

'You're always laughing my dear and seem chilled and relaxed.'

I finish my sandwich and drink and reach for my serviette, which I notice I have dropped. I bend down to pick it up and to also take some extra tissues out of my handbag, which is sitting in-between us on the floor.

'Shit,' I whisper to myself. 'Shit!' This is not what I expected to see. On his bare leg strapped to his calf is a gun. I can see a clear outline of this as his Arabic dress clings to his legs. I sit up and pat my lips with the serviette.

I am intrigued by this man. 'I do not understand, why not just introduce yourself? I would not have put you down as the timid reticent type of guy. In fact I would say you are the most presumptuous man I have ever met!'

He chuckles at my forwardness. 'I have my reasons.'

Very strange, I think to myself. What possible reasons are so important for him to hold back all this time? For months even! And what about this blessed gun strapped to his leg?

He takes a few more gulps and his pint glass is now empty.

I let things drop for now as I've made my point. In fact I have made it very clear to him how weird and disturbing it feels to have been watched for months.

'Going back to me laughing and enjoying myself Mojat, I have good boundaries when it comes to work — it's easy for me. I enjoy socialising and feel lucky that I have learnt the art of sailing.'

'Your life was not like this in England? No sailing club?'

I smile and say. 'No, my life was very different in England.'

I don't want him to pursue this conversation any further, not now. It's too soon and still feels raw and painful. This Arab man has no idea of the heartbreak I endured by walking away from Wisteria House in North Yorkshire. The wild moors and emotional bleakness where I would go for days without seeing a soul; where the locals would have thought a mojito was a foreign body of some sort! A wasp or gnat perhaps … something to swat!

'England has culture and some of the best architecture in the world,' says Mojat. 'I have recently bought a place in Knightsbridge.'

I agree with him about the architecture, trying not to raise my eyebrows on where he's made his latest purchase. 'Yes, English Heritage and the National Trust do a superb job of preserving our history.'

He begins to talk of his past. 'Janey, my parents had high hopes and expectations of me. They believed a good English university would set me up for life and there was always a sense of pressure growing up in our family. When you are a son over here it's your duty and role to support your parents later in life.' He then signals to the barman. 'Janey, tea, coffee or another drink?'

'Fresh coffee please.'

'A pot of fresh coffee for two. And cakes,' he adds at the last moment.

I make my excuses to go and check that all is okay with my friends, as I'm supposed to be spending the day with them after all.

Mojat's thoughts:
I watch her walk away. Her curves and provocative walk excite me. She moves with an air of confidence, which I like in a woman. Her dress shows off the fullness of her breasts and her firm skin has resisted any signs of ageing. I am magnetised!

Her cheekbones are flushed and her lips are full; I have an insatiable desire to kiss them. Desire is not the word, it's much much more! I am captivated by her Englishness, her naturalness. Her face has a faint tint of peachy pink and against her strawberry blonde hair — she is just so beautiful.

I return to the table and pour out the coffee for us both. There is silence as I pass him the white porcelain cup and saucer. He is deep in thought as he scoops up a sugar lump from the matching bowl.

Mojat's thoughts:
I reflect on the first moment of today when I saw her chatting to one of the crew, then she turned around at the bar and proceeded to walk right past me. She did not look my way at all. In fact, it's fair to say, I don't think she even noticed me!

I could not help myself staring as she passed by me, her hips gliding and swaying with her every step. For a few seconds I was a young man again, with a high voltage electricity charge running through my veins and down into my penis.

CHAPTER THREE

Pearls of Loyalty

The jealous sun moves down the skyline bringing a glow to my face. We have been in conversation for three hours.

Inquisitively I ask. 'How often do you sail?' I can't remember that huge yacht of his ever moving out of the marina.

'My dear, not as often as I would like, but this is now going to change.'

The noise of my friends and their children overwhelm us as they arrive at the next table. There is a brief interaction before they say their goodbyes and leave the club. It is 5pm and neither of us has realised the time.

'I have to go too,' I say to him touching my dress, my bikini still feeling damp underneath. It's uncomfortable in fact and I can hardly wait to get in the shower and wash the beach and salt off me.

We both stand up and politely I say. 'Thank you, it's been interesting getting to know you.'

'The pleasure is all mine Janey.'

He scribbles his telephone number on a serviette for me then gives me a warm smile and, as I go to shake his hand, he grasps it firmly and holds it up to his chest for a few seconds. Then he pulls my body close to his.

I can smell the heady remnants of his morning Cologne. He kisses me on the cheek. 'Please will you accompany me to dinner tonight? Say eight thirty?'

I hesitate looking into his eyes and before I can say anything.

'Janey I will pick you up.'

I gather my beach bag and walk back to my car. I can hear familiar voices calling me.

'Janey, Janey.' Simone is leaning out of the car window. 'Tell me, did you enjoy his company?'

'Yes I did, but I think he is a little too old for me. I have agreed to have dinner with him tonight, but I am not sure.'

David smiles as he puts the car in reverse gear. He leans out of his driver's car window, raising his voice slightly over the engine noise. 'Janey, you would be crazy not to go. He has never been seen in the club with a woman before.'

I look at them sun beaten and tired. The girls chatter on the back seats.

'We will see,' I say. I am thinking that I will probably change my mind.

'Enjoy your evening Janey, we will speak tomorrow.'

I can't remember the drive back to my apartment as I was in a trance, on autopilot. I open my familiar front door and the realisation of accepting a dinner date with a local Arab begins to hit home. Why am I doing this? There are too many unanswered questions about him!

Mojat is not just a local businessman — who is he frigging kidding! Owning a small sailing club does not buy you a super yacht of the like that Aristotle Onassis and Jackie Kennedy would holiday on! Something is not quite right. He read Politics at Cambridge, what happened to this? He drinks alcohol in public. Unheard of! He is much more like a European and certainly acts as such, almost English. Of course how can I forget the gun? Jesus, that bloody gun?

Many questions are circulating around in my head. No, I say to myself. No! I am fine — I do not need any complications in my life right now. I've been living here for several months on my own and it's been a healing process.

I pour myself a gin and tonic and start to run a bath.

On the other hand he seems a lovely man. Well educated,

entertaining and he makes me laugh — that's a first! David is right; he is a true gentleman of breeding, so why am I hesitating?

It's not the gun. In fact the gun, dare I say, intrigues me! I also find his bold impertinence flattering. I will call him to say I have had a change of heart? Yes, I will call him now!

Where is that serviette with his number on? I reach down into my beach bag and remove everything. Funny, I can't find it. I am in a good place right now with my job and the occasional date. I don't need him. I will cancel!

My beach bag is empty. I tip it upside down and shake it — there is no sign of the dratted serviette!

My stomach is in knots and I have just two hours to get ready. I did not give him my address or telephone number, but he owns the club of course and will have my details on file.

That's another thing that feels strange, the fact that he's been watching me for months with my friends. Creepy! Why did he not make a play for me months ago? What was stopping him? After all he is a very forward gentleman. In Yorkshire they have a saying: 'He is not backwards in coming forwards!' My God he isn't!

Too many unanswered questions!

I stand in front of the full-length mirror and give myself the once over. It's hard to choose the right dress on a first date. I decide on a pale pink chiffon cocktail dress, it's one of my most expensive and an inner lining — a special lining — as the lady in the shop referred to it. I call it my 'if all else fails dress.' In other words, when I am feeling hot, bloated, grouchy, depressed and sad and nothing feels right on me; I take this treasure of a dress out of my wardrobe and my smile returns. This little beauty would make Hylda Baker look like Brigitte Bardot! At this point ladies I would say, Google Hylda Baker! This dress makes me look slender with curves, elegant and so very classy. Why hasn't every woman got one? Or maybe you have?

Yes, you are all thinking right now, where did Janey purchase this? Who designed such a dress? Good question — it certainly wasn't 'Top Shop!'

The length is also perfect, being just below the knee with a hint of cleavage and, of course, I must cover my arms. Even though he seems quite westernised we are in the Middle East and it's respectful to cover your arms, so the long silky sleeves are perfect. Of course all the ladies of a certain age will know of other reasons why it has to have long sleeves, but I won't say any more on the subject!

My mobile is now ringing.

'Hi Janey, just to say we are five minutes away, we will see you soon my dear.'

'Fine Mojat.'

I close my mobile. 'We? Who is the royal we?' I say to myself.

I feel a mixture of emotions and, whilst finishing off my G&T, I put the final touches to my hair and face. Then I wrap my pashmina around my shoulders, pick up my handbag and walk down to the entrance in my matching heels.

I step out of my apartment block into the heat of the evening and, thankfully, there is a slight breeze. Down the steps and directly in front of me is an immaculate, highly polished burgundy Bentley that looks as if it has arrived straight from the showroom.

Holy Moses, I never expected this! Thinking about it now, I would not have missed this experience for the world!

His driver waits by the rear door ready to open it for me. He is in uniform, dressed in a dark suit and white shirt. His shiny brunette hair glistens as I walk towards him. 'Good evening Miss Janey.'

Before I can reply to him, the car door opens and Mojat leans across the luxurious leather seating, smiles and offers me his hand. I sit down and take in the sumptuous surroundings.

Maybe this is what Queen Elizabeth must feel like sitting in the back of her beautiful cars. He lifts my hand to his lips and kisses it.

'Janey you look enchanting.'

Mojat's thoughts:
I could not take my eyes off her. She is everything I imagined she would be in evening dress.

Her skin smells of musky oil, her blonde waves fall over her shoulders and I notice the only jewellery she is wearing is a pair of Arabic design diamond earrings.

'Janey, I want to introduce you to Kulpreet my driver — his family are from Kerala in southern India. He has been my driver for, oh, must be fifteen years now.'

'I am pleased to meet you,' I say, looking around the interior of the car feeling imperial and noble, forgetting for a brief moment who I really am!

Kulpreet is concentrating and does not take his eyes off the road as he manoeuvres the car away from the apartments. Driving in Jubai city any night of the year is hectic, especially at the weekends.

He glances in his central driving mirror at me. 'Thank you ma'am.'

I glance out the window to check the car is moving, as I cannot hear the engine.

I look across towards my apartment as we begin to accelerate away. I have to smile as my neighbours are enjoying a glass of wine on their balcony and just happened to see me getting into the car; their faces are a picture. Since I have moved into my new apartment we have enjoyed a friendship around the pool and they have never seen me with a man, let alone an Arab with such a prestigious car.

Kulpreet is taking the familiar route to the sailing club. I feel a mixture of emotions, but all my nervous feelings have disappeared and I'm pleased now that I didn't change my mind. At the end of the day I am curious and, if I'm honest, I am attracted to Mojat for all the right reasons.

'Janey, I hope you don't mind, but I thought tonight we would dine on my yacht as it will be more private.'

'Of course, sounds lovely!'

The journey is smooth as we glide down the main road. Everything inside this luxurious Bentley is shiny and highly polished.

I step out into a clear night sky, the stars are out in all their full glory. The club is decorated as usual in its evening fairy lights around the alfresco dining area. All the doors have been folded back so that the outside tables can feel part of the fine dining and entertainment for this night only. There is a man visiting each table singing and playing his Spanish guitar to the guests.

Mojat's yacht takes prominence in the marina, mainly because of its size and also the wonderful display of decorative lights on the deck area, which I have never noticed before whilst dining late at the club.

Mojat gives his driver instructions on when to return. I am relieved to hear this as it had occurred to me that he may have had other ideas. I am relaxed and feel good, knowing he is not going to try and take advantage of this private meal together.

We walk up the pontoon together and he holds my hand to steady me. 'You look beautiful tonight Janey, I have only seen you in casual dress before.'

I accept his compliment and look around the yacht as I step on to the deck — his captain emerges with three of the crew to welcome us aboard.

'Janey I have a full-time crew that have been with me for many years.'

I am then introduced to each of them in turn and, finally, the man in charge.

'My captain, Herman, is ex Royal Navy. His father is English and his mother is Austrian.'

Herman wears a blue uniform and on his jacket sleeve he has the gold captain's insignia.

We then move further up the deck and perch on a very comfortable white contemporary sofa.

Singing in Silence

'I didn't know your taste in food my dear so I have asked three restaurants to deliver at nine thirty. Lebanese is my favourite but I have also asked for Italian and French. They will send us all tonight's specials.'

'Mojat, I like my food but I don't really eat that much.'

We laugh and chat, which helps relieve all the nervous tension. I thought that maybe he would have some food delivered from the sailing club, or a chef would cook on his yacht; but I never expected him to order from three restaurants! It's like a grand takeaway!

One of the crew arrives from below deck with an ice bucket of chilled champagne for our side table. The dining table, a few yards away, has been laid with white linen. I notice the cutlery is silver with the crest of a falcon.

The champagne bubbles are going up my nose and I'm enjoying every sip. Many large candles flicker around the deck. He really has put so much thought and effort into our first evening together and in such a short space of time.

We chat and laugh about our sailing experiences and the various characters in the yachting world.

I like the energy around him. I look into his heavily lined eyes and sense a story behind them.

By the time we finish our second glass, Herman walks over and asks if I would like a tour of the yacht.

'Please go my dear,' says Mojat. 'Look around and the food will have arrived by the time you return.'

I stand up feeling a little light-headed. I love the fizz, but it has a tendency to go to my head.

Mojat's thoughts:
She slips off her high heels to go below deck. I like the fact that she is not fazed by what has been presented to her tonight. I noticed her reactions to meeting my chauffeur and the crew. I want a woman who is not dazzled or over impressed by wealth. I have had plenty of women in my life but all but one was fickle! I have learnt over the years that you cannot trust

a woman who is magnetised by power and status.

Herman walks me around downstairs. It is luxurious and sophisticated. Each bedroom suite — and there are ten in total — has an elegant white porcelain bathroom. All are lined in light solid oak and have a very contemporary feel with modern sofas and lamps. Pieces of modern art hang on the walls in each suite. Persian rugs have been carefully laid out on the wooden bedroom floors. All the suites lead on to a central ballroom that has a small stage, which, again, has a highly polished wooden floor.

I stand in the middle of the dance floor imagining wonderful parties with live bands playing. To the far side of the ballroom I notice three very large gold-framed photographs displayed on the wall, sitting side by side. I'm intrigued, as I look for clues of his past life.

I walk over and, to my amazement, the first photograph dated 1980, is of Mojat in this very ballroom with his arms around Frank Sinatra and Dean Martin. Mojat is wearing European clothes and there are several glamorous ladies around the three of them. The second photo was taken on deck, again Mojat. This time he's in his formal Emirati dress and headdress pictured alongside Ronald Reagan and Margaret Thatcher. This photograph is dated 1982. The third, taken in a house, shows a large round dining table in a circular room and the decor is very opulent. At the table are Sir John Major, George W. Bush and Mojat, again, in formal Emirati dress. There are other guests around the table, none of which I recognise. This photo is dated 1990.

'Amazing!' I say out loud.

Herman stands behind me and agrees. 'The last photograph Janey is in Mr. Mojat's house; this was a very busy time in his life.'

I didn't expect to see such status in the photographs. I had sensed earlier that there must be another side to him and I am right. He is a politician! So his studies at the University of Cambridge did not go to waste. Interesting!

Herman continues to discuss the photographs, saying that Mr. Mojat used to entertain all the time, until three years ago. On saying this there is sadness in his face, as if there is a painful memory.

As I climb up the stairs back on to the deck, the food is being carried in large silver terrains to the dining table. The waiters that deliver the food are now laying it all out. It's a small banquet.

'Janey are you ready to eat?' asks Mojat.

We sit at the table and the staff disappear. Mojat pours us both another drink; the ambience is perfect, dining under the stars on such a magnificent, palatial yacht. Though, of course, I have only seen part of it.

'Janey my dear, what do you think of the yacht? I call her *The Falcon*.'

'As we say in Yorkshire, it's proper grand!'

He laughs. 'Of course you are from Yorkshire.'

'Very grand indeed — elegant and fit for royalty. And the ballroom was a nice surprise!'

'I am pleased you like it Janey. I used to entertain royalty and other famous guests here and at my home, until quite recently.'

I take another sip of my drink, I have sort of sussed him out and intuitively I say. 'Yes, I noticed your framed photographs. You have an interesting life and what is extraordinary, is that it's hidden, almost clandestine.'

'Yes, it looks that way my dear.'

I was waiting for a 'but', and then he begins to explain everything to me.

'Janey I am the foreign minister for my country. This is my political role, although it's all going to change as I'm about to enter semi-retirement. My work will take on a more ambassadorial role.'

'I knew there was another side to you.'

He sits nobly, upright and smiles at my comment. He clears his throat and begins to talk. 'The Peace Treaty in the Middle East is close to my heart. I am one of the former founders and, over many years, I have worked tirelessly to keep it together with many other countries' leaders.'

I listen to him and respond quite calmly. 'Yes, I knew there was a secret about you, but I couldn't quite put my finger on it.'

He laughs. 'My dear, most people think I am just a businessman, owning a club and dabbling in the stock market, with maybe a few other ventures. I would be grateful for your discretion as I need to keep it this way, for now anyway.'

We look intensely at each other and I nod. 'Of course Mojat, I understand. So the club is your little secret haven of tranquillity?'

'Yes, it is.'

'Men in Yorkshire have a garden shed, but you have your sailing club!'

'Do they really? A garden shed!'

'Yes, at weekends men enter their sheds never to be seen again until Monday morning!'

'What's all that about?' he says, not having the faintest clue.

'Good question,' I say. 'What men get up to inside beggars belief. In fact there is a TV programme in the UK dedicated to men and their garden sheds!'

'Staggering,' he says.

We then return to our previous conversation before I'd diversified!

'You see Janey, here no one knows or recognises me and, even if they do, no one has ever said. The club knows me as Mojat; it's been my nickname since my university days. My full Arabic name is confidential. We are all here to relax and when I say *we*, I mean I am a sailor at heart like the rest of them in the club. I love to sail, so politics is left behind and this keeps me grounded. I enjoy mixing with Europeans in the club, which keeps me in touch with the side of me from my university days; that's where my love of England comes from.'

In the centre of our dining table is an elaborate silver candelabra that holds four duck-egg blue candles. I watch the flames waver and flicker as he talks.

We sit next to each other under the stars sipping champagne and eating from a variety of dishes. He leans over to me and kisses my cheek and again lifts my hand, pressing it to *his* cheek. In the background I can hear the Spanish guitar singer from the club and the sailing crowd applauding.

The second bottle of champagne is opened and he reaches across the table for a bowl of Lebanese food.

'I love this,' says Mojat. I spend several weeks a year in Lebanon as part of my work and have many friends there. In fact my closest friends live in and around Beirut. I adore the people, salt of the earth and so hospitable.'

He tells me more about Lebanon and how beautiful the country is, with its stunning diversity from Beirut up to the mountains.

The conversation moves on and we talk about our lives with openness. He tells me amusing, interesting stories that again make me laugh.

'Janey, like all young Arab men I had an arranged marriage following my studies at Cambridge. I have been divorced over twenty years now and have several children.'

He does not elaborate on his first marriage or children.

He then informs me of a previous love, a German girlfriend, Gretal, which lasted seven years and ended nearly three years ago. 'I will tell you the story one day. She is the only woman I have ever loved, but tonight is not the time.'

I then reflect on my life, the heartache of my divorce from Geoffrey after twenty years, my work and my children and how hard it was, and still is, making a new life for myself.

We both arrive at the conclusion that the journey through life can take many detours, twists and turns.

'Janey, I call my life *The Good, the Bad and the Ugly*!'

His sense of humour appeals to me. Whilst laughing I say, 'It was one of the first films I ever saw at the cinema, I remember it so well.'

'My dear, wasn't it just a brilliant western? One of the first spaghetti westerns directed by Sergio Leone who had such a brilliant mind. 1966 I think. You remember this Janey?'

I get a little carried away after a few glasses of fizz and I am such a film buff, always have been. World subtitles, erotic French, all the Woody Alan's — anything offbeat. 'For sure I do Mojat, the plot was so good. I remember it revolved around three gunslingers competing to find a pot of gold amid the violent chaos of gunfights, hangings, civil war battles and prison camps.'

'Now, I am not sure *The Good, the Bad and the Ugly* is quite the metaphor, but it is interesting that it appeals to your sense of humour,' says Mojat.

I can see from his expression that he likes the fact that the metaphor on his life has not gone to waste. He senses I am in tune with him.

Finally, he looks at his watch. 'Janey it's 11:30 and my driver will arrive at midnight.'

'I feel like Cinderella.'

He laughs. 'Cinderella, Yes! Well, I think very soon that Cinderella must go to the ball.'

He then excuses himself to go to the bathroom. I am then alone for a few minutes; there is no sign of his crew. I guess they must have had strict instructions not to bother us.

I soak up the last few moments of pleasure under the moonlight, stretching my legs out. The candles flicker in the gentle breeze. I can still here the flamenco guitarist playing something rather lively at the clubhouse.

Mojat returns on deck and as he approaches I notice a slight lameness in his walk, stiffness, maybe an old injury? The outline of the gun holster is still there, which I can clearly see as he sits down.

He is a very handsome man. I can see his dark hair greying around the sides of his headdress; it's just set back enough for me to catch a glimpse of his thick hair. His clean-shaven olive skin does not match his pale well-manicured hands.

He lowers himself tentatively down on to the sofa as though he feels pain, this time he sits much closer to me than before. I feel the gun as it brushes past my leg. Maybe this is normal for someone of his status to carry a weapon?

There is a fragrance of earthy cinnamon wood oil on his skin. He takes a clean white linen handkerchief out of his pocket and wipes the glistening beads from his brow. He then he reaches back inside his pocket and takes out a small oyster-coloured silk draw purse. 'This is for you my dear.'

He places the delicate bag in my hand; I am surprised to receive a gift on a first date. I hold it for a few seconds.

'This is unexpected.'

'Open it, my dear!'

I pull on the silk cord and I lift out a string of pale pink pearls. On closer examination there are four pure white diamonds set in the clasp.

'They are beautiful; stunning!'

I am overwhelmed by his generosity. He fastens the diamond clasp around my neck. They sit perfectly just above my breastbone.

'Janey, in Arabic tradition pearls represent loyalty. A man gives a woman pearls to ensure she always comes back to him. I believe it's also an English tradition.'

Our first kiss lingers tenderly. He eventually rouses himself from my lips and, still only a few inches away from my face, his deep ebony eyes pierce my soul.

I almost forget to breathe as he runs his fingers through my hair, gently stimulating my scalp. He then lifts my hair up away from my neck and pulls me towards him, gently kissing my neck. Tingles are pulsing through my ears into the back of my throat, down through my body. He then caresses my ear with his warm moist lips and whispers to me. 'Janey, I want you in my life. I need you. I have waited a long time for this moment.'

There is a silence as he holds me close. I have tears and he passes me his handkerchief. I wipe my eyes and look up at him. He takes the linen back and wipes away *his* tears.

'You are a breath of fresh air my dear; I have not felt this excited for many years. I am fifty-nine and had almost given up looking.' His words touch a part of me, the part that I have kept hidden away from the disappointments of the past.

I touch my pearls.

'They suit you Janey.'

He takes my other hand and gives it a gentle squeeze.

'Gosh Mojat, quite a speech.'

He holds me tighter. 'I mean it Janey.'

Kulpreet's footsteps can be heard in the distance as he climbs on deck. Mojat stands up and wraps my pashmina around my shoulders and we wander back to his car. He phones Herman to leave instructions and then he drops me back at my apartment.

As I climb into my bed, my thoughts are fixed on this chance meeting.

The end of a beautiful and surprising day.

CHAPTER FOUR

The Office

The next day I arrive at my office glowing, thinking how magical the previous evening was.

After all these months of living in solitary confinement trying to nurture and heal my aching heart, I never expected to have feelings for a man after only a few hours. I must stay clear-headed and focused for the sales meeting with my team.

Part of me wants to be left alone to daydream and to reflect on the last twenty-four hours, but there is no chance today as Sunday is usually my busiest day. I am surprised I managed to sleep at all last night.

I look down at my desk to see the usual paperwork and my PA, Prasitia, arrives with a coffee and one of her mother's home-made biscuits.

'Janey, I have sorted the mail and updated this week's diary and …' She abruptly stops talking as her eyes zoom towards my necklace. With a gleaming Indian smile, which is a picture of delight she says, 'Are they real? Your pearls, are they?'

'Yes, I believe they are.'

'So beautiful Janey.'

'A present actually.' I feel them and smile, whilst reminiscing.

The expression on her face says it all. She lifts the pearls slightly away from my neck and begins to stroke them. 'Ooh, I have never seen pearls like this, they are so lovely.' She lets go and the heavy string rattles back on to my neck.

My boss Sam is now on the phone and wants to attend our sales meeting this morning. I walk through the reception area into our large office at the back. I stand in front of the team, who are all sitting at their desks, and loudly announce why the meeting will be delayed by thirty minutes. They briefly look up from their computer screens and mobile phones, then all resume their phone conversations. I then accept a couple of calls regarding ongoing deals, most of them are problematic and that's why I get involved. I smile to Martha the receptionist whilst I am on the phone. She can see through the glass door and is pointing to my pearls.

The outside door opens into the reception, I look up thinking Sam has arrived early, but it's a man delivering a huge arrangement of flowers. He places them on the reception desk and I suddenly lose sight of Martha. She walks around the desk and signs a delivery note and, within seconds of me finishing my phone call, Prasitia and Martha enter my office in a flurry of excitement. They announce that the flowers are for me.

I am amazed! 'Is there a card attached girls?'

Martha rushes over and picks out a small card that is tightly sealed in a white envelope and hands it to me. Before opening it, I step out of my office into the reception to take a closer look at the flowers. They are impressive! Within seconds the scent fills the office.

The arrangement is made up of a breathtaking array of different colours and types of flowers, but what stands out the most is my favourite, the old English scented roses called Gertrude Jekyll.

'Gosh, they are stunning.'

Prasitia and Martha are bright-eyed and bushy tailed and so excitable.

'Janey who are they from?' they ask.

I open the envelope whilst they peer over my shoulder. They read the note aloud. Before the words leave my mouth, Prasitia loudly proclaims, 'A Mr. M has sent them.' She reads the note. 'To my English rose, yours M. Who is M Janey?'

I smile as they both look at me.

'Is he the one who has given you the pearls?' asks Prasitia.

'Yes, my date last night.'

Martha looks astounded. 'Ma'am, after just one date he sends you flowers of this magnitude and gives you real pearls! He must be crazy over you?'

Prasitia agrees. 'Yes, he must be super crazy over you?'

I am overwhelmed, how does he know about my favourite old rose? I lean over the arrangement again to take in the wonderful scents.

'Yes, I know girls, unbelievable isn't it? I am still trying to get my head around it too! Now back to your desks, Sam will be arriving anytime now.'

I put the small card on my desk and I watch the girls lift the arrangement together, as it is so large. They move the flowers to the main table in the centre of the reception area, and then Martha informs me that there are one hundred of them!

The aroma is overpowering and soon gives the sales office a heady feel. A few of my agents arrive in the reception area to investigate what all the fuss is about. Then the banter begins.

Thomas one of my bestselling sales agents takes one look. 'Janey, whoever he is for sure he is wealthy. Do you know how much flowers are in this country?'

The office suddenly comes alive with gossip about my flowers and the identity of the man with the initial M. Their inquisitive minds start working overtime.

Lola, my sexy Brazilian agent, is always up for fun and a good gossip. She walks over to the arrangement and lifts a pure white stemmed rose and places it in her long brown hair. She tucks it behind her ear and starts to dance around the office swaying her hips, imitating a Hawaiian dancing girl. In her Brazilian accent and enjoying the whole office as her new audience she says, 'I have never seen such a bloody large arrangement of flowers; it's like a wedding ducky. For sure he is rich, Janey. Is he good-looking too?'

Lola is a close friend who often spends the night with me at my apartment. Whenever I am out with her it is a sure thing that we have a good time.

I could not help but laugh at her. The agents give her a round of applause; she has stirred everyone up this morning and has put my team in a good mood.

Sam arrives and looks great with her short platinum blonde hair. She is long and slender and has a boyish look about her, dressed in a trendy trouser suit. Sam likes to work out most days, it's part of her de-stressing routine. She is the sales director, South African and forward thinking, direct and straight to the point. I love working with her — she is dynamic and has a strong Pretoria accent. 'Hey, Janey, what's happened to the Marina office? It's turned into a florist — and who the fuck is M?'

'Sam you have read my card! He was my date last night.'

'Wah! Some date chick! If he can afford flowers of this magnitude in this desert.' She then gives me a more serious look and places the card back on my desk. 'Chick, a small bunch of roses is more than a good bottle of champagne here.'

I laugh. 'Actually Sam I have never seen flowers sold here. I wouldn't know.'

'Exactly chick! That's what I am saying! He will have flown this arrangement in from Holland especially. This guy is serious and obviously very confident about you.' She looks me up and down for a few seconds in a knowing sort of way, woman to woman, then speaks in a more serious voice. 'Janey, please be careful, if he's a rich local, he's probably got several wives already. He is obviously a man of status. Umm … usually rich locals don't send flowers.'

'Sam, how do you know this?'

'I've worked here for over ten years and have mixed socially with plenty of local business investors. Trust me I know!'

'Anyway Sam, what makes you think he is an Emirati?'

'Honey, just a feeling, just a gut feeling.'

Her knowing expression returns and for a few seconds my mind is ticking over at a hundred miles an hour; but how could Sam know anything? It has only happened over this weekend; how could she know about his status and the fact that he is Emirati?

She puts her arm around me and gives me a tight hug. 'Hey chick, I just care about you that's all and don't want to see you get hurt.'

Sam is taken aback as she walks over to the arrangement then, thankfully, she is sidetracked by a few of my sales agents that have started to chat about their deals and a new building called, Inferno Mansions. It's just been released for sale by a celebrity developer, a famous footballer called Trevor Rivestar. Right now he is the talk of the town — to my relief!

I start the meeting amongst all the noisy banter from the agents. I quieten them all down and, as I stand in front of them, all the serious talk begins. Sam often sits in on the meetings — usually at the beginning of each month to go over last month's financial figures — particularly if our office has done well. It's a good motivational skill. We talk about sales targets and how well the Waterfront office is doing. Good for me, I think to myself, I am obviously driving and leading my team in the right direction.

One hour later the meeting comes to a close and Sam and I then get an opportunity to discuss a few things privately. She is thinking of implementing a new commission structure within the next three months. I'm not sure if this will go down well with my agents, but this is the downside of my work. Of course all jobs have their downsides. I just present the orders from above in a positive way. The skill of a good manager is to always back up and support your team. I will expect eruptions at my next sales meeting, something I am not looking forward to!

I walk back into my peaceful office. It is now 1pm and I'm feeling a little hungry. Prasitia pops her head round the door and kindly offers to order some lunch for me. She knows when I shut the door it means I need solitude for a while. The office rule is that when my door is kept open it's a signal to all my agents that I am free, but when I push it shut it means I need my space.

The international sales team are from all walks of life, the majority being very well educated before coming to Jubai. For example my lovely Irish Kerrie used to be a speech therapist. I have two bankers from a well-known Singapore bank, a Polish dentist, a professional singer, Denny, who was a famous celebrity in Sweden, an entrepreneur who owned nightclubs there but he originated from Iran. Also on the team is an English midwife, a Russian diplomat's daughter, a Turkish girl whose father owns a local yacht building company and, Godfrey, a former English broadcaster for the BBC. I feel honoured that I have been given the opportunity to work with such an incredible and motivated team.

The property market is booming here so the lure of making big money tax-free for a few years gives people a chance to acquire cash in the bank. They work purely on a commission basis, so they have to be fairly astute and hungry for deals. The thought of implementing any commission structure change will cause problems for the managers. Good sales agents are money orientated, that's why they are here for one thing only — to get rich!

I sit at my desk enjoying a sandwich whilst reading the local *Gulf News*. I look up from my paper. I have to pinch myself as I glance at my arrangement of flowers sitting in a glory of colour. I am flattered by his gifts and the attention he gives me. I then touch my pearls, a reminder of his kindness and words of loyalty and eternity. A frisson of excitement runs through me.

I must take a few deep breaths and keep calm as my anxiety levels are going up and down like a pair of tart's knickers! One minute I feel ecstatic, as high as a kite. The next I am hesitant, especially after Sam's words of warning earlier this morning.

After work I drive to an Australian beach bar called 'Down Under' to meet my *Sex and the City* girlfriends. Their nickname is appropriate as when we all meet up each week it reminds me of an episode from the famous American drama of the same name. In the series there is a group of good-looking women who care about each other and all have something interesting to say regarding life, men, sex and relationships. They're always eager to give advice on these particular subjects.

I order a stiff drink upon my arrival, as I have a strong feeling I will be interrogated regarding the flowers and, no doubt, they might have heard about the pearls too by now.

Sabrina, who is Moroccan and very exotic looking, is married to a guy from Cornwall in the UK. Laurel is blonde, beautiful and South African, with aqua blue eyes. She is a keen investor in the property market and is married to a man from Devon, also in the UK. My other friend, Sophia, an Essex girl, looks just like Christine Keeler from the Profumo affair scandal in the early 1960s. She is an ex-model, dark and petite, who prefers to remain single. She has her reasons for this, her opinion of men being quite low. And, of course, there is Simone who is my lifeline and more like a sister to me.

Sophia has an Essex accent. She lights up a cigarette, deeply inhales and looks at me in a rather stern way. Unfortunately life has dealt her a cruel blow regarding one man in particular. For all her beauty and brains she has never got over him. 'Well,' she says, taking another drag of her cigarette. 'If you are so sure that he is not married and he is as attractive as you say he is, why is he single? What's the catch Janey?'

I look at Simone as she orders her shisha pipe from the waiter. She sits quietly being very discreet, especially about the sailing club, not breathing a word.

Sabrina is inquisitive, her feisty Moroccan temperament is always getting her into trouble and she pushes the conversation whilst Laurel and Sophia look at me intensely.

'How did you meet him?'

'Work,' I reply. My first white lie!

'When did all this happen? Do you know what part of Jubai he is from? Who is he anyway?'

Sabrina has lived here now for a very long time and likes to think she knows everyone in town, especially anyone who she believes to be rich and powerful. The interrogation has started.

'Well,' I say to Sabrina. 'Which question do you want me to answer first?'

Laurel is more laid back, swigging down her vodka and cranberry juice. 'Ah, maybe he is a cad, a playboy? Let Janey have some fun! I can't remember the last time she had a date. Yonks ago, bloody yonks!'

I grin like a Cheshire cat. 'Listen girls, you are all fired up over flowers and pearls. I am allowed a date occasionally!'

Sabrina is still on my case, even though I had given all good answers to her inquisitive nature. 'Well honey, looking at those pearls and hearing about the hundred flowers sat in your office reception, he must be loaded, absolutely loaded!'

The girls discuss me like I'm not there, whilst Simone carries on smoking her pipe, keeping right out of the banter. The shisha guy turns up with his copper pan full of burning fire to renew her coals and, as he bends over to clear her ash away, he gives us all a smile. Each week he enjoys listening to our girl talk. Then the girls turn to Simone.

'Have you met this Mr. M?'

I could sense what she is thinking. The *Sex and the City* girls will invade her cosy sailing club. The club is important to her and her family and she doesn't want everyone coming over to check the talent. I have to step in as this Spanish inquisition is finally getting to me.

'Ladies, ladies, you are supposed to be my close friends.' I decide to tell my second white lie! 'Okay, I will tell you.' This is to the utter relief of Simone, who I can tell was trying to conjure up something. 'He is an investor. I met him months ago and just occasionally we meet for lunch and chat on the phone. He finally asked me out after many months of chasing me.'

Suddenly they all sit bolt upright to attention, glued to my every word. Well, I had to make it sound exciting!

I could tell that Sabrina was turned on by the idea of a man chasing a woman as deep down she would like to be chased and, yes, she would enjoy a love affair or a sexually erotic encounter with a man. Or, I think, she might also consider a woman! Unfortunately her sex life at home has gone stale or, to put it in her exact words, like mildew. 'How come you never mentioned this Mr. M and his chase before?' she asks.

I then take a deep breath and, before my brain really kicks in, another white lie rolls off my tongue. 'You see, two things ladies. Number one, I haven't mentioned him as I think he's too old for me and, secondly, he's too rich and powerful. It scares the shit out of me!'

They all look at each other in utter amazement! Simone chokes on her drink and Sabrina's eyes light up. This is not what they expected to hear from Janey Green, Sales Manager of the Year and someone that never dates. Well, you can't call the Scottish redhead who works for the Kuwaiti government a date. I ended up paying for myself as he was as tight as a duck's arse, as we say in Yorkshire.

Sabrina's green envious eyes look me up and down. This is her dream. She has mentioned to me on several occasions that many Moroccan women want wealth and status and look for an older man.

Laurel laughs and laughs. 'Oh Janey, I love it! So you have met a rich old crooner then! Well good luck to you. Enjoy some good sex!' she says, as if it's a fading memory for me.

Sophia, still concerned, just has to say more. 'Janey just be careful. Rich, good-looking men come at a price and I should know! Are you sure he's not married? I do know a guy here who will check him out for you — he is ex-British CID.'

'No, I don't think I need to, but thanks anyway.'

'The offer stands Janey, whenever you are ready.'

Sabrina and Laurel agree. 'To be sure, it might be a good idea to check him out, don't you think love? What do you know about him?'

All eyes are now on me.

'He divorced back in the eighties and subsequently dated a German woman called Gretal for several years. They broke up three years ago.'

There is silence while the information is digested.

Sabrina's fiery temperament is like a pit bull terrier; once she gets her teeth into something juicy and exciting she can't let go of it. 'What nationality is he?'

I pick up my drink, take a gulp and then another … a fuzzy feeling comes over me. Eventually I say. 'He is an Emirati who was educated at Cambridge in the UK.'

'I knew it! knew it! He had to be a local … is he in oil? An oil baron?' asks Sophia.

I laugh. 'Oil?'

Simone, who had been sat quietly trying to keep out of the interrogation, nearly chokes on her drink again. 'An oil baron? Come on girls, you've been watching too many re-runs of Dallas.'

All the answers regarding Mojat barely satisfy them. This is why I call them the *Sex and the City* girls, as they enjoy nothing more than a tangled web of curiosity. Today it's me in the web! This makes a refreshing change, as it's usually legs up to your armpits Lola who's the centre of attention!

An Egyptian waiter brings our food and re-arranges the table. The energy changes quite quickly as we all dip our Arabic bread in the various bowls of meze. We chat about Laurel's potential developments on a house she's having built back in South Africa.

The girls are always fun to be with and our conversations are usually interesting and stimulating. Simone eventually gives me a look across the table signalling she is ready to leave. I'm feeling quite tired so we pay the bill, give each other hugs and say our goodbyes.

The roads are quiet as I drive back to the apartment. Simone follows me in her Jeep.

Finally we arrive at my place for coffee, enter the apartment, switch the side lamps on and draw the blinds to shut the world out.

'For God's sake Janey, ten out of ten for coming up with that story, you were amazing how you just slipped all that information in.'

'I know, I did my best not to mention the sailing club.'

'Thank the lord you didn't, as David would not have been impressed if they had all materialised at the weekend in their red lipstick and high heels, looking for a strapping sailor with a good pair of biceps!'

'Yeah, that would be interesting?'

'Not for David it wouldn't. He can only cope with all the girls together in very small doses!'

Simone's head sinks into my leather sofa and she closes her eyes, breathing heavily ... saying, 'I know chick, it was all a little over the top.'

'I'm just thinking, my marriage would be in serious trouble if the girls all turned up together at the weekends.'

'That will never happen.'

I change into my loose robe and return to the lounge with a large cafetière. I need to ask a few questions and I can see Simone is nearly asleep on the couch.

'Simone, wake up and listen to me and please be honest. Tell me everything you know about Mojat?'

'Janey, you're the one that's psychic — you should be telling me. Anyway I think you know as much as David and I.' She pauses for a moment. ' Okay, pour that bloody coffee as I need to come round a little.' She takes a gulp. 'It's quite straightforward. David and I have only had three or four conversations with him since becoming members, which is nearly four years now.'

She has another swig, her epiglottis moving back and forth giving a loud glucking noise in her throat as the hot coffee is gulped down quickly. She pours herself another and aligns the chocolate digestive biscuit over the top of the cup, then hesitates before she dunks it. 'Oh yes, there is one thing which seemed a little strange. A couple of years ago he walked with a stick for ages — maybe an accident? Bit of a mystery really!'

'Did anyone talk about it in the club?'

'Janey, it was strange really as no one seemed to know or say anything and if you mentioned it to anyone or … what's that waiter called, the little Egyptian guy who is always trying to chat me up? Samir, oh yeah Samir! He began to talk about it once, then stopped, before really saying anything. You know Janey he also travels extensively for weeks at a time and then just appears at the club again. He is always very sociable and, one thing, we've never seen another local Arab in the club, not one! You would think sometimes he'd invite a few friends along?'

'What about women Simone?'

'No, no female friends either, I've never seen him with a woman romantically.'

'There is Big Brenda, one of the members.'

'Who the hell is Big Brenda?' I ask.

'Double-barrelled Brenda,' she says, in a posh English accent.

'Who are you talking about?'

'Brenda Scott-Davies, a very competent sailor. Everyone knows her as she has sailed around the world single-handed.'

'Actually, I don't know her.'

'She talks with a plum in her mouth, obviously from a very titled and posh background. Janey you must have seen her in the club, she is always trying to allure Mojat with her big tits. It's a joke really.'

'How funny you telling me this.' I begin to giggle.

'Yeah, she struts up to his corner table in her white kitten heels, wearing her gaudy Hawaiian-style bikini top and the tightest shorts you've ever seen. She then provocatively leans forward, elbows on his table, sticking her arse right out into the next table whilst she tries her hardest to chat him up. How her tits don't fall into his pint?' Simone then pauses to dunk another chocolate digestive into her coffee dregs and pops it into her mouth quickly, as it's breaking up and wet crumbs are dropping everywhere. 'Anyway, David says her sixties backcombed brassy blonde hair would not be Mojat's style.'

This also amuses me and I want to know more. 'How does David know Mojat's taste?'

'He could tell by his lack of response, though I will say one thing, he is always very polite to her.'

'Bloody hell! How have I missed all this?'

Simone laughs. 'Janey, now that I'm talking about the whole situation, it's funny thinking about those poor people trying to pull their table discreetly away from Brenda's arse. Another thing Janey, she must be well over sixty-five!'

I am trying to conjure up a picture of this situation in my head.

'David says she is still stuck in the 1960s, a sort of Dusty Springfield look, wearing a sailor's hat!'

'Jesus, Simone, I can't imagine!'

'I tell you Janey you wouldn't want to.'

Simone tops up her coffee and attempts to dunk her third chocolate biscuit, but it falls in.

'Shall I get you a spoon?' She doesn't answer me, as she swigs it from her cup. 'Interesting!' I say. 'Who is his type then?'

'You are chick. David often comments when you are in the club that he follows your every move. Has done for ages. We were not surprised at all when he introduced himself to you.'

I think about this comment for a moment as I pour myself the last half cup of coffee. 'Simone, I can count on your discretion can't I?'

'Of course chick, don't worry.'

She leaves my apartment and I climb into bed.

Just as I am dropping off to sleep, my phone starts to ring. I pick up and the line sounds as if it's a long distance call.

'Habibie, how are you?' Habibie means my love in Arabic. It's a term of endearment.

I notice the time has gone midnight. 'Mojat, where are you right now?'

'I am in the States, I have just finished a meeting.'

'Who with?'

'The foreign minister, Mr. Jeremy Rosenberg, and other European diplomats.'

'You never mentioned to me that you were travelling to the States.'

'Janey, my work schedule is complicated and what I meant to say to you last night is that, for security reasons, it's difficult to talk.'

I decide not to push on this subject.

'Thank you for my wonderful arrangement of flowers! I love scented flowers.'

'I know you do.'

'How did you know this?'

'I made it my business to know.'

'But how on earth did you know that my favourite old rose is Gertrude Jekyll? The only person who knows this is Geoffrey, my ex.'

'Like I said, I made it my business to know!'

I decide not to pursue the matter on the phone right now. 'I've had a busy day at work and a lovely evening with my girlfriends. Of course my work colleagues and girlfriends all want to know who the secret Mr. M is?'

Mojat laughs. 'Hmm, interesting.'

'I know Simone and David just think you're a businessman who owns the club.'

'I know habibie, that is what most people think. Anyway, I know I can trust you.'

'How do you, we have only just met?'

'I would not make myself vulnerable my dear; we will talk on this subject on my return. You are in my thoughts habibie and I will call tomorrow evening. I just have one request. I want you to keep Thursday evening and the weekend free. And just one more thing, the lovely pink chiffon dress you were wearing last weekend, you mentioned you bought it recently from your favourite shop.'

'Yes, Betty Boo's Boutique. Why?'

'That's the one! I was trying to recall it.'

Before I could question him further, he makes excuses that he's running late for a meal with colleagues and hangs up the phone.

I snuggle down into my cool cotton sheets.

Erotic thoughts enter my mind for the first time in … well … let's just say a very long time. I stretch out full-length enjoying the coolness of pure cotton. It's been ages since I have been intimate with a man; I wonder what is underneath his Arabic dress? Other than the weapon attached to his leg and his hair that is always covered. It looks thick and wavy.

I sleep very deeply, waking to the sound of my alarm. I drive to work recalling the conversation from last night. He says he knows he can trust me; how can he possibly know?

CHAPTER FIVE

White Lies

The next three days pass quickly whilst I work and keep to my usual routine, with Mojat hidden away in my secret thoughts.

He phones me each evening at around 11:30 for a chat. He doesn't mention his work, and I don't encourage him to do so.

Thursday arrives and it's late afternoon. My anticipation has been building all day and now I'm just finishing up by writing a few bullet points for the Sunday sales meeting.

Simone arrives at my office; she sits at my desk and kicks off her heels. 'How much longer are you going to be chick, as my feet are killing me and my ankles are swollen from the heat?'

I look down at her feet. 'Haven't you any flip-flops or sandals in your car that you can slip on?'

She mutters something under her breath to the effect of she wouldn't be seen dead wearing comfortable sandals for work. I glance down at her Jimmy Choo five-inch heels and can tell she is tired. She groans as she rubs her ankles. 'This bloody heat gets to you when you are in and out of the car all day.'

'Yes,' I say, trying to quickly finish off everything.

'We are meeting David and the girls at the sailing club for an early tea,' says Simone.

I always keep another set of clothes at the office, mainly beachy lightweight dress and a pair of pretty sandals; just for these occasions when we all meet up straight after work. I finish my jobs, clear my desk and change — not forgetting to wear my pearls.

We arrive at the club, which is alive with energy. All the die-hard sailors are dressed in various coloured shorts, T-shirts and deck shoes — some are also wearing the traditional sailor caps. Everyone is totally engrossed in sea talk as they lean over maps rolled out on a large table. The race for Saturday is being planned as they plot their routes. I could not help feeling uplifted too; I wonder if this is what Mojat had in mind for us — to join the race?

I glance over their shoulders, this particular map looks quite old, dog-eared and creased at the corners. In bold black typeset letters it's headed, The Gulf of Oman. Lots of lines have been previously drawn as though many expeditions have taken place over the years.

A commanding deep voice takes me by surprise.

'Are you participating Janey?'

I turn to see George, one of the oldest diehards!

'I fear not, as I do not have much experience.'

'We will teach you. Why don't you come as crew on my yacht, The Endeavour?'

I look up and George smiles, a stout broad-shouldered man, with a thick shock of white hair. He is standing holding a very large whisky. As my mother would say, 'as brown as a berry' from lots of sea exposure over the years.

'That's kind of you George, but I'll have to decline. Perhaps another time as I'll need to prepare myself.'

'Nonsense my child! In my experience the best things that happen in life are the ones that have not been planned!'

Maybe he's right, but not this evening.

Simone and I eventually sit down at a large table outside with David and the girls. Opposite us are all the various sizes of moored yachts and, behind them, an orange-red sky that would impress any keen photographer.

David remarks to me about the flowers. 'Too large to get in the car then? Are they still decorating the office?'

I laugh. 'What else could I do? They will last for weeks and it has given everyone something to talk about, other than their property deals.'

I finish my light snack and enjoy the conversation with another couple that have also joined our table. Happiness is in the air and the weekend has now officially begun. I sit listening to everyone's chatter, when a strange feeling comes over me. A rush of excitement runs down my spine and intuitively I know … I hear a familiar voice.

'Dusk, my favourite time of day.'

I am daydreaming, fatigued after a busy working week. From behind I feel a firm grip on my shoulder, then another large hand on my other shoulder. It startles me.

'How is my beautiful woman?'

I turn towards the voice and look up; a wonderful smile greets me and he looks good in his starched white Arabic dress against the now dark red sunset in the background.

'Dusk is the perfect time of the day Janey.'

I have to let any negative thoughts go and trust spiritually for now that this journey will be a good one for me. I say spiritually as, for months, I have been praying for the right man to come into my life.

He looks me up and down then kisses my cheek. He sits down at the table and acknowledges everyone.

Our eyes meet.

'Sorry, I never answered you — I was miles away. I agree with you, there is something enchanting at dusk and sunset. When did you return?'

'Early afternoon; I have arranged a little trip for us. We are going to sail in one hour to Muscat in Oman, just down the coast.'

'Muscat, sounds fun. How long will we be away, as I will need to go back to my place and pack a few things?'

He leans over to me and quietly whispers in my ear. 'I have arranged a few things for you, so don't worry about clothes or toiletries.'

I can see his driver Kulpreet in the distance giving the marina workers supplies and parcels to take on board his yacht.

'That is why I asked you what your favourite shop was. So don't worry, everything is organised.'

Although I seem cool and calm on the outside trying to take all this in my stride, underneath I am thinking: Whoa! Betty Boo's, so extravagant!

'How do you know my size?'

He smiles and then draws an outline of a curvy woman in the air, which amuses me.

I am turned on by his forwardness and, more than anything, his thoughtfulness. A man has never shopped for me before, ever! I'm impressed!

Mojat speaks with David and Simone informing them we will be away for two nights, returning Saturday late afternoon, depending on the weather and wind conditions.

They are excited at my surprise sailing trip. Mojat chats to David regarding our destination in the Gulf of Oman. 'Not too far away,' he says. 'Mind you there is a strong wind forecast for Saturday; could be up to twenty knots.'

Simone gives me a hug. 'Enjoy yourself in Oman chick. I know how much you love sailing.'

CHAPTER SIX

A Surprise Sail

In the daylight the yacht looks magnificent — it seems much bigger. The deck is clear; no dining table or deep squashy sofa and any memory of a soft candlelit ambience has gone.

He gives the captain the okay to sail and, within fifteen minutes, we are out of the marina and pressing forward into the Gulf Sea. It is an exhilarating feeling; the sea breezes rushing through my hair. The night sky clouds drift towards us, the fair wind is behind us and we're soon cruising at around 15 knots.

We leave the blustery deck and he shows me to my suite.

'Habibie, my manservant has put your clothes away — I think you will find everything is in order. My suite is next door and I will go and rest now. We can meet for cocktails in one hour.'

The suite is mainly white with bright splashes of colour from the modern art adorning the walls.

He pulls me close and we embrace, enjoying a long lingering kiss. He then departs.

In the Middle East I have learnt that rest is important, as the heat dehydrates you. Mojat has flown back from Washington earlier this morning, so he will also be suffering from jet lag.

I look around and check inside the wardrobe. There are many items of clothing: Three dresses, several tops, one pair of casual white trousers and one of beige. I open the drawers and, to my amazement, there are four sets of silk bras and panties to match. I check the size. 36D cup — spot on!

The cabin suite is fresh and bright. I shower and put on a new coffee-coloured silk robe that I'd found lying on the end of my bed, all wrapped in pale blue tissue paper. I have a permanent grin on my face as I touch and admire the quality of the lingerie. Betty Boo's Boutique is where I shop for a special occasion; it's far too expensive for every day. I'm flabbergasted that he has organised all this for me.

I look down at my beach sandals. Yes, they are pretty and very presentable, but not to wear with the dresses hanging in this wardrobe!

I can feel the movement of the yacht and the waves lashing on its side.

I open another drawer to find three pairs of shoes, all designer labels, and two small clutch evening bags. Then I stand in front of the mirror and admire the silk gown. I take my make-up bag from my handbag and brush my hair. After this I choose a pale blue dress from the wardrobe, not a colour I have worn before.

I'm just putting the finishing touches to my lips and eyes when there is a knock at the door and Mojat walks straight in.

'Janey you look amazing, pale blue really does suit you and the pearls ... well ... what can I say?'

I'm grinning from ear to ear as I look down at my silver shoes and bag. 'You have good taste Mojat and you know how to make a woman feel special!' I enjoy the moment and stand and admire the dress in the full-length mirror; I am blown away by his generosity and his interest in women's clothes.

We walk to the ballroom and a dining table has been laid at one end. The lighting is low and, in the background, chill-out lounge music is playing.

Our evening starts with a fresh strawberry margarita. He talks about his trip and his meetings. Nothing too confidential, he just outlines the purpose of his visit. He then informs me that he flies with the airline, Royal Jet. A private airline for everyone working within the diplomatic and political service and, of course, they fly the royal family and their relatives all over the world.

'Janey, I have been doing a job over the last thirty years that has made me incredibly happy, although, at times, it's been frustrating. It all sounds glamorous but travelling can be very tiring and, for security reasons, I never talk on the phone to anyone regarding times and places of arrival and departure. I hope you were not offended?'

'I am only just getting to know you, why would I be?'

I enjoy listening intently to him about his lifestyle and business. Although he is a man of wealth and distinction I can relate to many things he discusses. I like his earthy personality. He is neither pompous nor full of himself and doesn't try to impress me. No, none of that bullshit!

We laugh together. He has a dry sense of humour and he is fun!

The meal is served by one of the kitchen staff, a young man dressed in a starched white blazer and trousers. The Arabic food is excellent and we polish off a variety of fish and vegetable dishes served with rice and local bread. A bottle of champagne is opened and the cork launches with a hollow pop!

'A toast is in order Janey.' Our crystal flutes chink together. 'To us!'

'To us!' I reply. I don't really know why I have concurred with his toast, but hey, at this moment it feels right.

He stands up and walks over to his music system. 'Habibie, I just want to put one of my favourite songs on.' As he returns he performs a little dance and a twirl. My eyes light up, I love a man that can dance. He opens his arms to me and says, 'This track is for you habibie.'

He leads me around the dance floor whilst singing along at the same time. He holds me so close, pressing his lips occasionally on my forehead. He has natural rhythm and is very light on his feet.

'You are such a romantic, and you can sing!'

'My dear, I am an Arab. Romance and love with the right woman is everything to us. I am nearly sixty years old habibie and had almost given up finding you.'

As we dance around the floor I think to myself, how can I not be blown away by this old-fashioned romance? Come on tell me? A man who buys you expensive clothes, who sings to you, who loves dancing and, as an extra bonus, is a good mover. Also he chases you, always making the phone calls and the first moves. A romantic at heart, what more could a woman want? I am literally being swept off my feet!

I suddenly remember Sophia's words from the other night: 'What is the catch Janey? Come on, there must be a catch somewhere?'

We sit down and he pours me another glass of fizz.

'How do you know that you have found me?' I ask.

'I know, I have had a sign.'

'A sign — really?'

'I have only loved once. With Gretal it all went tragically wrong, both quickly and painfully. She brought me to my knees!'

Any negative feelings evaporate. His openness is not what I expect from a man I have only known a few days. I feel empathy and resonate with him on some level. Deep down I didn't want to leave Geoffrey, but felt I had no choice.

'I have watched you for months in the club with your friends. I have to be honest, I wanted you, really wanted you.' He pauses before speaking again, this time with a slight hesitancy in his voice. 'Janey, before I could make the first move to ask you out, I had to have you checked out by government security. Sorry, if this is a bit of a shock, but I needed to know I could trust you or things could've been disastrous for me.'

I feel indignant and abruptly I reply. 'Disaster! That's a little over the top Mojat! I've been checked out? When?'

'Janey please do not get upset.'

'You are a politician, not frigging royalty!'

He takes my hand. 'I am part of the royal family, my nephew is our ruling Sheikh.'

'The Sheikh? Your nephew! Really?' I ponder for a brief moment. 'Well, who are you?'

'My Arabic family name is Bin Al Mohini; I am Sheikh Haitham Rashid.'

I am speechless. 'My privacy has been invaded Mojat, even if you are a Sheikh and part of the royal family.'

'I know Janey, it is royal protocol.'

'That must mean Lindsay, the owner of the company I work for, must know.' I suddenly feel a little rattled. 'My privacy has been invaded and for what?'

'Don't be upset with me, please trust me.'

'Trust you, I hardly know you! You had me checked out by government security before you had ever introduced yourself to me.'

'Do you have all the members of your sailing club checked out before becoming members?'

'No, of course not! I was planning a relationship with you, not the members of the club!'

After initially feeling my territory has been invaded, I begin to calm down. He pours me another drink.

At the club, he said he had his reasons for not introducing himself earlier, at least now I know why.

'So you're not a weird stalker then after all? All that time watching me you were planning a relationship?'

'Yes, am I excused now?'

I do not answer, as I am considering everything that has been put in front of me.

'Your brother?'

'My brother Omani stepped down five years ago.'

'Why?'

'Omani made his decision based on ill health to pass his leadership responsibilities and role to his eldest son.'

'Is he still suffering from ill health?' I ask, still trying to build a picture.

'Unfortunately it is a rare form of epilepsy which the medics are struggling to balance with medication. There are other things too which plague him.'

I sit and contemplate for a moment. 'Can you do that, just pass everything on to your son?'

'Omani can do anything, he has more power than a King or Queen in England. His son rules the country and gives the orders. I am one of his advisors.'

'You advise our ruling Sheikh?'

'Of course he is younger; in the Arabic culture age is wisdom and is highly respected.'

'That is how it should be. In the UK we have lost respect for the older members of our society. We should take a leaf out of your book.'

My brain is ticking over — imagine this in the UK? The queen has to die first before Prince Charles is crowned. I am now trying to learn and understand about other cultures and their traditions. Mojat is a Sheikh. For some reason this does not shock or surprise me.

I look at his dark eyes; he waits patiently for me to digest all the new information. Eventually I say. 'Where does the name Mojat come from?'

'It was just a name I conjured up at university, an abstract name and it has just stuck ever since with my friends.'

'Is there anything else I need to know about you? Anything at all?'

'Nothing that important.'

This chance meeting I now realise was nothing of the sort. He had planned all along to capture my heart. I am a sensitive creature, aware that my surroundings and dreams are at times prophetic. But I never saw this coming. I feel he is ready for love and, more importantly, he is willing to take a chance. His sensitivity and openness have touched me.

'Janey, I have thought about this moment for a long time. Whilst I was in Washington you were constantly on my mind.'

We begin to kiss and kiss and kiss …

Mojat's thoughts:
I pull her close to me; her skin has a sweetness as I kiss her lips. I stroke the downy hairs on her neck and quiver with excitement.

I take her hand and lead her into my bedroom suite.

We stand close and very still for a few moments. Our eyes are fixed, almost paralysed, staring at each other.

I gently embrace and explore every part of her.

His kisses change from a tender seductive embrace into a wild wind of masculine passion that ignites the most powerful flame.

We stand next to each other and I remove his headdress, revealing a mass of dark coarse hair that is heavily greying. I run my fingers through, then clasp his locks tight in my hands pulling his head back whilst looking directly at his face. He is a good-looking man with amazing eyes.

I feel his strength as he picks me up and carries me to his full-length mirror.

I am full of excitement as he begins to remove my clothing piece by piece. Sparks of electricity are rippling through my body into my solar plexus, spiralling down into every cell of my cunny.

He whispers, 'Habibie, keep your shoes on.'

He stands behind me cupping my breasts, enjoying the reflection.

Mojat's thoughts:
She is provocative and sensual in her French lace panties. I am hard, so hard, almost at bursting point! Her long blonde hair sits tousled over her shoulders. I remove her panties and am delighted to see her stocking tops held up by a fine silk band.

I move my hands over her womanly thighs until I feel the gap of skin just above the shear thread of her stocking tops. This excites me and, fuck, I am shaking from the anticipation.

I lift her up and place her on my bed.

I hold her breasts and feel the warmth of her caress as she showers me with kisses. Her nipples are large and bright pink, standing proud. I start to suckle them as she squirms and screams with delight. I suckle harder and she begins to twist and turn under me.

I explore her curvaceous lines whilst moving my hands downwards, nipping in at her waist and out over her hips. I reach down in-between her thighs to feel her outer lips — her moist secretions excite me. Then I spread her legs apart and feel inside her fanny. I am hard and pulsing and cannot contain myself any longer. I enter her, pushing deep and maintaining a hard powerful rhythm amidst her river of flowing juices. I look down at her pink nipples that synchronise to each rise and fall of movement.

She is my English rose. She screams out in pleasure. I am now a crazy man; she has made me so. I reach wonderful heights of pleasure as I explode within her.

Throughout the night I take her again. I want her and will not let her rest. I need to suckle, feel and penetrate until I am satisfied and exhausted.

Holding her close I whisper … 'Tonight with your kisses my life begins. We are like creatures of the wind and wild is the wind. Hug me my darling.'

It is our first night together and we fall asleep clinging to each other like souls who have been separated for centuries by war or disaster, finally returning to fulfil a past life promise to each other.

His sexual restlessness is what I have desired in a man for so long. He has regained his life force and I have gained my power as a woman, a spiritual light has entered our souls, an awakening. This is a deep love from another time, another spiritual plane, a higher dimension.

CHAPTER SEVEN

The Truth

I open my eyes to find Mojat staring at me, playing with my hair.

'I love your hair, the way it waves and falls around your shoulders. In Arabic we say antiii jamelaa jeddan, which means you are so beautiful.'

I enjoy the tingles on my scalp from his gentle touch.

'You make me feel good Janey.'

I lie next to him enjoying the moment and then I say, 'It has been such a long time since I have been this intimate.'

He kisses my forehead. I feel excited as he lays naked next to me cupping my breasts.

'Habibie, it pleases me that you have not been intimate; it makes me want you all the more.'

I smile enjoying his compliments.

'I want you, like I've never wanted anything before. I never want to be parted from you!'

I sit up in bed in shock. I look up at his face whilst I pull the white cotton sheets up around my neck. 'Whoa! That is quite a statement; do you realise what you are saying?'

His face lights up and a huge smile bursts forward. 'Of course I do. I never thought for one moment that you would take a chance on going out with me.'

'Why? Why are you saying this?'

'In the club I used to watch you circulating and chatting to people and, I have to say, you seemed totally oblivious to me.'

There is a silence between us. I sense his uncertainty and doubts regarding the challenge to capture my heart.

Confidently I say, 'You know, there were a few times when our eyes did meet and I do remember the feeling it gave me. But it is true, I was never aware of you watching me.'

'The feeling it gave you habibie, can you describe it?'

I linger for a few seconds, choosing my words carefully. 'Yes, it was a feeling that triggered some sort of memory, a knowing feeling I suppose like I had met you before — but that sounds a little corny. It's hard to describe.'

He cradles me in his arms and squeezes me tight. 'You're the one I have been waiting for — I mean it.'

'What about your work?' I say chuckling.

'I will take you with me.'

'What about my work?'

He grimaces then says. 'In love there are always compromises.' He raises his voice. 'If we are meant to be together. Inshallah habibie, Inshallah!'

I know Inshallah means if God is willing. Of course I know who will be doing the compromising; it will be me!

We shower and dress and climb back up on deck. We are now in the Sea of Oman, anchored off the coast of Muscat. It is breathtaking; a small pretty cove lies in front of the yacht. The long stretch of sand is volcanic, greyish, even black in parts. The waters around the yacht are crystal clear and turquoise. In the distance to the right of the cove is an interesting mountain range.

I look out from the deck and Mojat stands next to me with his binoculars. He passes them to me.

'Look habibie, see the mountains. They are called Al Hajar and the palace in the background belongs to the Sultan of Oman — a good family friend. If he knew we were here he would be distraught that we haven't visited him, but another time in future I will introduce you.'

The heavy dark mountains are impressive as they stand on the edge of the beach. In the background is a decadent looking hotel that looks like another Middle Eastern palace.

'I can see you are looking at The Omani Grand; it attracts tourists from all over the world. The chef is French and has an excellent reputation.'

'It looks interesting,' I say inquisitively as I return his binoculars. 'From the outside it certainly lives up to its name.'

We take a power dinghy to the shore and walk hand in hand up the beach just like any normal couple. It feels quite natural to have strong feelings flowing between us.

We stop at a cosy taverna-style café to have breakfast.

This morning I can't take my eyes off him as he looks so different in his knee length khaki shorts, leather Timberland flip-flops and a loose white shirt. His black hair is nearly all one length to just below his ears, with heavily greying streaks that wave. He smoothes it back with his large hands and tucks it behind his ears. His lined face and pronounced Roman nose are softened by his deep ebony eyes. In fact they remind me of a deer's — wide-eyed, kind and gracious. Having only ever seen him in his traditional dress before, he looks great right now.

My mind is overcrowded with thoughts as I listen to him talking to the couple that own the café, who just happen to be Spanish. I secretly like the fact that he has never lost his public school voice. I find it such a turn on and, considering how perturbed I felt at having been checked out, I am now on a high but composed from the pleasures of spending our first night together.

I relax into a seat and pick up the menu. I've let go of all the indignant feelings I had about him having me checked out by government security. It does not matter right now. Of course, if you have something to hide then that's different. But I haven't! I am just a country girl from North Yorkshire seeking happiness and a new life.

We enjoy a late breakfast of scrambled eggs with manakish, which is za'atar flatbreads, drizzled with a little of the local olive oil. This is a traditional Lebanese breakfast.

The coffee is good and strong, just how I like it. Our conversation begins to take on a more serious note.

'Janey want do you want in life?'

I smile, look directly at him and take a deep sigh ... 'Ooh, so many things are important to me, but desires are what I wish for.' I hold back for a few seconds then very confidently I say. 'I have been loved before in my life, I know this for sure. Even though the relationships have broken down, I want to be cherished. No one has ever really cherished me. Of course like most men and women I desire passion and a powerful love that lasts, but to be cherished is something that would secure my love until I take my last breath.' I pause, gathering my inner strength. 'And the next time I am not prepared to settle for anything less.'

He pulls a face as if to say, impressive bold statement. Perhaps he did not expect to hear me say this.

'Has that answered your question Mojat?'

'Yes, quite a speech my dear.'

I change the dynamic. I need to know about the only person he has ever loved. 'Tell me about Gretal?'

He sits for a moment almost resisting to speak. His voice deepens and his head bows for a few seconds, then he raises it and looks towards me. He is gathering his thoughts wisely ...

'Gretal, where do I begin? What can I say? I loved her, really loved her. It was true love; in fact it was the first time I had ever felt love. She was German, blonde, vivacious, loving and confident. We enjoyed seven years together.'

He falls silent for a few seconds as though he is thinking very carefully on how to present the story of the woman he loved so much and lost. He sighs deeply and heavily before continuing.

'You see, she always wanted a child, but at that time in my life I was busy travelling with my work and, remember Janey, I'd had children before from my arranged marriage. Somehow this was no longer a priority for me.'

I look into his eyes and I see his pain.

'In hindsight I should have gone along with her wishes, it was selfish of me not to have considered her needs more and I was a foolish man back then. I should have given her the child she so desperately wanted.' He picks up his cup and takes a gulp of coffee. 'This was a big mistake and I paid the price!'

I watch his mannerisms as he pushes his thick greying hair back off his face and tucks it behind his ears. He finishes his coffee then resumes his story with sorrowful energy.

'Janey, then an unexpected and terrible thing happened.' He pauses again as though it's too painful to talk. His voice breaks up.

'What was that?' I ask.

'I had not been feeling well for a while when one afternoon I collapsed with a sharp piercing pain. A headache — more than a headache — I'd never felt such pain in my whole life.'

There are tears flowing down his face. I feel terrible right now, but felt I needed to ask about Gretal.

'I lost my speech for a few days. It turned out that I'd suffered a stroke. I was frightened and it did cross my mind that I was either going to die, or end up in a wheelchair.'

I study his face — he looks a broken man. Tears are in his eyes and he takes a deep breath. 'Gretal did her duty. She stayed with me during my recovery but after this, well my dear, the story is not so good.'

'I am sorry,' I say, feeling his deep remorse. My inquisitive nature has obviously opened up deep painful wounds.

He wipes away his tears with his hand then continues. 'I was put on strong medication for a few months and our sex life deteriorated. Well, deteriorated is an understatement! I just could not perform, could not get a hard on. Nothing — not a flicker of manhood left in me.' He takes my hand across the table and squeezes it; he then gestures to the lady owner for another pot of coffee. 'You see Janey, I do understand. Gretal panicked, really panicked. She felt at forty years old her biological time clock was ticking away, so she left me and returned to Germany. Before she departed she looked after me until I regained my speech and could walk again, albeit with a stick.'

Mojat pauses to recompose himself. 'We kept in contact and six months down the line she rang me. There was a lightness in her voice — it was joy. She told me that she was going to get married and was pregnant. This all happened too quickly and left me feeling totally devastated! I was deluded in denial and had buried my head in the sand, believing deep down that she would return to me one day. Listening to how deliriously happy she was left me in quite a state of shock. I have never felt such heartache and after this my life was carnage.'

'What happened then?'

'Our seven years together came to such an abrupt ending. I was depressed for months and, of course, full of regret. If I could have only turned the clock back I would have. Of course Janey, I wished her well, a safe pregnancy and future happiness. My full recovery was slow mainly due to my state of mind. I had been living in cloud cuckoo land thinking that she might return. You see, I respected Gretal as she was not interested in my money; she knew I would have bought or given her anything. However, a child to nurture and love was far more important to her.'

I nod my head thinking, yes, I know that maternal feeling. The desire for a baby is so strong it can take over everything else in your life. I've been there.

'I had to walk with a stick for a few months, which made me feel old and decrepit.'

I feel for him. 'I am so sorry for your sadness, so sorry,' I say. 'Life can be cruel.'

'Janey, it was all my own doing and I blame myself. I was selfish and did not put her first. This was a harsh lesson for me.'

The lady appears with the coffee and glances at Mojat's obvious tears; she looks at me and shrugs her shoulders by way of acknowledgement. I smile and say, 'Thank you.' She leaves extra serviettes for my man.

The taverna is quiet with only a few other people eating. Mojat reflects quietly as he pours the fresh coffee into our cups.

I wait for a while, not wishing to make conversation. I am engulfed in sadness, but then I had asked about Gretal!

Mojat resumes: 'Janey, I cried for a year, yearning constantly for her, for the love we once shared. I wanted to ring her and say, come back to me with your son and I will bring him up as my own.'

'Did you call her?'

'No, although so many times I wanted to. I knew she was happy as she'd sent me a photograph on his first birthday. He was blond and blue-eyed, just like Gretal. He looked such a sweet child.'

'Would you really have brought him up as your own child if she'd agreed?'

'Of course, I loved her and from his photograph he looked adorable. I had to face the fact that her maternal need for a child was too strong. I could have given her anything but, after the stroke, not the baby she so desperately wanted.'

I feel overwhelmed as to how I should answer him. 'This is such a sad story Mojat.'

'The medication left me with huge side effects. I could not get an erection and could not feel aroused in any way. I had lost my sexuality. So we went from a full sex life to nothing, absolutely nothing. I might as well have been dead!'

'Oh God, please don't say that Mojat.' I can't bear to hear him say these words.

Mojat clears his throat. 'Emotionally I was on my knees! It was the lowest time of my life.'

His head bows as he wipes more tears away with his fingers. I pass him a serviette and feel the intenseness of his pain and desperation. Of course it brought back memories for me of when I first arrived in Jubai, leaving my family and Geoffrey at Wisteria House. God forgive me as that felt like a bereavement.

I swallow hard feeling a dry lump at the back of my throat,

trying to hold back my tears, my throat feeling sore from the suppression of emotions. 'Mojat, I really don't know what to say.'

He blows his nose hard and composes himself. 'You don't have to say anything my dear; it's the first time I have truly opened my heart to anyone about Gretal. I am fine, I really am. In fact it's almost a relief to talk to somebody about her and finally let go.'

'You've never talked this through with anyone before?'

'Never, but I feel such a release having told you.' He looks to me. 'One door closes and another opens.' He squeezes my hand. 'And now I have met you.'

'I can relate to Gretal's desires for a baby as I have had strong maternal desires myself in the past. Sorry Mojat, maybe that wasn't an appropriate thing to say?'

'It is nothing I don't know already.'

'How long before you weaned yourself off the strong pills?' I suddenly have a flashback to yesterday evening and say. 'As you were pretty hot last night!'

The twinkle in his eyes returns. 'Are you trying to flatter me Janey Green?'

'Maybe!'

'Yes, America, I can barely remember now but quite a few months.' His voice is stronger. 'In the end my full recovery was eighteen months. I flew to the States to see Dr. Richard Oriole, a well-known professor of neurology who lectures in New York. He helped me through the transition to get back to normal physically. When my body began to respond he took the decision to gradually reduce the dose of my medication. Then I discovered an amazing homeopath who restored me completely, emotionally and physically. Dr. Chan, my acupuncturist, worked in conjunction with the homeopath on my nervous system and circulation. These alternative practitioners are marvellous. I still sing their praises today as I see them three or four times a year, mainly as a preventative measure.'

'That's good; you're a man after my own heart. I also use

homeopathic medicine; it's wonderful and has no side effects like conventional treatment. I know of Dr. Chan too as I met him once at a workshop I attended on Chinese medicine. It was impressive.'

'You know Janey, time is a great healer and that was three, nearly four years ago now. I will be truthful to you. I have slept with many women since, but no one has interested me. I'd almost given up looking and searching for real excitement, until the day I saw you standing in the club. At that moment my life changed from mono to colour!'

I laugh joyfully; it feels great to have such a compliment. 'I am relieved you have turned your life around physically and emotionally Mojat. I just want to say if you only knew the pleasure you gave to me last night.'

'Really Janey, that pleases me. A man has to keep his woman happy and satisfied in the bedroom. I don't want you straying.'

He is so old-fashioned in many ways; can you imagine a young man saying these words?

'I am almost semi-retired now and will be passing my full responsibilities on to the next foreign minister, as we have been working in tandem for a few months now. The Peace Treaty in the Middle East is a gradual process. I have a duty to my country and will remain as a foreign diplomat and ambassador. Politics has been my life; it's a love that fires me and gets me up in the mornings. It gives me that fizzy buzz and, of course, it's in my nature to try and fix things.'

I listen intently as he analyses his life's work. His strength of character resonates with me. His openness is refreshing and his emotional feelings run deep.

The midday sun is stifling and there is a stickiness in the air. We decide to head back to *The Falcon* for the cool offshore breezes.

The crew help us climb back on board. They are all such a friendly bunch and we spend the next thirty minutes chatting.

I am being shown and taught many things by Herman as we wander around on deck. I learn about the tides and wind directions, also the changes in atmospheric pressure regarding weather patterns. Herman is capable of navigating via the stars, something he learnt from his father, who was also a Navy man.

I am hot and sticky so excuse myself to go down to my suite to shower and change.

I shower in tepid water to cool myself off, then wrap a towel around my body and return to the bedroom feeling the need to find something cool and casual to wear. I go through the drawers and place all the beautiful underwear on my bed, stroking the pure silk bras and panties. I still feel excited about my new clothes.

I open the wardrobe to look for a light cotton dress and decide to wear my own dress as worn last Thursday, as the other dresses are far too good to wear on deck. I am just about to shut the wardrobe door when I notice at the back of the closet something strange, some other opening made of steel. On closer inspection I realise it's a false door.

Once again my inquisitive nature gets the better of me. I pull the hanging clothes to one side and lean in and carefully try the door and, to my amazement, it's not locked! It is heavier than I anticipate and I cautiously pull on it until it's completely open. Fuck me! I'm stunned and almost paralysed for a few seconds at what I'm seeing. My heart races and I can clearly hear it pulsating loudly in my head.

There are several guns — three of which are large machine guns, four are revolvers. Next to them sitting on the floor is a large heavy canvas satchel. I lift it out and push firmly on the weighty metal clip to release it and then I pull the flap back. Jesus Christ — bullets! Dozens of them and several magazine rounds.

'What the hell?'

It begs the question — why does he need all these guns? Pirates maybe? I don't think so! Or protection of another kind perhaps?

Nerves engulf me as I quickly close the satchel, replace the clip and put it back very tentatively. I swiftly shut the false door and secure the handle firmly before closing the wardrobe.

I sit on the edge of my bed and breathe again! What a discovery! I can hardly calm down. I adjust the towel that is wrapped around me to cover my shoulders as, suddenly, I'm feeling chilled to the bone!

I quickly put on my familiar dress and slip on my sandals, brush my hair and head back on deck.

Herman and Mojat turn to greet me.

'There you are my dear,' says Mojat. 'We were just wondering if you'd fallen asleep.'

Herman and the crew return to their duties.

'We women like to take our time,' I say, trying to appear casual. 'Anyway, you look fresh, radiant and very natural.'

Mojat has noticed that, in my panic, I had forgotten to apply any lipstick or make-up.

I wander around deck, trying hard not to think of the can of worms that lay behind that false door. There is danger around this man! Do I want this in my life? Would I want to live like this?

Mojat's thoughts:

Having now released my burden and explained about Gretal, not only do I feel a weight lifted, but I can also see that Janey is a woman who can empathise compassionately with me.

She shows integrity as she wept feeling my pain and of course I understand, she has also lost her love Geoffrey. Even though I do not fully know her circumstances I feel her decisions have had repercussions.

I smile to myself now as her warm confidence infatuates me. I have been trying to think who she reminds me of, a certain look she has. When her lips are painted red and her hair is groomed into soft waves. Yes of course, Kim Basinger! Just a certain look about her.

Looking at her now I think, why oh why did I waste all those months just looking at her in the club? Of course, before I approached her, I had to be sure about her and felt that there was no choice but to have her checked out. I needed to know that she is a woman of integrity, a sincere honourable woman with no hidden spiders in the closet!

Singing in Silence

As she talks to my crew, I find myself gazing at her breasts. She turns to me and notices that I am watching her. She smiles and provocatively moves towards me, the sway of her womanly hips tantalising me. I am totally besotted!

I am turned on and ready for her again. I take her arm and walk her back down the steps into my suite. I shut the door and lock it!

I am burning on fire again and as hard as a rock. There is no time for foreplay; I have to take her now!

CHAPTER EIGHT

Behind Closed Doors

His forceful kisses make me delirious and he is holding me so tight I can hardly breathe.

He pulls and yanks my dress up to my breasts, then lifts me up with my legs around his waist and proceeds to carry me over the room to his large mahogany dressing table, placing my bottom right in the centre. My legs are now sprawled apart.

I look up to his face and down to his manhood; he is virile and energetic and ready for me once more. My reflection in the full-length mirror in this position I find disturbing, it's unfamiliar territory.

I am on the edge of a precipice, still thinking about the guns hiding in my room behind the false steel door and, at the same time, I'm so sexed up and turned on from the fantasy of living a dangerous life with him. I now thank God that I didn't light a candle or smoke a cigarette in my suite, as the whole yacht could have ignited!

I've never had a fantasy before, not like this anyway. This one is too near the truth, which in itself stimulates all of my sexual senses. I am high on danger!

The dressing table has three large mirrors, a central one and one on each side that are adjustable to curve around. With the three mirrors now reflecting on to the large full-length mirror opposite, I have to say, it's a bit of a shock! I have never seen my naked body at every angle before, having lived such a sheltered life back in Yorkshire.

I am now perched on the edge of the dressing table.

Metaphorically I'm in a dangerous and precarious position. Not just physically, as my moist bottom slides around the tabletop, but mentally. I am dicing with death whilst at the same time lubricating his mahogany antique. I am enjoying my first real fantasy.

He unzips my dress with eagerness, only it sticks half way down. Aggressively he rips my beach dress and throws it on to the floor, casting it off like an unwanted rag.

'Shit! My dress!'

His animal energy is crazy as I am pulling and holding on to his hair, trying to stabilise myself, keeping my bottom from sliding right off his antique. He is so absorbed in the foreplay he does not seem to notice that I am hanging on for dear life!

We are both erotically entrenched in sex, enjoying every second, never before has anyone turned me on so much. I have never known this erotic side of life before, a dangerous life that he is leading me into.

I am just a country girl at heart. The most sexual thing that has ever happened to me is making love with Geoffrey in a barley field in broad daylight!

Another surprise, well it's more like a jolt to my system. He is arousing me so much that I find my personality changes ... I am now 'a bitch on heat'. I could be anything for him: a French maid, a high class call girl ready and waiting. You name it I think my imagination could now accommodate.

His wide penis fills my palm; it's hard to imagine an organ more magnificent as I grab his balls with my other hand. This now sends him over the edge, his eyes are closed and he starts rambling loud in Arabic ...

He lifts my bottom up and finally disposes of my panties, ripping them apart too. My French lace knickers are in two parts lying on the floor on top of my dress and, as he glances back towards the torn heap, this seems to really excite him.

I have never in my life experienced sex with such destructive behaviour, it's as if he can't get enough of me.

My bottom is now sliding back and forth and my man is in a frenzy of excitement. He enters me, holding my legs apart, pushing deeper, forcing me back hard against all the mirrors. I watch him glancing at our reflections and this is turning him on more!

It's disconcerting for me, seeing my naked body reflected in the four-way mirrors and my clothes lying on the floor like tattered remnants.

He looks down at me, staring and scrutinising. His large hands grip my thighs on his path of discovery, moving up and down he squeezes the folds of my skin, shutting his eyes and talking loudly in Arabic, as though he loves my fleshy bits. I have spent most of my adult life trying to firm them up; I have never been a skinny lady. I am a woman who is extremely comfortable with her curvaceous body and remain relaxed when he discovers a few fine folds of flesh on my thighs. This I now realise turns him on more.

He presses his lips on to my cunny's delicate mounds and then pulls back and stares. He is fixated. He calls it fanny — his fanny — which makes me feel as if I am taking part in a Victorian play, re-enacting a scene from Madame Bovary.

'Habibie, I want to know every part of you. I want the curves of your body and the fragrance of your flesh embedded in my memory.'

My long strawberry blonde hair sits across my breasts like a pair of curtains. He parts them and suckles me forcefully. I push him away yelling, 'It's painful!' I squirm and squeal and try to force him away. 'You're hurting my nipples. Get off you fucking beast!' My language is terrible. I rarely swear. With all my strength I am trying my hardest to get him off me, but for some reason this only excites him more. He is now crazy, grabbing me hard, pulling me right to the edge of the table and pressing my thighs wide open to the point of pain. Again he enters me; he is the Arabian stallion I have been waiting for.

I look into his eyes as he stands in front of me. I see a wild, delirious man who's enjoying every part of me. Still attached he lifts and moves me on to his bed.

Thank God, I think to myself. I could not have stood another minute of sliding around on my arse!

He then positions my body to suit his needs, his needs only!

I used to think that sex was a distant memory for Janey Green, the middle-aged woman.

A new life brings new experiences and I feel like a human contortionist. I can see myself grinning in the four-way mirror system we have got going on in here and did not realise how athletic I am. I had little idea, before today, that I'm so agile.

He is certainly wild and passionate and, I have to say, I'm addicted to this mercurial sexed-up man!

We enjoy the rest of our time and the two days pass very quickly, swimming in the sea and chilling on deck. We leave the yacht to sample the local fresh fish and seafood whilst indulging in Mojat's finest wines.

The nights are blissfully spent enjoying each other's bodies and eventually falling asleep heavily exhausted together.

CHAPTER NINE

A Time of Reflection

Mojat's arms are around my shoulders as we stand on the deck taking in our last view.

The anchor is lifted and we sail away leaving Muscat, this beautiful bay and the imposing mountains of Oman behind us. His crew are on full steam ahead and Herman is in control of the yacht from his power room.

This weekend will certainly live long in the memory. After several months of living dry in the Middle East I have finally met a lover who stimulates me mentally and physically. I am happy that fate has brought me such an exciting partner — the intrigue, adventure and danger all being part of the attraction.

I left Wisteria House in an emotional state of bleakness. I recall how I would gaze out from my bedroom window to the rugged moorland of purple heather and trees bending over from the sharp north-westerly winds. I would sometimes think; is this it? At the time I lived with a husband who would occasionally drop in from his busy working schedule to grab a meal that had been keeping warm for hours in the bottom of the Aga. Then, thoroughly exhausted, would fall asleep in his chair to *Match of the Day* on TV. Is this what my life was to be about?

I was a barren, desolate woman trying to conjure up the energy to love myself again and, yes, don't be shocked — I still love Geoffrey. He is the father of my children. When you are with someone for twenty years, there are feelings that never disappear. Time begins to heal and you then remember what attracted you to your partner in the first place.

Relationships are strange; you are constantly fine-tuning and balancing the emotions and preserving what is good between you. Talking of relationships, there is much more, there always is. As my mother used to say, nobody knows what goes on behind closed doors, and, of course, she was right. Cohabiting couples and married couples, live, breathe and love each other for better or worse! Don't they?

Muscat fades into the distance and the winds start to whip up. *The Falcon* is a magnificent yacht that glides over the waves with ease.

I feel exhilarated by the sea. Sailing and the salt air have always been good for me. I am in that fuzzy state of bliss from the closeness and sexual experiences that we have shared over the weekend.

I would never have thought that sex with a man ten years older could be so hectic and thrilling, but it is amazingly so. I do not use the word 'thrilling' lightly. His touch signals sparks of electricity throughout my body and his public school voice is a huge turn on. Over his many years he has mastered the art of exciting sex by taking his time to play and enjoy me. And singing to me is real old-fashioned romance!

Mojat is old school in many ways; for sure he knows how to sweep a woman off her feet.

Imagine, going to my favourite clothes shop and taking the time to buy me almost a new wardrobe of dresses, lingerie, matching bags and shoes.

Physically, I am now embedded in his memory.

CHAPTER TEN

The Power of the Sea

Fifteen minutes out to sea and the surf's spray is now hitting our faces. The waves are growing larger in size and the crew pass Mojat and I waterproof lifejackets. I can now see the usefulness of my deck shoes, as they stop me from slipping over.

This is real sailing; the storm clouds are dark and satanic and the waves must be twenty feet high, smashing over the edge of the deck. It's getting a little hairy and I need to go downstairs to pee … nerves I feel. We have hit a storm and now, of all times, I need the loo!

I fall over as I try and perch on the toilet, the yacht rocking from side to side. I hold on to anything I can to steady myself before tentatively making my way back up on deck. I can't stay below or I'll be sick. The need for fresh air takes over.

Mojat shouts across the deck. 'It's just a temporary storm, hold on tight or go down to your suite.'

Go down to my suite, who is he kidding! I could barely stand down there!

The wind is strong and the looks on the crew's faces are nervous and apprehensive. I feel a sense of panic as we sail right into the storm.

Mojat scurries out of Herman's power room, reassuringly shouting to us all. 'The storm won't last for long; twenty minutes tops!'

This is the longest twenty minutes of my life. The swell of the angry sea and the vicious huge waves are breaking white foam over the deck. The salt spray is drenching us all. Mojat is screaming orders and it's all hands on deck.

Herman shouts across the yacht. 'The Meteorology Centre gives a forecast of moderately rough.'

'If this is moderate,' I scream in reply. 'I can't imagine what extremely rough feels like.'

I am holding it together just fine until I witness two of the crew making the sign of a cross over their chests. I give my man a look. I need a little more comforting.

'It won't last long,' says Mojat. He takes me to the power room and points to the radar image.

I shelter with Herman as we head directly into the waves. He smiles in acknowledgement as he concentrates at the helm. It's unnerving and scary and I am trying to be brave!

'We should never take the sea for granted, as we are always at her mercy,' advises Herman.

'Yes, I suppose we are,' I reply. 'I had never thought about this.'

Herman's words stay in my mind as we emerge from the storm and enter the moderately choppy waters of Jubai, the aftermath of which is calm in comparison to what we had just experienced.

The wind is blustery as the crew let go and lower the sails. Very soon we are moored safely.

Mojat informs me that the Middle Eastern shamal brings changeable currents at this time of year around the Gulf area.

What a turbulent end to a perfect weekend.

CHAPTER ELEVEN

The Truth

Back at my apartment my mobile phone rings. It's late.

'Habibie, are you still swaying?'

'I am slightly, it's a strange feeling when you first walk back on land.'

'I was just a little worried that the storm had put you off sailing forever?'

'No, it has not put me off. But I don't mind admitting I was scared.'

'You didn't seem fearful?'

'I just hide it well.'

'Janey, when you are ready I would like the opportunity to teach you everything I know. I have sailed for over thirty years and have experienced many countries. I want to share my love of the sea with you and I'm happy that you have a strong sense of adventure. Some women would have been hysterical as it was extremely choppy out there. It's the shamal season after all.'

Mojat finishes off the conversation. 'I just wanted to hear your voice and to say goodnight. I miss you already. Remember you are my love.'

I drift into sleep thinking about the weekend: the emotional sadness regarding Gretal, Mojat's stroke, and the stormy sea on our return. My mind goes back to the false door and the can of worms that lie in there. I am still trying to figure out why he has so many hidden firearms. This is serious stuff!

The next day it's back to normal and I'm busy working in the office. There are buyer and seller contracts to be signed, a meeting with a potential developer at 3pm and afternoon tea with my boss Sam.

All day thoughts of Mojat's secret false door agitate me.

I arrive at Sam's office looking very businesslike, wearing a blue pinstripe skirt, fitted jacket to match and a cool crisp cotton shirt.

Sam and I discuss most of the usual business such as sales targets, motivational techniques and the latest city news regarding developers and new buildings. Then there's the ongoing saga with Inferno Mansions, Trevor Rivestar's building. When I say saga, it is a development that has initially taken its time to get off the ground, presumably because of finance or local opposition. The building has now reached the sixth floor and it's taking on a very futuristic look.

The good news is that Trevor is holding a meeting for our sales teams to give his project an extra boost. There is nothing like an international footballer to generate new business. Our marketing team have been busy organising a photo shoot. Posters of Trevor will be distributed to our offices and a wider network of interesting places around the city.

Our official meeting is coming to a close. Sam is looking quite relaxed for once and, as she leans back in her black leather executive chair, she smiles at me. I know what this is leading up to. In her usual strong Afrikaans accent she says. 'On a personal note chick, how's your secret Mr. M?'

'Fine,' I reply. 'In fact, good.'

'I've been thinking, I sense he must be quite a big shot in Jubai.'

'Are you asking me Sam or telling me?'

I know Sam is a discreet woman. In the past when we have been on our own, she has talked very openly to me about personal things in her life. I know she has trusted me and I also know I can trust her.

I clear my throat and look directly at her. 'Yes, he is. He does have an important position.'

Sharply she says. 'How important?'

'He, he … is the foreign minister about to take on a more diplomatic, ambassadorial role. He is heavily involved in the Middle East Peace Treaty.'

Her eyebrows arch up nearly touching her hairline.

'As it turns out, he is related to the royal family.'

She is aghast! Her shocked expression says it all. 'How related?'

'Well, quite related I think.'

'You think? You must know!'

'Well.' I pause, thinking I must get this right.

When Mojat told me all about his royal connections and, in particular his brother's seedy life and illnesses, I was in a hazy state of shock. He wouldn't have seen this in me though as I cover up well!

His eldest brother comes into my mind. Mojat told me in confidence that Omani is always in scrapes of one sort or another and is often reported back in the UK's *News of the World* but never, never in the local *Gulf News*. So I speak up, choosing my words extremely carefully.

'Yes, Sam, I am thinking.'

'What is there to think about Janey? You know or you don't know. Spit it out girl!'

Shall I mention to her that his oldest brother is Sheikh Omani? No, not now. I notice Sam's eyebrows rise again.

'Come on, who is your Mr. M?'

'His friends call him Mojat, but his family name is Bin Al Mohini something? I can't remember his last name. It was long, something beginning with S I think?'

'Is he Haitham Rashid?'

'Yes that's right.'

'For fuck's sake Janey, that means our ruling Sheikh Shaheed Ira is your guy's nephew. Or, to put it another way, your Mr. M is the uncle to our Sheikh.'

'Yes, he is.'

After initially choking on her tea, Sam then looks at me and says, 'Omani is his brother?'

'I'm afraid so.'

I then speak in a way that defends my man. 'Mojat is a humble man, not like his elder brother Omani, or Jimi as he's known to his friends from his university days in the UK.'

Sam looks shocked. 'Jimmy?'

'Yes Sam, but spelt J-I-M-I, as in Jimi Hendrix. Anyway Omani is another story, shame they're brothers!'

Tea arrives and I pour myself a cup. I help myself to one of her chocolates from a designer box laid out on her desk.

When I mentioned Omani, Sam shrugged her shoulders and pulled a pained facial expression. She now leans towards my face and picks out two chocolates. Before she stuffs them in her mouth she stops to look directly at me.

'Of course Janey, just between you and me that brother of his …' She hesitates for a moment. 'Is a devious, womanising, arrogant shit!'

'Between you and I Sam, I believe this to be true.'

'Janey, a word of advice; stay clear of him. He is evil! Don't let his good looks and charm fool you. He is a sheep in wolves clothing!'

I enjoy the tea and another chocolate whilst I think to myself. Fuck, she knows something! A secret insight into Jimi's ways perhaps? But this is not the time to discuss Jimi. I think many good-looking women in Jubai will have succumbed and had dealings with this man. For sure he has looks, power, influence and the big one; stacks of money!

'Your Mr. M, or Mojat as we now know him to be …'

I wait for Sam to finish her sentence. Her voice is now taking on a more understanding tone. She walks quickly around to my side of the desk and looks out through the office door window. She then opens the door and looks around the outside office before immediately shutting it again. Then she opens her drawer and takes out a small bottle of single malt whisky and pours a large measure in each of our cups.

'Just in case anyone is hovering around Janey.' She puts her hand on my shoulder as she walks past me and gives it a firm squeeze. 'Jesus Janey you're quite a woman. How on earth did you meet our Mr. Mojat, the foreign minister? How did you pull this one off? You're something else — you really are something else!'

I then tell her everything: Where we met, how we got together and his long infatuation with me. Also Mojat's Cambridge education — which gave us both common ground. Not, of course, in an educational way, but English life and humour. For example there were shared memories of the pop scene at the time and the swinging sixties. And the last, but most important thing, that romance is in the air. I tell her of our sailing weekend and our mutual love of the sea.

'Yes Sam, I think he is falling in love with me.'

'And you chick, are you falling for him?'

'All I know is, there is something very powerful going on inside me.'

'Chick, you're well and truly in the Arabic world now.'

Restlessly she stands up again and walks around the office, then sits back on her chair, twitching and fidgeting.

She then changes her expression and her facial persona turns to stone. Cold bloody stone! She is speechless, concentrating hard on what to say next. She then picks up the phone and asks the tea boy for two strong fresh Arabic coffees.

Her eyes suddenly enlarge popping out of her head in disbelief, like an anorexic toad. And her voice takes on a gruff excitable whispering pitch, as though she has seen the light.

'Janey, I knew it! I knew something was strange a couple of months ago.'

'What do you mean, strange?'

'A government official turned up without an appointment one day asking to see Lindsay and the head of HR. He said he needed to confirm your passport details and your previous address in the

UK. When the official saw Lindsay's alarmed look, he advised her that there was no need for concern as this was just a routine residence check. When Lindsay walked into my office afterwards she was flabbergasted. She told me that in all the years she'd owned Arabian Homes Investments, this had never happened before! Of course, Lindsay wanted to know if everything was okay with you and whether I knew of anything different in your personal life? Or anything other than your work?'

I dwell on her words.

The Indian tea boy knocks on the door and enters with a stainless steel tray sporting teak handles. The staff nicknamed him 'Indian Prince' after the 1950s tea merchant. The tray has a small white linen cloth with lace on the edges. On top are two large Italian white porcelain cups and saucers, plus a cream jug and a bowl of brown sugar. There is a matching coffee pot. He smiles displaying his sordid yellowing teeth. 'Anything else ma'am?'

'It's okay Prince, thank you.'

He very quietly leaves her office.

'Sam, can't the company pay for a dentist for Prince?'

She looks up. 'I will mention your suggestion at the next general meeting, but I fear his teeth have gone too far for any treatment?'

Sam excitably carries on our conversation. 'Janey Green you are a dark horse! The morning I walked into your office and it was like a florists I did begin to put two and two together. I said to you before, those flowers in this country are worth a stack. I knew then you were seeing someone well connected, but I never considered the frigging foreign minister! Or even better, royalty!'

Sam pulls out her filing cabinet drawer and removes a box of chocolate-covered figs. She then pours another shot of whisky into our coffee cups. She looks at her watch and comments that it's just past five o'clock. Most of the staff are leaving and Sam proceeds to hide away the spirit bottle.

We sip our coffee and chat. She then drops a bomb on me!

'Chick, I have to say you're not going to last long here. You know this don't you?'

'Sam, what do you mean?' I feel flushed, hot and suddenly very het up and nervous. All my insecurities flood back from a previous life. 'I love my job. It's the best job I've ever had and I'm so happy here!'

She stares at me and in a harsher tone says. 'Come on Janey, get a grip. Think about it!'

I swig the last dregs of coffee from the bottom of the cup, which brings tears to my eyes, as it's more whisky than coffee. I look back at her, waiting for a response. She takes her time as if she feels the need to tread more carefully, as she can plainly see I'm hot, flustered and upset.

'There is no getting away from it, you're living on a time bomb!'

'What time bomb?' I suddenly feel sick in the pit of my stomach.

'He knows, your guy, how it works here in the United Arab Kingdom.' She takes my hand firmly. 'Now listen carefully to me Janey. It's important you understand how it works here too.'

I nod and she carries on.

'Mojat, has taken his time, fully checking you out first. When all was good he stepped up to the mark, to woo you and, of course, he can't run the risk of losing you. That's why he has not created any sense of urgency yet!'

'Urgency?' I ask.

'Yes chick, he has made it clear how much he wants you, so you know ... gently, gently!'

I finish my chocolate date, sitting listening and watching Sam torturously explaining the so-called 'plot' in her head.

'It sounds to me that he's made it very obvious he wants you by his side and has proclaimed his feelings.'

Still nodding my head, I wait for more.

'His status means that things have to move quickly Janey, mainly for security reasons.'

Singing in Silence

'Sam, I have been naïve, it just hadn't occurred to me why he was so forward. He said he had been watching me for months.'

Sam refills our cups with another large measure of whisky. 'There you go girl.' She pours the rest of the coffee. 'Janey, once he'd received the okay from the officials, that's when he made the play for you.'

'Yes, I know all this.' I am beginning to feel a little irritated. 'You have just repeated yourself Sam!' My voice is beginning to break up a little now. 'Think about it, how would I have known anything? My friends confirmed to me that he owned the sailing club — just a businessman they said! A real gentleman they said! That's what they all believe at the club.'

'Of course yes,' says Sam nodding in agreement. 'Of course. Chick I have lived here for over ten years and I know the Arabs. Once they set their eyes on a woman they want, that's it! Your guy has huge status within the royal family and you can't mess him around. If he has fallen for you and is free, as in divorced, then you will be secure for the rest of your life. Shit Janey, what an amazing opportunity! Forget your freedom though!'

Her last four words reverberate in my head. Alarm bells are ringing and the word freedom for me is like a red rag to a bull. Freedom is getting louder and louder in my head, over and over again … freedom, freedom.

I'm becoming dizzy and disorientated and start to feel slightly giddy. Maybe my blood sugars are dropping sharply? I'm shaky and my vision is blurring. Sam's voice is fading and her face melts into the distance. I'm fainting ... then nothing ...

'Janey! Janey! Are you okay? Can you hear me Janey?'

I come around to Sam slapping my face and Lindsay, the big boss, bending over me. I can smell the salts right under my nose — such a putrid odour!

Lindsay's office suite is next door. She heard Sam's raised and panicky voice and came rushing in.

'Honey you're as white as a sheet,' she says in her Canadian accent. 'What happened?'

Sam has her arms around me. 'She is in shock. I think I pushed her over the edge.'

'I am not surprised she's in shock,' says Lindsay in a raised voice. 'Now, come on honey, you're going to be just fine. You have nothing to worry about; you're a very lucky lady.'

I look up and smile with relief.

'You fainted honey. You gave Sam and I a shock too. Come and see me tomorrow morning at nine. Please don't worry about anything; you are gonna be all right honey.'

Lindsay's final words are comforting.

After several minutes, I compose myself. I take my compact from my handbag, open it and look at my pale face. I look terrible. I remove a tissue from the box and wipe my eyes.

'Sam,' I say, still shaking. 'It was when you said forget my freedom that my whole past life stood in front of me. How hard I have worked to find a place of independence and now, well, I don't know! It's been so hard to start a new life post Wisteria House. Only you know my story Sam. The truth! Only you!'

Sam knows all about my pain, the separation and divorce from Geoffrey. My independence and the money that I now earn helps to bring my children here to visit. It's their only holiday.

All my guilty feelings regarding leaving my family behind to start a new life come to the surface. The independent life I now enjoy has not come about easily and when she spoke about the potential loss of freedom, it just tipped me right over the edge.

Sam is a woman after my own heart, we are survivors in life and share secrets from our past that have tormented us both. Secrets of survival and pain, which has given us common ground. We've confided in our struggles and have wept together. It's all confidential and will remain so.

CHAPTER TWELVE

The Burning Bush

Lola is one of my *Sex and the City* girlfriends and also a sales agent from my office. She has received some good news on the phone, which she wants to celebrate. With Lola I have to really concentrate to understand her broken Brazilian/English accent, especially after she's had a drink.

She arrives at my place early and rings the doorbell. I answer standing in the doorway, a huge towel wrapped around my body.

'You're earlier than I expected Lola!'

She looks flustered and rushed. 'Yes I know, but we have some interesting news.'

She walks in dressed in a full evening gown holding a large Louis Vuitton carry bag.

'Lola, who is we?' I ask inquisitively. I'm half expecting her lover, the designer tennis coach, to be following behind carrying a few more of his designer bags. I stand half-naked clasping my towel straining my head around the doorway to peer down the corridor, thinking someone else is behind her.

'Ducks you have to put on your bestest dress now Janey. Hurry up!'

Lola is fun. She lives up to her 'showgirl' name. Since our first meeting I have laughed more with her than anyone else in the past year. She is full of drama and nervous excitement.

Lola speaks to me whilst lifting a handmade card from her Chanel handbag. 'Look, we've had a personal invi … vi … a personal paper to my friend's club.'

'You mean an invitation Lola.'

I smile at the way she mixes her words around.

Lola looks classy and stunning, wearing a lovely black evening dress to the floor with shoestring straps decorated in delicate silver flowers. She has an elegant cream shawl around her shoulders and matching silver bag and heels. Her long dark brown hair shines heavy and straight, almost touching her waist.

I stand with my towel around me wondering what on earth I'm going to wear that would match Lola's standards. I left Yorkshire having only attended a ball once in my life. God only knows what happened to that ballgown?

She sits down and opens her powder compact to check her lips. Every two-seconds she glances up at me, still in conversation. She re-coats her lips with a bright fuchsia pink gloss, at the same time watching me dry myself off.

She shouts loudly at me as I walk into the bathroom. 'My God ducky, what is that bush?'

I stand looking at my face in the bathroom mirror, holding my mascara rigidly, not daring to move. I have to think for a moment as I go about applying my first coat of Maybelline's long lash. I shout back to her. 'What bush?'

Where the hell outside in this desert city is a bush? Moses and the burning bush springs to mind for some silly reason.

The next minute she's standing at the side of me looking down in a disapproving way at my pubic hair. Then she gives it a light tug with her long polished manicured fingernails. 'This bloody bush ducks.' She looks horrified. 'Ducky this has to go!'

'Does it, why?'

'My Godfathers, you English women and your bushes. Always want to hold on to your bushes! I will take you tomorrow to my special lady in beauty parlour, where all Arab ladies go. Here in Jubai and Brazil ducky, no one has bushes or any hair other than on their head, and it is, oh … so much lovely pleasure. Very pleasurable with my special lady. She has good touch, you see — very fresh feeling!'

What on earth is Lola talking about? Through all her jumble of words, I can't imagine for one moment how removing years of thick pubic hair can be remotely pleasurable. Yes, of course, I am sure after removing it all you might feel fresher afterwards. Lola is so amusing.

'Now Janey, what will we wear?'

'Lola I hope you don't mind, but I need to help you with your English. You say what will *you* wear tonight, not we.'

Very flustered, she says: 'Yes not we, but you … I am dressed already see!' She points to her beautiful gown. 'And you need dressing still. Anyway my darling, I have something just perfect.'

I resign myself to her pidgin English. 'Okay Lola, sounds good to me.'

She lifts a midnight blue Crêpe de Chine ballgown out of her designer carrier bag. 'This will fit you English curvy shape. I bought this when I was pregnant.'

'That's nice,' I say smiling. 'A pregnancy dress! Seriously though Lola, I can see it is a beautiful ballgown.'

I hold the dress and the fabric is exquisite. I check the size on the label half expecting it to read just for English women with hips, boobs, a bum and oh yes, of course, a bush!

I smile as I slip it over my head. To my surprise, it's a good fit and I locate a pair of strappy cream heels from my daughter's wedding last year. Lola provides the evening bag to match. I wrap a pashmina around my shoulders and we head off to her friend's club, 'by invitation only'.

CHAPTER THIRTEEN

When In Rome

The following afternoon Lola drives me to her beauty parlour, as she calls it. The salon is situated at the other end of Jubai where all the local, not so well off Arabs, live and shop and run their daily lives. The more affluent people in Jubai call it, 'The Other Side of Town.'

We park outside a double-fronted salon called, 'Beautiful Ladies' and, on entry, we're immediately greeted by several Filipino women.

'Hi Lola, hi ma'am,' they say.

As they all begin to fuss around us I think to myself, Lola obviously tips well.

It's a very large beauty and hairdressing salon that's extremely busy; every chair seems to be taken. There are at least twenty hairstylists cutting and dressing women's hair; the noise from the dryers is loud to almost deafening.

I look around and notice that the clientele is mainly local ladies with just a handful of Europeans and Indians. At the back of the salon is the beauty area. As you walk through an archway there are a line of cubicles to one side and, on the other, are several luxurious large leather couches that recline for pedicures and manicures. These are all occupied.

'Very busy place Lola,' I say.

I meet Frances, Lola's beauty therapist. She nods her head, looks at me and smiles. Lola begins to give her instructions on what she needs to do to me.

'Frances, ducky, I want you to give my friend Janey a *very special*

Brazilian.'

'Okay ma'am, yes, *very special*.'

I chip in. 'Why the emphasis on *very special*?'

'Ducky, you will feel so much better once your bush has gone.' She speaks as though this has caused me such pain and discomfort during my life.

'Frances, ducks, just one more thing. It's her first time!'

'Very well madam.'

Lola leaves to have her hair washed and styled.

'Miss Janey, please follow me.'

I am led into the end cubicle. She closes and locks the flimsy hardboard door behind her. I can hear all the background noise of hairdryers and conversations in Arabic, Indian and, of course, the banter between the Filipino beauty therapists conversing whilst they groom and massage their clients in a slow methodical way. Every type of cheap perfume smell is floating around from the array of hair and beauty products.

Frances switches on the machine to heat up the wax, then begins to tear off white cotton strips from a large cloth, adding them to a pile that is ready on one side. 'Are you sensitive ma'am to essential oils?' she asks.

I confirm to her that I have no allergies or skin problems. A clean white towelling robe neatly folded is placed on the massage couch. She then leaves me for a few minutes whilst I undress and then informs me that she's going to mix her oils after her diagnostic techniques on my skin type. I feel apprehensive, but resigned to the situation. 'When in Rome,' I think to myself.

Frances I would say is in her late thirties. She wears a white uniform dress and her black long hair is secured back with a large tortoiseshell slide. I am almost relieved to be lying on the couch as I'm feeling tired after a late night of dancing. Frances enters the cubicle and secures the lock.

'Madam Janey, I want you to relax and enjoy.'

I nod at this point and just want the pain over with. I almost want to ask for an anaesthetic!

The cubicle is small and clean. I remove my robe and she covers me with two heavy warmed towels, one for my top and the other covering my waist down to my knees. The wax is ready to go, as the machine clicks off.

She lifts my hair away from my face and fastens it behind a hair band. Then she wipes my face and neck in methodical upward strokes with steamed pieces of cloth.

'This ma'am helps to relax you.'

I feel like saying, just give me an anaesthetic now and wake me up when I'm hairless. But actually, this facial cleansing is working a treat. I soon enjoy being cleansed and am now entering a meditative state.

The waxing procedure starts. She removes the bottom towel and lifts white flannels out from a steamer she has next to her. Gently she opens each cloth and presses firmly on my pubic bone. She then releases it and presses again rotating all over my pubic area, my inner thighs and right up to my tummy button. This feels incredible, as I love heat applications. She repeats this a few times, paying special attention to my more sensitive areas. I close my eyes thinking this feels wonderful, the scent of lavender and a faint fragrance of tea tree oil seem very therapeutic and cleansing.

'Ma'am this opens all your pores and makes your hairs release very easily.' As she speaks to me she is smiling all the time.

I then chill out and shut my eyes, not yet knowing what the full impact will be. She lifts my right leg first and puts it over her shoulder, leaving me wide open and exposed; thank God she locked the bloody door! She proceeds to put the warm wax over my hairs with a large spatula, then presses a dry strip of cloth very firmly over the wax area, ripping it off in a flash.

'Jesus Christ!' I proclaim noisily.

I can hardly contain myself, the rip comes and the pain follows one-second later. The next strip is firmly lined up and the ripping process starts again. It's all done at quick speed with no time to

Singing in Silence

scream out and demand that she stops. She works quickly, sticking on the wax and, within a jiffy, ripping off the strip. She repeats this with precision, just taking very small areas at a time. It makes me shudder at first but she assures me it's less painful doing it this way. I have to say the pain diminishes as I somehow get used to the process. After the first dozen strips are quickly removed the shock soon disappears. I am okay!

She repeats this procedure for around fifteen to twenty minutes. Then she gets a little more intimate. My knees are now bent, feet on bed and legs wide open. Now she has to remove the hairs from my vulva, clitoris area and outer lips. This takes real skill as she lifts and moves my outer lips around in a gentle way, teasing out every last hair.

'Ma'am just checking, are you good, okay ma'am?'

I reply affirmatively as I am now drifting off.

The background noises are fading, as I am so relaxed. I have never had anyone touch me in this way as part of a beauty treatment.

Frances then pours a few drops of warm oil on to my pubic bone and gently massages all around my cunny in circular movements. She lifts my legs again in turn placing them on her shoulder and massages down my thighs, pressing harder all around my groin area. She tells me these are pressure points used in the Philippines for pleasure.

I am beginning to realise this as her smooth hands and fingertips finally massage in circular movements again on to my outer lips, paying special attention both to this area and also my vulva. It's an amazing feeling having this special Brazilian. A few more drops of oil are added on to my tummy and she smoothes this down to my cunny again, but with a more unusual movement. I say unusual as she is now gently rubbing and plucking away at my clitoris, over and over. Her other hand also massages at the same time from my anus up to my inner and outer lips. God, it's ecstasy!

I open my eyes to see her concentrating and working hard on me.

'Is it a good feeling ma'am? You enjoy?'

I can hardly get my words out. 'Yes, amazing Frances.'

'Good ma'am, I need to make you feel fresh.'

I am not sure what her 'fresh' really means but I am now beginning to get the idea. Her slim fingers are circulating, firmly pressing and massaging my clitoris and her final touches then pleasure me. I reach a special Brazilian moment.

She looks at me, and says, 'Now you feeling fresh ma'am?'

I've never experienced anything like this before, well not from a woman anyway!

'Yes, very fresh feeling.'

I feel myself pulsing deep inside. She moves her hands and fingers for a little while longer in and around my wet outer lips to prolong the 'fresh feeling', then covers me up again with warm towels. She washes her hands in the corner sink and looks at me.

'I will leave you now ma'am' to relax for ten minutes and dress. No hurry, just take your time.'

She leaves me and I lay drifting in a trance, trying to get my head around this special waxing process. I really had no idea what was going to take place in this little cubicle and that is the truth!

She returns with a bill for me to give the receptionist for my waxing. On it she has written 'Brazilian bikini wax' 70 dirhams. I pay the girls on reception and leave Frances a tip, then sit and wait for Lola to return.

A young Indian girl brings me a cup of tea whilst I read a riveting glossy magazine of real news, which informs on what's happening in the world of glamour and celebrities. Peering up occasionally from my page I think about my new enlightenment. Is this what they refer to as fresh? Or is it a 'Special Brazilian?'

Lola is now standing next to me, looking just as gorgeous as the women in the 'Who's Who' magazine I am reading. I compliment her on her hair and she touches and flicks a few strands around, then double checks it once again in one of the empty mirrors.

'My stylist is good isn't she?'

'Yes, she has done a great job Lola.'

She pays the receptionist and we leave the salon and head for her car, which is parked outside. She turns the ignition on and looks at me.

'Did you enjoy your Brazilian?'

'Yes I did, not quite what I expected.'

'Yes ducks, Frances gives the best treatment. It's an amazing fresh feeling with her.'

I am now inquisitive to know a little more. 'Have you tried Brazilian waxing with some of the other beauty therapists?' I'm thinking maybe it's only Frances who obliges Lola, she being from Brazil and all.

'Oh yes ducky, many. But I find her to have the best touch by far. You are clean now?'

'Well yes,' I say. 'Not one hair left. Very clean!' I start laughing, thinking about my bizarre experience. This waxing technique will stay with me for a long time.

'Ducks it was my local Arab friend, Mona, that introduced me to this. The women here remove all their body hair at least every ten days.'

'And this is good business?'

She looks at me as if to say, are you stupid or something? 'Of course very big business here, especially if they don't have their own personal maid!'

'A personal maid?'

'Of course,' she says.

Maybe this has some significance, but I do not pursue it. I've had enough to take in on my day off.

I spend the rest of my day with a different perspective of life for women!

CHAPTER FOURTEEN

The Star of Hope

Over the next few days our relationship grows deeper and deeper. He wines and dines me and, like a true gentleman, always drops me off at my apartment late at night in one of his chauffeur-driven cars, which are mainly Bentleys.

It's Saturday evening and I'm dressing for dinner. It feels very special tonight, as this is the first time we are to dine at his home on the outskirts of the city. I have no idea what to expect. Kulpreet, his driver, is picking me up in half an hour.

Mojat has informed me that he is travelling tomorrow for four nights, visiting Iran and some other Arab countries. I feel that he wants to show me his life from another angle, other than sailing and a few exclusive select restaurants we have dined in since returning from Muscat.

I finish arranging my hair and have pinned it back off my face. My eyebrows have been tinted and I have a more natural look tonight. I brush my lips with a light pink gloss and slip on a floaty dress and strappy low-heeled sandals. I do my usual check myself in the full-length mirror routine, then make my way downstairs to the foyer. I only have to wait a few minutes before Kulpreet arrives driving another car. It is a pristine white newer-looking Bentley. Why should I be surprised?

He opens the door for me and I get myself comfortable in the back. The car pulls away.

'What happened to the other car Kulpreet?'

'Miss Janey it has gone in for a service and repair.'

He makes polite conversation for the first ten minutes of the

Singing in Silence

journey, then there is silence as we pass through the main part of the city. He has to concentrate harder as the traffic gets busier with five lanes of crazy drivers weaving in and out of the other cars. There appears to be no respect on these roads.

We follow the signs inland towards Fujairah as though we're heading towards the desert, passing places en route where tourists would never go. These areas are where the less well-off and poorer locals live. There are villages, but not like any we have in England. Small collections of run down off-white villas of various sizes, some quite decrepit, with just a few solitary Arabic grocers placed in-between. Many families are sitting outside on old settees and odd wooden chairs. Neighbours share makeshift seats, basically old boxes, with cushions placed on top. A few men smoke sheesha pipes. The odd dog and cat mooch around. Children kick a football on the rubble verges, then all stop and wave at us in awe of the car. The tourist would not be interested in this side of Jubai.

I smile in amusement as we drive past a grocer, sitting outside his tiny shop amongst his aluminium pots and pans on a well-worn sage green velveteen armchair. He is watching a portable TV that has been precariously wired up to the open mains above his shop, almost hanging by a thread! Highly dangerous I would have thought.

After another ten minutes we pass a few larger, more established villas set in good-sized gardens. On the roadsides are tall palm trees. Shortly we turn off the main Fujairah road into an opening of large galvanised steel electronic gates — it's the start of Mojat's driveway! It looks leafy and tropical. Unbelievable — he has his own oasis!

The gates automatically close behind us as we embark on a long sweeping drive. Tropical bushes, plants and long grasses spread back into his garden, which lays out a carpet of vibrant colours. Tall green lush palm trees line each side of the driveway. Bright red, fluorescent pink and orange flowering bushes, typical of this part of the world, sit amongst other beds of smaller delicate flowers.

Kulpreet eases off the accelerator almost down to a crawl, as there are peacocks wandering on the lawns and across the driveway. He is annoyed and mutters something under his breath in Hindi. I have never heard him do this before.

I am astonished! Mojat has managed to grow an emerald lawn, the first I have seen since leaving the UK.

His house eventually comes into view. In front of me is a very large white circular villa on two levels with water fountains in front. This is a precious commodity in Jubai; only the richest people can afford such ornate displays of water.

The car stops outside the grand entrance. A large heavy turquoise and gold Arabic wooden door sits behind a set of four large Egyptian-style marble pillars, on the side of which is a small engraved plaque. The old door opens gently and Mojat walks through towards the car. I am overwhelmed as I stand outside surveying the scene. The noise of so many peacocks distract until Mojat wraps his arms around me and kisses my cheek.

'Hello my dear. Welcome to my home Janey.'

I walk towards the gold-inscribed plaque, written in Arabic. Mojat translates. 'To my dear friend Mojat from Mohamed Al-Fayed, Egypt 1988. He had the marble pillars made for me as a present.'

'What a lovely gift.'

'Yes my dear, another story for you one day about my friend Mohamed.'

I soon realise Kulpreet is not just a driver, he is his manservant too. There is also a male cook and a few gardeners who all reside in small houses within the grounds. The peacocks are large and noisy; I am not sure how I feel about them? Why does he have them? I love birds, but have always thought peacocks to be somewhat strange.

We walk through the entrance into a large hallway with an open staircase leading off the centre of the hall. It is a contemporary arrangement inside; not what I expected. There is an ultra-modern chrome and glass table with a large exquisite display of scented flowers.

Mojat shows me around the hallway; it is more like a gallery. In a clockwise direction he leads me around. The walls are decorated with large framed photographs of presidents, royalty and other foreign dignitaries. The photos are of him from the late 1960s up to quite recently, shaking hands, or walking on red carpets with important men and women at his side.

One magnificently framed photograph in a prominent position in his hallway draws me in. The picture is of a red carpet leading out of a plane with him and President Hrawi of Lebanon embracing each other.

'Now I can see what kind of a life you have been leading,' I say.

'Yes, I am a fortunate man.'

His thirty something years of working closely with the sheikhs and presidents in the Middle East have mounted up to at least a hundred pictures, all in contemporary frames placed throughout the house. His large circular hallway is more like a gallery of humanitarian peace work.

'Janey, my work is now winding down and I look forward to the next instalment of my life. A new adventure!'

I am looking all around me. It's such an unusual hallway, and it's a mixture of old Middle Eastern with contemporary furnishings.

'It's very impressive and I can view you throughout the different stages of your life, so interesting,' I say, as I study each picture with interest.

There is one photograph that I feel more drawn to of Mojat. In it he has long black hair and a moustache and is pictured in an informal setting on a racetrack. It looks like the 1970s and Mojat leans against a Formula One car with his arms around World Champion driver, James Hunt.

'Whoa, amazing photo, I love it!'

He smiles. 'I have very fond memories of James, we were such good friends.'

'He was a good-looking man Mojat.'

'Yes, I have been blessed to have known him.'

We walk around the ground floor. Off of the hallway are many rooms. We enter the lounge and sit down. I expect the decor to be very decadent and palatial, with gold here and there but, to my surprise, it's all very modern. There are marble floors, large modern sofas and quality Persian rugs, exquisite lighting by a German designer and, overall, quite minimal.

Kulpreet serves us our gin and tonic with the usual slices of lime. I walk around his lounge holding my glass, admiring pieces of modern artwork.

Mojat's thoughts:
Her rose complexion captivates me, she does not realise her own beauty. I cannot stop looking at her. She is the sexiest woman I have ever met. I want her so much.

'Mojat you are staring at me.'

'Yes I am, you know what affect you have on me. Janey … Janey my dear … come and sit next to me.'

I walk over. He looks edgy and excited as he begins talking to me. He moves closer, putting his arms around me and gives me one of his familiar heavenly long drawn-out kisses. He pulls away from my face and touches my lips with his forefinger.

'Beautiful full pink lips that match your wonderful pink nipples.'

I flush.

We kiss and hold each other, I sense that he is aroused. His stare is intense and there is a silence as we look at each other. He moves his hands throughout my hair, lifting pieces up, fingering the texture and letting it fall again. Whilst doing this our conversation becomes more intimate.

'Habibie, there is so much I want to say to you.' He pauses for a few seconds. 'I love you Janey — I love you so much. When we are apart I cannot sleep. I'm restless desiring you next to me.'

Mojat's eyes are glazed, shiny and full.

At this very moment, I'm flying high like a bird. He's said the words, the most important words. Overwhelmed I say. 'I believe I love you too.'

He pulls me close. 'I have been waiting to hear this, patiently waiting to hear that you love me.'

I raise my voice slightly. 'I do, I love you Mojat.'

I feel his heart pounding; he looks into my eyes again as we embrace. He squeezes me hard, whispering so very excitably. 'Habibie don't move, stay where you are, don't move.'

'Okay, I won't move an inch! I promise, I won't move,' I say whilst giggling.

He stands up and walks towards a writing table in the corner of the room. He pulls out a drawer and lifts out a small dark blue box. Intensely I watch him grinning as he walks back to me.

'I do hope habibie that you like my choice.'

He has never said this before when he has given me a gift. Mojat perches himself on the edge of the sofa at my side. He kisses my forehead, then wipes his eyes with a linen handkerchief.

I have not moved, still sitting in anticipation. Mojat lifts up his white dishdasha dress and kneels down on one knee in front of me. He carefully opens the box and inside, on a white satin bed, is a large pear-shaped ruby ring surrounded by the whitest diamonds. He lifts it out and places it on my engagement finger.

'Janey, will you do me the honour, will you marry me?'

Without hesitation I reply. 'I would love to marry you.'

We kiss and embrace each other; he then lifts my hand just as he did when we first met in the club and kisses it but, on this occasion, many many times. I hold out my left hand in amazement at this stunning ruby.

He then asks me a question as though he needs some sort of

reassurance. 'Have I made the right choice, as rubies represent the eternal love?'

'It's perfect, what a surprise, I am blown away.'

He holds his head to one side, 'I know it's only been a few weeks but I am sure, very sure.'

'I never expected a proposal of marriage tonight. I am amazed!'

'Janey, you know in this country, we don't live together.'

'Yes I realise that,' I say, holding my hand out, still admiring my beautiful ring.

'I need and want you in my life now. The first time I saw you it was powerful and I was conscious then that I wanted to marry you. I have been waiting, waiting for you to feel the love that I felt for you.'

'You have not wasted any time Mojat. I really do love your choice of ring, it's stunning! I realised my love for you after last weekend, when we'd returned from Muscat. I cried to Sam, my boss.'

'Janey I know Lindsay the owner of your company. I called her on Sunday morning to advise that we're seeing each other and that I'm very serious about you.'

I had a flashback to Sam's office and when I came round from fainting. Lindsay's Canadian accent was very reassuring when she said, 'Honey you are in good hands.' At the time I was not quite sure what she meant. So Mojat had called her in the morning and I'd subsequently had my meeting with Sam. Now it was all fitting into place.

Mojat looks at me from head to toe. 'Habibie, how are you feeling now that we're engaged to be married?'

'I am deliriously happy.' I look down at my pear-shaped ruby, the size of a red wine gum. It is surrounded by the purest, brightest diamonds.

I start to cry ... my heart is an open chalice. Pure love flows out like a carpet of shining light covering the desert sands. He is offering me his hand in marriage. It's a hand that appears from the clouds. A divine gift, this time bearing a jewel-encrusted ring to form a loving union.

He has never seen me cry like this. At first he looks concerned, then he begins to laugh. 'It's good to know I have this effect on you too, it is usually me that turns on the waterworks.'

'I have to admit you are a very emotional man. Please take this as a compliment — you are in touch with your feminine side and I like that.'

'Janey, Arab men are indeed emotional. We feel deeply and are not afraid to show it.' He holds out his hand for me as I stand up. 'Dinner is served.'

We walk to his dining room, he gives me his handkerchief and I gently wipe away my tears.

I am floating with the angels on a cloud throughout dinner. We briefly embrace, showing our love for each other. Beside us is a table laden with fine food and wine. I look around me at the opulent surroundings and sense a mutual feeling of emotional nourishment and sensual satisfaction.

He pours me a glass of champagne and proposes a toast. 'To our future happiness; to us Janey.'

I raise my glass. 'Yes, to us.'

'Now on a more serious note my dear, I travel to Iran tomorrow for four days. On my return, I will take you to meet Saheed Ira if he is in town. I will call Lindsay before your meeting and explain that we are now engaged and that this must be kept highly confidential for your own security.'

On hearing the word security, I have a sudden vivid memory of the false door and his collection of guns on the yacht. Now, however, is not the time to broach the subject.

I listen intensely as he makes a plan, whilst I enjoy the food his chef has prepared for us both. Dinner consists of chicken and almonds in a wonderful sauce, with vegetables and rice on the side. I sip my champagne.

'Habibie, you will have to keep our secret for just a few more nights.'

'Umm, yes,' I say. 'I will be singing in silence.'

'You will have to my dear. Of course, I am not promising to keep calm and act normal myself. How can I? It's the first time in my life that I have ever proposed to anyone.'

'What about your first wife?'

'No, Janey, that was arranged.'

'Did you ever propose to Gretal?'

'No, we never even got engaged.'

'So are you really saying to me at your time of life, I am the first?'

'Yes and I feel so amazingly happy, ecstatic in fact!'

On hearing this I feel like singing and dancing with the angels. At this moment I have quite forgotten what normal feels like!

'I am so pleased I am making you happy. Janey, I have to prepare many changes for you. Once I have confirmed our engagement to the Sheikh, it will then be made public by announcement. You will have to move from your apartment before it is formally announced. I will find you a suitable place to live so you can be protected until we marry.'

'Why will I need protection?'

'Janey, are you kidding me? You are now my fiancée and very soon to be my wife, I cannot risk anything happening to you.'

I look and listen to him as he struts proudly around the dining table, holding his glass of champagne high in the air. He takes the occasional sip in-between his verbal diarrhoea. He is as excitable as a puppy dog, trying to organise our lives. I sit at the table smiling and laughing — we are both on an emotional high.

He stands at the opposite end of the large table to me, in front of his French doors and tops up his glass. 'I want to tell you a true story.'

I have never seen him so tipsy. 'Go on then, I am all ears and waiting — tell me a true story!'

He walks over and tops up my glass again, still strutting around like one of his male peacocks!

'Can you remember on our first date a few weeks ago, I mentioned to you that I knew you were the one for me? I told you that I'd had a sign.'

'Yes I do, you never said what it was.'

'Just before we met I was walking around my garden one night feeling quite low. Well, actually, very low! I felt spiritually dry, starved of love and not in a good place. Even the peacocks looked at me curiously, watching my every move. I had been doing some soul searching and had all but given up of ever falling in love again.'

He sips more of his drink still positioned at the end of his grand table.

'I was standing in the middle of the lawn and it was pitch black, the night was crystal clear and I was stargazing. They looked amazing. Suddenly, as I peered skyward, a shooting star flashed into the atmosphere and landed in the lake behind my house.'

'You have a lake? In this desert?'

He nods and carries on talking. 'For a split second this star lit up the house, the lake and all of the surrounding grounds. It was dazzling! So bright, in fact, that it hurt my eyes. The star Janey has always been a spiritual emblem of hope and promise and, of course, guidance. In the Old Testament it is seen as a light to steer by. If we lose hope we lose the point in life. You have probably gathered by now Janey that I am not a religious man at all, but on this night I felt a presence from this star and a sense of purpose for my life returned. It was a sign and, after this, I felt a renewal of my life's force. Previously I had been so low, almost, dare I say, depressed.'

I am waiting for the next instalment, as he sips a little more from his glass. I am giddy from the drink and giddy from the excitement.

'Then what happened? Come on tell me?'

'The next day was a Friday. Kulpreet took me to the club for lunch and there was a lady there I had not seen before. My heart stopped beating and I could not take my eyes off her. I asked around, as I wanted to know her identity. I was told that this lady is Janey Green.'

I laugh. 'Was she hot this lady?'

'Oh yes my dear, blew my mind away. She was a classic English rose.'

We laugh together as the fizzy bubbles get the better of us.

'Seriously, Mojat, what an amazing story.'

He unlocks and pushes open the French doors to his garden, the noise of which startles his peacocks. We walk around the grounds holding hands and looking up to the stars.

CHAPTER FIFTEEN

A Wise Woman's Words

It's hard to keep a secret, when you are singing in silence from the rooftops. There is nothing quite as powerful as your inner voice. The feeling of falling in love that encapsulates every minute of every hour and every hour of every day. It's frustrating that I can't share this feeling with the world just yet.

I drive my car to work with thoughts of me as Maria Von Trapp, running through the Bavarian hills bursting with happiness, singing for the love she feels in her heart: 'The hills are alive with the sound of music.'

I arrive at Lindsay's office promptly at 9am. She has natural warmth and a calm energy that comes from the wisdom and experience that age brings to you. I admire her professional approach to business. Her company is sponsored by important Arab businessmen who are often in her office for meetings. She has brought up her own children here and now they are in their late thirties, enjoying their mother's fruits and that is fine.

'Well honey — congratulations on your wonderful news. I have spoken with Mojat earlier. I've known him for such a long time, though not as a close friend. Our paths have crossed so many times at business functions and parties over the years.'

'That's good to hear,' I say.

'Janey you will know about his life by now as you have been dating for several weeks.'

I sit down and capture the sea view from her office window. 'Yes, I know about his political position and that he's related to the royal family. I'm also aware of his stroke.'

'So you know about Gretal?'

'I do.'

'And Haya, his first wife?'

'A little.'

'I can vouch for him. He is a man who can be trusted. He is honourable and known for his integrity. I know this all sounds a little old-fashioned, but what I am trying to say is that he's solid. He chose not to come to me first when checking you out with the authorities. I do understand his predicament. If anything untoward was in your background it would have been embarrassing for both me and him.'

Lindsay continues to sing his praises. 'You know Janey he was always very close to Gretal. I met her many times at functions around the town, but she just disappeared about three months after his stroke. To my knowledge he never discussed with anyone the circumstances surrounding their break up.'

I answer her sympathetically. 'Yes it was a difficult time for him — very tough.'

'I hope you can bring him the happiness he deserves.'

I smile. 'I hope so too!'

Lindsay orders coffee and toasted muffins for us both and then picks up her phone to instruct her PA not to disturb her until further notice. I sit looking at the enchanting view of the Gulf Sea and the various portraits of Sheiks adorning her walls, including the UAK Saheed Ira.

'Janey I want to help you.'

'In what way?'

'I want you to understand about life and marriage here in the UAK, marriage to someone with status, not just political, but a Sheikh. Of course he downplays it as he is a humble man.'

I'm relaxed on an easy chair taking in everything she's saying to me. 'Okay' I say. 'Tell me what I need to know.'

'There are certain rules if you like and if you follow these with a good heart your marriage will be a splendid affair.' Lindsay

Singing in Silence

pauses for breath and composes herself. 'Rule 1 — discretion. Your life together is of no importance to anyone else, only the gossip columns! And the world's press are always looking for weaknesses. Rule 2 — loyalty. Stand by him. He will need your full support. And, finally, rule 3 — arguments! Yes we all have them, but never air your dirty washing in public.'

We continue the meeting for a further half an hour during which time she gives me a true insight into how to enjoy a life here, when you're not an expat living amongst mainly Europeans and Americans.

CHAPTER SIXTEEN

Life is Full of Surprises

I arrive back at my office mid morning. My diary looks good, not too many things to do today. I sigh with relief as it'll be good to have a stress free day for a change. My team are rushing around as normal. With potential deals there are a few clients in the office creating a buzz, which is good for the adrenaline.

My good friend Simone enters my office.

'Hey love, what a nice surprise, I was going to call this afternoon to see if you wanted to go out after work?'

Simone also works in sales in the same company, but is based at another office. She has a huge grin on her face as she sits down at my desk — two frothy coffees arrive.

'Your tea boy.'

'What about our boy?'

'Just to say, he is great in your office, he makes the best coffee in town.'

'That's because he is well trained,' I say jokingly.

'Well, Janey how was your sailing weekend?'

'Of course I have not seen you for days.' I smile at her. 'We were caught in a bit of a sea storm.'

Simone had heard news from the sailing club that the waters had been rough around Oman. 'David and I were concerned for you. Gosh! that was a whole new experience for you Janey.'

'I've had a few new experiences over the past few days.'

I have to keep my silence regarding his proposal last night. In fact I will not even mention going to his place, not tonight anyway, as it might slip out of my mouth. I am no good at keeping secrets,

Singing in Silence

not happy ones anyway! It's hard; I want to burst it out from the rooftops and shout — 'I am getting married!'

Janey Green, Sales Manager of the Year, the naïve woman from Yorkshire. Yes, can you believe it? I am marrying a Sheikh! Royalty! A multi ... well, lots of money! Not sure how much, but loaded! For now, yes, I am singing in silence. I must remember — Janey Green, keep your mouth shut!

After work we head to our usual beach bar 'Down Under'. It's just after 6pm and the place is heaving. There is an international football match showing on the TV later. Part of the club is a sports bar, which explains why it's so busy. We find a free table and order a drink, a homemade burger and a fatoush salad. Simone is eager to hear about the weekend.

'The weekend was great, there were a few surprises.'

Simone looks intrigued. 'What sort of surprises?'

'Well, first of all he had bought some clothes for me to wear, which were already in my cabin suite.'

'How lovely is that? How did he know your size?'

'Good question,' I say. 'When we first met, he commented on a dress I was wearing.'

'Which one?'

'The pink chiffon.'

'That is one of my favourites, glad to hear you wore that as you look so good in it.'

'I happened to mention where I had bought it from and also that it's one of my favourite shops.'

'Which shop?'

'You know it Simone. You've been there with me before — that little boutique on the beach road.'

She blurts it out. 'Ah! Betty Boo's.'

'That's the one. As it turns out he knows the owner there.'

Simone's face becomes a beacon of light and her eyes begin to bulge. 'Really? I bet he does chick — that Mandy the Minx is a man-eater!'

'How do you know she is a man-eater? Are you sure we are talking about the same woman?'

Simone seems eager to tell me. 'When I say Mandy the Minx, that's what the guys in David's office call her.'

'You are now gossiping Simone, it doesn't become you.'

'I'm just telling you.' Her voice goes up a notch and becomes a bit whiney. 'But if you're not interested?'

'Of course I am bloody interested, I want to know how Mandy the Minx got her delightful name and how she became famous with David's office colleagues.'

David works for a well-known computer software company, MBI International.

'Well, according to David one of the guys at his work, you know Pete?'

'Not really.'

'Anyway Perky Pete, as he is now known since visiting Betty Boo's, went to buy some sexy lingerie for his girlfriend's birthday.'

'What is wrong with that?'

'Well, you know what she did? She only bloody modelled the outfits for him. Can you get your breath Janey?'

I am listening, trying not to laugh.

'One of the sets was a thong and a nippleless bra. One thing lead to another ... anyway he said, she is red hot! His actual words to David in his Devon accent were — like a frigging furnace is that Mandy. Since that day Perky Pete has been his nickname as it perked him up no end after that incident. According to his girlfriend, Pete was a like a new man in bed since her birthday. She couldn't understand what had happened to him.'

I try to control my giggling. 'Jesus Simone, who would have thought this of Mandy.'

'That's not the end chick, there's more. The following week one of Pete's mates, Gary, decided he wanted to try his luck too and went in to buy some silk undies for some bird he was trying to impress, a fancy lawyer who works at Morgan Sisley's. He ended up watching her model several sets of very unusual lingerie.'

'Unusual Simone? You mean French lace or something fancy like that — not just bras and panties then?'

Simone's voice gets higher and louder. 'No chick, much more interesting. Listen to this — she was willing to demonstrate how useful the crutchless panties are.'

'Useful? Crutchless! Easier to pee you mean?'

'No Janey, what is wrong with you? Don't they sell crutchless panties in North Yorkshire?'

'I've never seen any in *House of Fraser*.'

'Bloody *House of Fraser* won't sell these. Jesus, Janey, what planet are you on? For sex! More sex than Gary had experienced for months! He thinks she is great, a real hot firecracker. Cost him though.'

'How much?'

'Three silk sets. He said it was the best buy of his life — never had sex like it!'

I sit flabbergasted for a few seconds. 'Well what did she do to poor Gary?'

'Poor Gary! What are you on Janey?'

I laugh. 'I think I lived a very sheltered life for twenty years in North Yorkshire.'

Simone tuts at me and shakes her head from side to side, despairing of me. Loudly she says. 'Poor Gary had the time of his life. She tied him up with a Wonderbra and performed some sort of sexual erotic act on him. Eventually he left the shop around midnight.'

'No bloody way, you're kidding me aren't you?' I continue to eat my salad for a few seconds then curiosity overcomes me. 'What sort of sexual erotic act?'

'Gary says,' ... she was just about to blurt it out. 'Sorry chick, no, I can't tell ya. Not while you are eating Janey — wouldn't be right! See it's a bit, well, not to your taste. Not mine either! Well some people like that sort of thing, so I've read in David's magazines.'

We finish our meal and I decide that I don't want to hear anything sordid. So I do not pursue the details of the erotic sexual act — not tonight anyway! Maybe I could laugh when we are with the *Sex and the City* girls, but not on a full stomach of burger and salad!

'Who would have thought Mandy was ...'

Simone interrupts. 'A man-eater Janey, a red hot one too!'

'You know Simone, every time I have been in her shop she always comes across as prim and proper. Just like the demure Miss Jean Brodie's crème de la crème, in her twin set and pearls.'

'Janey, so sorry we have digressed a little, anyway yes, the Betty Boo's Boutique and Mandy the Minx.'

'Yes Mojat had obviously been into the boutique to buy some lovely dresses and ... '

'Janey, did he buy silk lingerie for you?'

'As a matter of fact, yes, a few sets ... oh for God's sake! I wish you hadn't told me about Pete and Gary with Mandy. Anyway it's too late to worry about Mandy the Minx, Mojat was in a rush to get back to me.'

'Of course he was chick, of course! I bet he busted a gut to get back to you, why would he want her? Although she might have been an old flame!'

'Jesus! Simone, I don't want to hear that right now, stop trying to wind me up when I'm trying to be serious with you and you're just ...'

We both burst out laughing, it was really hilarious this conversation, especially after the second gin and tonic. I lighten up a little from my loved up silly dizzy feeling.

Simone suggests I should start again.

'I don't want to imagine Mandy in a thong thank you! Or her performing strange sexual acts. Her of all people!'

Mandy wears A line skirts to the knee, the sort we made in our third year at high school and always a top with a coordinating cardigan. Her shoes are sensible and polished. I just can't get my head around the fact that she's a sexual firecracker!

'Okay, carry on chick,' says Simone.

I then tell her about my fainting spell in Sam's office and everything that took place yesterday afternoon.

'He was so forward with me, he wants me to give up everything to be at his side.'

'Gosh Janey, you didn't mention that to Sam did you?'

'No not quite, but I did say how pressing he was regarding a decision to be with him, and then the whole royalty thing came up and how I would need to be protected. And then there was the last thing that Sam said to me before I fainted.' I give a big sigh and pause for a few seconds.

'What, royal family? Have I missed something here, the man that owns our sailing club is what? Royalty? That can't be!'

I look at her. Oh bloody hell, I have let the cat out of the bag. I might as well get it all out now I have started! 'He is also a politician.'

'Is he? Are we talking about the same man? Are you sure? What is his position?

In the end I have to come clean with Simone, so I tell her everything — yes absolutely everything!

Simone sits there, now wide-awake, taking in the whole picture of what I'm describing to her.

'I know it's a shock Simone, a real shock, and still is for me too. When he informed me that he has another life it kind of made sense.'

'Why chick?'

'Come on Simone, that bloody super yacht! Do you know how much they cost? Didn't it ever occur to you and David that he could never have made that sort of money from his backwater sailing club? He is our ruling Sheikh's uncle and the foreign minister, soon to take a step down to ambassador.'

Simone mumbles. 'Hardly a step down!'

'Now you know everything about him.'

Simone takes a deep breath, 'You must have been in shock too?'

'I was. In fact I still am.'

I tell her everything except the marriage proposal and last night.

'I can't imagine you fainting, you're one of the tough survivors in life.'

'Simone, please don't breathe a word, not even to David, just for three days until Mojat returns.'

She nods with a sincere expression. 'What made you faint in front of Sam?'

'Well, Sam said ...' I begin to cry — blubbering from the heart and powerless to get the words out. I turn my back to the people on the next table and look into Simone's eyes.

'What did she say?' asks Simone.

'Well her actual words were, chick, you're not going to last long here, you know this don't you? The next few words she uttered just tipped me over the edge and I passed out.'

Simone's face becomes a picture of intenseness; she is absolutely glued to my every word. 'Forget your freedom chick, but you will have amazing security.'

'Sam had given me a reality check. So ridiculous, I have never fainted in my life. I have given birth to five children, one in the back of a Ford Escort — without any pain relief! That's how chilled I am.'

'You've never told me about giving birth in the back of a car?'

Simone is spaced out, concentrating on my every word. Silence falls upon us for a few minutes whilst we take stock.

'Wow Janey, all this has happened since Thursday evening, it's bloody bizarre how things can move so quickly in life.'

I feel an ache in my heart, a pang, a tightening in my chest as I sit next to my closest friend. I take the serviette that had a few meat juice stains on one side, fold it over, wipe under my eyes and then blow my nose.

Then the energy changes between us as she speaks quite frankly and calmer. 'Are you happy? Happy that he wants you in his life — marriage and all that?'

I smile at her not speaking, then nod my head whilst wiping away another flood of tears.

'He is much older than you Janey and I once saw him walk with a stick. His face looked grey and old. In fact he looked pretty awful then — sad and depressed. That was some time ago now I know — but you have to be sure Janey.'

I recount to Simone the story of his stroke five years ago and about his love for Gretal and how she left him — the whole story.

'Janey how sad, so sad. That fits in with when he walked with a stick. It must have been terrible for him, having a stroke and his long term girlfriend leaving and finding someone else to give her a child.'

I sit there thinking. 'Yes when you say it as bluntly as that, it is just awful!'

'Janey are you really in love with him?'

'I am.'

I sigh and then so does Simone.

'I know it all sounds very dramatic but, over a long weekend, it was romantic and blissful. We both felt so much happiness being together.'

I breathe deeply as I confide my true feelings. 'He fulfils my needs and is sexually charged and takes control.'

'Is he? Does he?'

'You know Simone, I am now shocked that I am even saying this to you. I have not told him this yet.'

Simone looks intrigued and serious and smiles enjoying my openness and honesty. 'What have you not said?'

'How much he sexually excites me. I have never experienced such erotic, wild, intense passion in my life. And the chase! I love his chase!'

Simone looks astonished by what I am saying, as I never discuss anything so personal with my friends, especially regarding sex. I am the one that usually listens, the one who keeps quiet in the background, maybe because I don't really have relationships that often and, if I do, it's just a few dates — nothing more.

I have had plenty of younger guys chasing me, but since my divorce with Geoffrey I have not been that interested and secretly, very secretly, have never felt anyone was good enough for me. It's a haughty statement, one that I would not readily admit to my friends, but it's true! Most men are not good enough! I have just not found anyone that makes me sit up and take notice, inspire me or make me laugh. One that I can feel respect for.

Simone's thought processes have been ticking over. 'You like this do you, him controlling you sexually?'

'Yes I do, does that surprise you?'

'Well ... yes, it does. And in what way is he sexually charged?'

'He blows my mind away. Never before have I been taken in so many ways.'

'Wah! sounds amazing. They say variety is the spice of life! Anyway you have never mentioned your sexual needs before — I'm shocked to hear you speaking this way.'

'I think I have only just realised that I have needs, as I have blocked them out for months.'

Simone looks down with a huge sigh and says, 'I can't remember the last time David and I had sex. I am quite envious.'

CHAPTER SEVENTEEN

The Transition

The morning sun is out in all its glory. I open the door on to my balcony and step outside carrying my breakfast tray. There is a stillness and in the distance a funnel of wavering air, the beginning of the heat haze.

The sweet small voices of the birds are singing beautifully today. I look up to see them hopping from palm to palm, busy building and pruning their nests.

It's early morning and all my neighbours hurriedly leave for work, carrying their laptop bags, files and papers. It seems that everyone is on the business treadmill here. There is a knock on my door. As I walk through my lounge, I can hear Simone chatting outside on her mobile phone. I open the door just as she finishes her call.

'I know it's early chick, but ...' She looks at me. 'You're in your robe — aren't you working today?'

'I am. I will be going straight to a meeting this morning instead of the office.'

Simone is finalising a deal, actually one of her best. She has sold two whole floors in Inferno Mansions. She proceeds to walk into my kitchen, rubbing her hands with glee as she picks up a cup and pours herself a coffee, then sits down next to me. 'What's up?' she asks.

'I went for a meal at Mojat's house before he left the country, which was a surprise.'

'You never mentioned this last night?'

'I know.'

'Why?'
'I was holding back I suppose.'
'Wah! Janey, this is getting serious. Does he live in a palace?'
'Of course he doesn't.'
'I just imagine him in a palace that's all.'
Simone becomes giddy and laughs as though she's connected to my internal energy. I also feel that same giddiness, but mine is nerves, thinking about all my future life changes.
'No not a palace, but a mighty fine circular villa on the outskirts of Jubai.'
'Circular?'
'Yes, surrounded by peacocks.'
'Bloody hell, can't stand those weirdo birds! Why does he keep peacocks for God's sake?'
I shrug my shoulders.
'So you're a free lady for the next couple of days are you?'
I look at her and smile; in fact I can not stop smiling, as I now resemble a cat that has just lapped up its first taste of cream. 'Yes I am free for now.' My silly grinning now morphs into uncontrollable laughter and I'm feeling as though I am going to burst. I glance at my mobile and it's just past 8am. Simone looks at me as though I have gone mad, in fact I feel as if I am in the process of going insane!
'What the hell is wrong with you Janey? Come on tell me — you're acting so strangely?'
I glance at my watch again. 'We have time,' I say audibly under my breath.
'Time for what Janey?'
I put my arms around her and give her a big hug. She is now getting very frustrated with me and shrugs me off like a child who doesn't want to be cuddled, as if a cuddle has a double-edged meaning.
'You have something to tell me, don't you?'
'Yes, I do have something to tell you. You arrived here with

your good news about a deal that's going to make you a lot of money.' Frustrated looks are coming my way. 'Yes, well, I have some good news too. I am free for the next few days and then my life is going to change.'

'It's already changing Janey.'

'But really change I mean! I want to tell you that Mojat proposed to me at his house the other night.'

'Proposed? Wahey! Fab news. He hasn't wasted any time. Wait until I tell David.' She stands up. 'That will mean I am going to lose you, my closest friend.'

'Please do not breathe a word — you're not going to lose me.'

Then I talk to her of his plans, introducing me to the Sheikh, a wedding date, etc. And then there's my protection and Lindsay, our boss, in contact with Mojat. Simone is concentrating and listening to me, but has a stunned look about her!

'Jesus chick, Jesus! So who knows?'

'Just you right now. Lindsay and Sam will be told before the end of today.'

'Lindsay knows him, they have met at various business functions over the years.'

'That's a coincidence? I have a meeting with Lindsay this morning; I will have to move somewhere where I can be protected.'

'Then what chick?'

'I don't know?'

Simone gazes into her cup. 'Well all these years we have just thought of him as a businessman, the owner of the sailing club — the local with the huge yacht!'

I fill her in, regarding his foreign minister duties around the world, and his ties to America and the other Arab states. Wherever he travels he has an entourage of people at his side.

I feel better for explaining all the finer details to her, even though I now find it exhausting. I am talking far too much. I am usually the listener.

'Well, a foreign diplomat's wife,' says Simone. 'Who would

have thought that just a few weeks ago?' She is still trying to grasp everything, when the phone rings and it's my man.

'Habibie, I am just about to take off. I have spoken with Lindsay at length this morning; so enjoy your meeting and the last few days in your apartment. I love you my English rose.'

'I love you too,' I reply.

'I will call you tonight habibie — I must go now.' He hangs up.

Simone expresses sincerity. 'You know you can trust me, you have my full confidence.'

'Thanks love.'

I want to tell her about the secret false door in his yacht and the stash of guns it contains, as it's causing me some anxiety. I have never been very good at keeping anxious things to myself. In the end I could not confide in her.

She leaves my apartment with a glazed look.

I shout to her down the corridor. She looks back and I signal with my forefinger on my lips.

'Don't worry chick,' she replies as she enters the lift.

A woman I have never seen before is loitering around. Funny I know just about everyone here, maybe she's just moved in? I was going to say hello, when her mobile phone rings.

I close the door and decide to have a quick shower. I shut my balcony doors, as the desert heat is sticky as it enters my lounge. I put the air conditioning on to cool things down whilst I organise myself for the meeting.

The head office is just off the beach road. Lindsay has the most gorgeous office suite. Her furnishings are modern and on her walls hang expensive pieces of art.

Lindsay is well known for her deals with dignitaries and royalty all around the UAK and other Arab countries.

She is now seventy, blonde, Canadian and one of the nicest women I have ever met.

I knock on her office door. I can hear her talking on the phone like before at our last meeting. She finishes her call and speaks to me in her Canadian accent. 'Come in Janey and take a seat.'

I take my jacket off and she continues. 'Well, Lady Al Mohini, I think congratulations are in order, you must be feeling excited and so happy.'

'Thank you, it feels very strange, wonderful and also a little scary.'

'Now where do we begin?' She moves her work to one side and closes a folder full of her own handwriting. 'I've had a long conversation with Mojat earlier today and, by accepting his proposal of marriage, you've made him a very happy man. He is bubbling over with excitement.'

I smile as I envisage his face in my mind.

Now Janey, for the next few days, discretion is the key.

'Sam will have to know and that's all.'

'Janey, in my business you have to be discreet, or the local community will never deal with you. I knew Mojat when he was married to Haya. They have a large family — the children are now grown up. They divorced so long ago now and I always wondered whether or not he would ever take another wife, as nothing ever materialised with Gretal.'

She pours me a glass of water. 'Honey, you are such an English rose. Since you started working for the company I've always thought that any man would find you such a catch. Please take this as a compliment. You are bright, strong, confident and warm-hearted; all the right characteristics.' She continues. 'I am pleased for you both. I know your backgrounds. You are a survivor of life and you both know the pain and suffering of divorce. His marriage to Haya was arranged and this is normal here. Unfortunately true love only came to him when he met Gretal. He is a good man.'

'When you met her what was she like?'

'Gretal you mean?'

'Yes.'

'She was a beautiful tall elegant blonde. Very natural looks and an air of confidence about her — like you Janey. Arab men find confidence in European woman so stimulating.'

She picks the phone up and orders a light breakfast for us both.

'Lindsay, you have lived here a long time — is there anything I should know? I feel anxious about my engagement to Mojat and all the things that are going to change in my life. I hope that he will give me a little time to adjust.'

'Honey, you are now entering an exclusive Arab world. Rule number one — Arab wives do not work. I will be losing you very soon. You will not have the time anymore, as you'll be with him travelling by his side. He made that very clear to me today. Rule number two — always be discreet and protect him, never let any words roll off your tongue without thinking first! Rule number three — for the rest of his life, you will be his confidant. Words and conversations between engaged and married couples here, and in all the Arab states, stay behind closed doors. He will put all his trust in you. I am sure he has already tested you over the last few weeks, where he met you and the relationships around your social life. Think back Janey.'

I try to but my brain feels fuzzy. 'Since he proposed to me I have lost all clarity of thought.'

'This is what falling in love does to you. Arabs are very proud private people. Mojat has status, yes, but he is also a very humble man who has earned great respect from world leaders over the years.'

'God you're frightening me now, I can't live up to all this!'

'Don't be fearful, I trust you will be perfect by his side and I told him so.'

'Did you really say this?'

She nods in her organised business way.

'Lindsay there are things that …' I stop and hesitate for a moment.

'What things — what are you frightened off?'

'It's silly really, just one thing. Maybe you can put my mind at rest as I have not mentioned this to anyone.'

We eat a little before she pipes up. 'Well, are you going to tell me what is troubling you?'

I recount the story of our lovely sailing weekend and how perfect it all was. Then I tell her about the false door, the stash of guns and ammunition.

'An interesting one Janey!'

Surprisingly she doesn't seem fazed or shocked by this.

'It's what I would expect. In fact if he did not have this kind of protection he would be very foolish and extremely vulnerable.'

'Oh, I see. I have felt so anxious, but machine guns Lindsay ... why?'

Lindsay has a surprised look, as if she's thinking — get a grip Janey.

'He has a bodyguard you know.'

'Does he? I have never seen one.'

She tuts. 'Is this your only concern?'

I nod my head. 'Well, it feels a big deal to me.'

I now realise I've lead a sheltered, secure life back in Yorkshire, growing strawberries and runner beans in my Victorian kitchen garden and busying myself listening to BBC Radio 4, whilst cleaning and organising the running of the family home.

My boss continues speaking as though having armed weapons is acceptable for a man of his status. She tucks her blonde bob behind her ears and in a business-like manner says. 'Where was I? Oh yes. He would not risk choosing a woman who could potentially let him down and damage his reputation. You are strong, a survivor. He will prepare you in so many ways for your new life. It's my bet that he wanted you to see the guns — another test!'

'Maybe he did.'

'That is why the door was unlocked, so you could ask him? Think about it, why would he put the guns in your bedroom suite?'

'Umm, yes why?'

'He could have hidden them anywhere on the yacht, think

about it Janey? Coincidently this brings me to the final rule, number four. It's protection and security issues. He will have you trained.'

'Trained!' I say on a higher decibel, trying not to lose my sense of humour. 'Trained for what — SAS, CIA?'

She smiles. 'Yes, very good Janey.' she appreciates my sense of humour whilst conscious that my nerves are taking over. 'It is not for me to say, I'm a businesswoman not a government security agent! Honey, Mojat has bodyguards. There is one in particular, a personal bodyguard, who will train you up.'

'I have never seen any bodyguards?'

'Give it time honey!'

We finish our breakfast meeting and, by the time I leave Lindsay's office, it's nearly midday. I get into the car.

I have lots to think about. My head is spinning and it feels as if I'm in a dream and totally spaced out.

This will be the last time I drive a car in Jubai.

CHAPTER EIGHTEEN

The Spinning Wheel of Fortune

Whilst driving back to the office, a call comes through on my mobile phone. It's Simone and she's in celebratory mood. Her deal has gone through, all signed and sealed with the developer.

'Wow!' I say. 'Congratulations, drinks are on you later.'

She insists I come over to their apartment tonight and have a meal with the family, so we arrange a time.

I park in my Arabian Homes reserved space in the underground car park. I have plenty of work waiting for me and I like the fact I'm so busy as this all helps me to feel less nervous about my future. I need to stay focused at work.

So many changes are entering my life and I have to keep pinching myself as it all feels like I'm living a dream. Any moment I'll wake up in my bed at Wisteria House!

When I arrived in Jubai I had no job, just one suitcase and £5,000.00 in my bank account. Within three weeks I managed to secure a contract working for this company and I have kept my head down ever since.

My team are waiting for me. There are deals to discuss, letters to check and contracts to look over and sign before the buyers and sellers turn up for their meetings. In-between all this the phone doesn't stop ringing. It is a great, hectic environment and, I am proud to say, lots of business is generated in this office. I know in my heart that I will miss this so much.

It is now 3pm and I need some lunch. I walk out into the reception area to stretch my legs and ask my PA to order me a sandwich.

I stand in the reception admiring the office's new lush fig trees, whilst deciding on my lunch order with Prasitia. I glance through the impressive floor to ceiling windows out on to the road outside.

'Your usual tuna salad Janey with mayo?'

'Please.'

'Do you want crisps with your sandwich? You English like your crisps.'

'Just plain,' I reply, slightly fazed.

Many cars are parked and a few heavy trucks are passing full of building materials destined for a construction site two minutes down the road. Another prime plot has been bought by a developer at the waterfront.

I am distracted as there is a large black Mercedes C Class parked outside. I can here Prasitia is on the phone ordering lunch. The car looks shiny and new as if it has just left the showroom. The driver, formally dressed in a suit, is a very familiar looking man. I stare at him as he shuts the car door and starts to walk up the pathway to our office doorway. Suddenly it dawns on me, it's Kulpreet!

He smiles at me. 'Good afternoon Lady Janey.'

'Christ!' I say under my breath. My PA looks up from her desk startled, to say the least, that a handsome Indian gentleman has walked through the door calling me Lady!

I move him quickly from the reception, away from everyone's prying eyes. I almost push him into my office and shut the door. For God's sake — why is Kulpreet here?

My girls Prasitia and Martha are hovering around the reception area, glancing towards the see-through glass door of my office. I'm trying to keep my private life private, so I pick up my office phone and ask not to be disturbed for five minutes.

Why is Kulpreet here when Mojat's out of the country?

'Please sit down Kulpreet. What can I do for you?'

'Lady Janey, I have been given strict orders by Mr. Mojat to be your driver.'

'Strange, as he's not mentioned this to me.'

'Until he returns to Jubai ma'am, he has given me full responsibility.'

'Full responsibility for me?' I say as if I need this!

'His orders are to pick you up early in the morning and drive you to work and all your meetings and socials. This is until he returns from Iran. Also ma'am, I then have to return you home safely last thing at night.'

I try to be diplomatic, which has never been one of my finer qualities. 'That's very nice I'm sure, but there really is no need.'

He looks indignant. 'It's my orders.'

'Kulpreet, that's lovely, but I can assure you that I can look after myself.'

I stand there face-to-face with him, thinking about my meeting earlier with Lindsay. 'I suppose I do not have a choice?'

He smiles at me, relieved that I've agreed.

I pause for a moment. I am slightly put out but not really surprised. In fact I have had so many surprises over the last few weeks, this is just another to add to the list. I look at him and he looks slightly tense. I thank him. He gives me his number.

'Please ma'am, you must ring me next time you leave the office and I will be waiting close by.'

He looks drained the poor man.

'Kulpreet, are you okay?'

'Yes ma'am, I am used to driving, it's just, I was supposed to be at your head office earlier to collect you from Miss Lindsay's and drive you to this office after your meeting. But so many problems with traffic. Now I know where you work, everything will be in order.'

I look him up and down and can see perspiration running down his brow. 'Would you like a glass of water?'

Prasitia brings him a long glass of water and they smile at each other as if there's a little bit of chemistry there.

'Ma'am, now I know all of your company's offices everything

will run smoothly from now on.'

'Don't worry,' I say reassuringly. 'Of course I will ring you.' What more could I say? I will be speaking to Mojat later and just wish we could have discussed this.

Kulpreet nods showing his ultra-white teeth against his dark skin. His Indian-English accent was endearing and he nods his head several times, like many lovely Indian people I work with. The nodding head is how they communicate, like the Arabs with their hands. I have agreed — or submitted — to having a driver.

'Your secretary is very nice ma'am.' He smiles. 'Yes, earlier on the phone, Miss Prasitia, she gave me all the office locations and telephone numbers. One more thing Lady Janey, this car is for you. Your use only.'

'For me — as in mine?'

'It has special number plate, Arabic for diplomatic. So police or traffic police know it is diplomat.'

I thank him and he leaves.

My PA brings in my sandwich. 'You know Janey, that man?'

'Kulpreet you mean?'

'Yes, he is very good-looking.'

'Don't get any ideas,' I say.

I eat my tuna salad sandwich and munch on my crisps, accompanied by a fresh pot of tea. I am flicking through today's *Gulf News*, trying to keep calm and taking every hour as it comes — as we English say. I am three pages in and my eyes turn to the International Business section: 'Iranian talks with the UAK, Minister Bin Al Mohini visits Iranian leaders to discuss further developments in the peace process in the Middle East. The United Arab Kingdom is stepping up their security.'

There is a photo caption of his previous visits with the Persian Shah Karima and Mojat plus a few other Iranian diplomats. I continue reading the whole article.

Sheikh Bin Al Mohini, what a mouthful for a name I think to myself. Am I really going to be Mrs. Janey Green Bin Al Mohini? It does not flow — Mrs. Bin Al sounds better!

The words written in the article sound troubled, lots of problems to be solved regarding a uranium plant and the US are also in discussion. It takes up about a quarter of a page. As I finish my lunch, I wonder what else I could possibly learn today?

The rest of the afternoon goes by very smoothly and I chat to one of my agents as she leaves the office at five thirty. I am overwhelmed and tired at the end of an emotionally exhausting day. My car is safely locked in the underground car park and one of the security guys for the building helps me remove all my personal belongings. I ring Kulpreet and, within a few minutes, my car is waiting outside.

Kerrie O'Neil leaves the office with me and in her Irish lilt she says. 'Shit Janey, since when has Arabian Homes paid for a fricking driver?' She watches Kulpreet open the car door for me.

Embarrassed I say. 'The car belongs to a friend.'

'Nice friend Janey. I don't suppose it's the one that sent you the flowers is it?'

She then walks off towards her VW Golf, still jesting with me about my moving up the ranks of society!

I sink into the cream leather seats in the rear of the car. The engine starts and we drive away from my office. The windows are slightly tinted and it all feels very comfortable. I want to say swanky. Yes, it definitely feels swanky sitting here.

'Where to ma'am?'

'Simone's please Parker.'

'Parker?'

'Just a private joke,' I say.

I give him the directions and we safely arrive at our destination.

'It's okay, you can go home now Kulpreet. My friends will give me a lift home — they only live two streets down.'

'Ma'am, I am supposed to see you home. It's my duty, my job.'

Oh dear, many thoughts are rushing around in my brain now. That's a shame, that's a bloody shame! I can hardly get a little drunk anymore with friends, get a taxi home and fall into bed fully clothed. Not that I make a habit of this behaviour, but if I did want it to become so it's nigh near impossible now.

I imagine the following scenario: 'Sorry Parker, I'm a little tipsy, please excuse me. Well, actually, I hope you haven't noticed that Lady Janey is pissed out of her brain and has lost one of her shoes in her favourite nightclub!'

I stand outside the car gradually learning more of what it will be like in my new Arab world. 'That's fine Kulpreet, I will call you when I am ready.'

Sam's words are now echoing in my ears — forget your freedom. Well it's gone, bloody gone! This is just the start, so Janey, just get used to Parker. I have to imagine I'm Lady Penelope sat in the back seat ... Thunderbirds are go! I never missed an episode as a child.

We all sit down awaiting a traditional roast chicken dinner, cooked to perfection, and the table is all laid out with white linen serviettes and Simone's best set of cutlery. Candles are lit on the table and there is a bottle of champagne in an ice bucket. Their daughters are sat colouring at the table waiting for Simone to dish up. The family are totally oblivious to how much this deal means to their mum. A light dessert of lemon mousse follows and, after the children have gone to bed, all three of us sit down for a brandy and a coffee.

'Your deal Simone, how much is it worth?'

David and Simone hold hands for the first time.

'Well it means we can now buy a villa without selling this apartment. We will rent this out for an extra income.'

'That's good then,' I say.

We pass the chocolates around and enjoy our drinks.

'Good Janey,' says David. 'It's wonderful — she has done well. I'm so proud of her deal.'

'Janey.' David seriously fixes his eyes on me. 'Will this new life suit you?' He doesn't wait for my answer. 'It's one thing dating and being wined and dined but to then take the next step. What I am trying to say is — do you realise the implications of entering the Arab world? It's your freedom Janey. Will you have any?'

I am tired but also very happy and can understand both his and Simone's concerns. I take a deep breath. 'I hear what you say.'

Simone sits next to me and puts her arm around my shoulders. 'I know how hard you have worked Janey since arriving here. You are an independent woman, proud that you have turned your life around since leaving the UK. Think carefully my love, you will be entering ... well, what I am trying to say is, not even a normal Arab world.'

I nod. 'Yes, I know.'

David seems very compassionate. 'You'll be right in the political throws of the Middle East. It's a dangerous world out there. Think about it!'

'I am beginning to realise this.'

He pauses for a few seconds. 'Mojat is right love. Once this becomes public knowledge you will immediately be at risk!'

'So Simone has told you everything?'

'Well I guessed something. But it will stay with us only. We care — we are your friends.'

David sits in his high back chair holding a large brandy goblet, swirling the drink around to warm it. I reassure them that I've given a lot of thought to the concerns they've raised this evening.

I inform them both that I now have a driver and very shortly I will have a change of address once Mojat returns.

David smiles with relief as if he was carrying the entire world on his shoulders. I'm sure he feels responsible for me, being so close to his wife. He then stands up and says. 'Sorry Janey, I did not want to appear all doom and gloom. You're planning the rest of your life with a man you love and here I am, well, putting a dark cloud on your plans.'

Before he has a chance to finish I walk over and kiss and hug him, thanking them both for their concerns and frankness. I am touched. More brandy is poured and we continue to chat.

'Well,' I say. 'Your deal Simone — well done!'

David agrees with me and we both then toast to her. They announce, as we clink our brandy glasses. 'To our new home, wherever that might be?'

'Invest in property that's what I say,' holding my glass up to the sky, laughing and enjoying these precious moments with my closest friends. I'm happy that they can now purchase the villa they've craved for such a long time.

When I think back to their previous life in South Africa, having to flee leaving all their possessions behind, letting go of the security they had worked for for so long! Their inherited family farms. White farmers suffered as their farms were burnt down under the tyrant Mugabe's command. It was terrible and despicable! So, yes, for a few moments I share their joy.

I like to think that God's guiding principle of his world seeks justice and balance to establish equilibrium, giving fairness and reason — a Buddhist would say it's karma! What was taken away from them has now been given back, albeit via another channel.

A further hour passes and I suddenly think of Kulpreet, waiting for me, perhaps sat in a small Arabic café, tucked away in some little side alley that only the manservants and drivers visit. I have seen many cafés like these. There always seems to be a small gathering of men huddled around a portable TV in the corner and a few chairs surrounding small Formica top tables. The men smoke shisha and cigarettes as they chat, drinking Arabic coffee from tiny cups. Some play backgammon or read the local news.

This is the start of my protection process. My friends were right to be concerned that my freedom would disappear overnight. Well, of course, today it already has. I now have a driver, so there will be no risks taken. I wonder if Kulpreet has a secret space in the car to hide a gun? I have to accept that I need full protection.

I am glad to return to my place and, as I lay in the bath, I think about Mojat's duties to his country and the risks he takes visiting the States and all the other Arab nations on his peacekeeping missions. All that David was concerned about he was right to mention. I know at times Mojat has been in difficult and dangerous situations. He has already briefed me, but I've never felt put off. I am looking forward to the adventure of travelling with him as his wife for his final years as foreign ambassador.

A new path in life — beginnings and opportunities beckon me. It's a time to feel hopeful as I embark on this mad adventure — an idealistic quest for fulfilment that falling in love does to you.

As lovers, we gaze into each other's eyes while Cupid flies above with his bow and arrow, poised to strike. Rubies in my engagement ring symbolise the purest eternal love of a future life together. I follow my heart and intuition taking a leap into the unknown. Departure, closure, death; the end of a life-phase — a necessary ending. You break outdated ties as you enter another transition in life, new people and prospects are free to enter your world and change is coming. I will embrace it rather than resist, as it is a blessing in disguise to make way for the new.

I feel excited and loved, so loved. The wheel of fortune turns around, the forces of Jupiter bringing change. Our chance meeting; a twist of fate, luck — whatever you want to call it. It is my turn now to benefit from the joy of my new pathway and I will appreciate this halcyon time, never forgetting the struggles and financial burdens that I endured throughout my life back in North Yorkshire. The seasons change and our fortunes fluctuate — the light and dark sides of the world come to the force.

CHAPTER NINETEEN

The White House

It is Wednesday evening, my final night in my one-bedroom apartment. I've purposely stayed in tonight to organise my personal things and start packing.

I remove some of the family photographs from the shelves and can't help but reminisce as I look at my children at the various stages in their lives. Tears roll down my cheeks as I enjoy all the memories. I miss them so much.

I reach for an old mahogany frame that is damaged down one side, turn it over and find that it's a happy picture of my parents when they were courting. The photo shows them walking together hand in hand on a beach promenade, probably on the east coast of England. I turn the frame over and on the back is written 1946. I sigh and wipe my eyes as I wrap it up, placing it carefully in my case.

I check all my bills are paid up to date and file them. Then I collect all my confidential documents from my drawer — my birth certificate, divorce papers, passport and, most importantly, my residence papers.

Mojat's timing is impeccable tonight. He usually calls me every evening just as I'm climbing into bed, but this evening it's earlier. I think he senses my anticipation as it's only 9:30pm.

'Habibie, how are you? Are you at your apartment?'

'Yes, I am packing and getting myself organised for tomorrow.'

His deep raspy voice is full of excitement this evening. 'Tonight habibie I haven't stopped thinking of you. So many feelings are whirling around my head.'

Singing in Silence

I wonder where he is in Iran but I never ask questions over the phone concerning his overseas visits, as it might be risky. Since my meeting on Sunday with Lindsay my brain is now on full security alert, as she has brought so many issues to my attention.

I sense Mojat's need and strong desire to get back to me.

'Janey, has Kulpreet been fulfilling his duties as your driver?'

'Yes, he has been very cautious and a true gentleman.'

'Are you enjoying your new car?'

'It's fabulous, is it really mine?'

'Of course.'

I want to say I wish we could have discussed the matter first, but right now it seems inappropriate.

'I thought that maybe it's just a temporary vehicle whilst you're away. I have to say, I was a little shocked at first when Kulpreet arrived at my office calling me Lady Janey.'

Mojat laughs down the phone. 'My dear, I like to keep surprising you.'

'Well for sure you do, you are keeping me on my toes and I love it!'

'I will be coming to collect you tomorrow from the airport so please be ready. I only want you to pack one case with your personal things. Just your jewellery, photographs and any private papers and, of course, your passport and clothes for two days.'

'Okay, I will be organised.'

'Janey, the remainder of your clothes will be packed by a member of my security staff. Your apartment, with your furniture, will be locked for now. I will be taking you to your new temporary home until our wedding day.'

'I am weak at the knees with anticipation and have butterflies in my stomach, wondering where you are going to take me?'

'Trust me Janey.'

In a mischievous manner I reply. 'Maybe, just maybe, I should have had you checked out by the British embassy.'

'Why is that my dear?'

'Well I don't want to be taken out into the middle of the desert to stay with the Bedouin tribespeople! Or end up in a harem of veiled wives that you've omitted to tell me about.'

He is now laughing so much he begins to choke and can barely get his words out.

'I only like nice surprises Mojat. No shocks please!'

'You're so funny at times. Please do not worry, I have arranged a nice apartment and I'm sure it will suit all your needs.' A sense of urgency enters his voice. 'I want you close to me habibie, always by my side.'

'I will be by your side always. I just hope you won't find it too claustrophobic?'

'Please habibie — don't say this! I have been waiting for this moment. I have said many times before to you, I had almost given up on ever falling in love again.'

'I am just nervous that's all. You don't give me a time you will arrive and I have no idea which part of the city I will be living in.'

'Janey you have to trust me!'

'I do, I do.'

We say our goodbyes and the call ends. I feel so touched that he has arranged all these changes whilst he was out of the country. It gives me a warm, secure feeling.

I try not to think of him out in Iran right now. Of course you usually only hear of the negative problems in the capital Tehran. I have four Iranian sales agents in my office and they are hardworking, family orientated people who are kind and very generous. Many times they bring Persian food into the office for us all to share. They talk of Tehran as though it's run by a dictator of a man who is now old and losing his mind. I don't know about this, but what I do know is my Iranian work colleagues are lovely people.

I decide to ring Lindsay at home; I would never normally do this, but on this occasion I just wish to leave a voicemail. I say on the message that, as I'm moving tomorrow, could I please take the day off to organise myself. I also ask if she can arrange cover for me. To my amazement she calls me back straight away.

'Don't worry honey, Mojat has called me too as he was concerned that you would not have time to arrange everything and go to work. His security people are all in place and you will probably find they were instructed a week ago.'

'Really? What do you mean a week ago?'

'I am sure you have been protected since the night you accepted his proposal of marriage. Why would he risk losing you for an extra few days whilst he is out of the country on business?'

'Lindsay are you sure? I have not seen anyone different around here.'

'Of course not my dear, they will be working undercover. Do you think for one moment a car is going to be permanently parked outside your apartment?'

'No, well I hadn't thought.' My mind goes blank as I listen to her voice.

'I will arrange cover for your office first thing tomorrow. Sam should be able to step in. It's a big day for you — enjoy the moment and I will see you on Sunday.'

The call finishes and I feel a sense of relief. I am usually organised at work and always take my responsibilities seriously. I don't want things to slip at this stage. Mojat was in touch with Lindsay too. Was that a surprise? Well I think not right now. And what is happening Sunday? What did she mean, see you Sunday? Of course — the weekly sales meeting.

I then call my PA knowing full well that she never goes to bed early. I inform her about my decision and reassure her that I am not sick. I just need to catch up quietly with some paperwork. She does not question me and accepts my explanation.

My mind is buzzing. I switch off all the lights and look outside to the front of the building. I cannot see anyone who looks different, or anyone hanging around.

I then open my apartment door, stick my head outside into the well-lit corridor and glance up and down. Bloody hell, there's that woman who I've seen before. She's pacing around whilst chatting on her mobile phone and is now aware that I've seen her. She smiles in acknowledgement whilst she continues talking. I observe her for a few seconds as she continually brushes her hair away from her eyes.

To my surprise my neighbour arrives at the top of the stairs in his gym clothes. He gives the mystery woman a once over then smiles at me when he realises I am scanning the corridor. He walks towards me.

'Hey Janey I have not seen you for ages — are you okay?'

'Yes, I'm fine thanks. Do you happen to know who that woman is?'

He briefly glances back. 'Not really, I think she might have moved in quite recently — not sure which apartment though.'

'James, what makes you think that she has moved in here? Have you seen her at the pool at the weekend?'

'Not at the pool but I have seen her around quite a lot in the last few days.'

'Really?'

We chat for a few minutes at my doorway. He looks tired and is still wiping the sweat from his neck and forehead from his gym workout.

'James, do you think she is Arabic?'

'She was speaking Arabic on the phone as I past her. Anyway why the anxious look Janey, we do live in their country after all?'

'Nothing really — just inquisitive that's all. You find her attractive do you? I saw you giving her a good look over.'

'I did, until I saw that nasty scar down the side of her face.'

'She has a scar?'

'Yes, though she tilted her head to one side. Maybe you could not see from here.'

I glance up again and she has vanished. We then wish each other goodnight and I walk back into my apartment and switch on the lights, lock the door and sit down for a moment. It was probably a coincidence that she just happened to be there as I opened my door. Relax Janey, relax, I think to myself.

I feel everything is falling into place as I climb into bed. My head touches the pillow and immediately I feel lighter as my mind begins to drift.

The alarm startles me — it is 7am. I switch it off quickly as it's a silly cockerel crowing, which irritates me. God only knows why I set this on my phone! I guess at the time it seemed better than some bland electronic tone.

I lay still for a while trying to recall my dream, snuggling back down into the sheets for a few more minutes. I remember having conversations with people whom I didn't know and then being pursued down streets and dark alleyways. It was night-time and I did not even recognise the streets, but I suppose this could be quite common in a dream when your life is about to change. I did not feel any fear, so not to worry, it was just a dream!

The morning is going smoothly. I shower, style my hair and arrange a few clothes by my case.

To my surprise Sam turns up at my apartment door. I look at my watch, it is 9:30am. I feel so pleased to see her.

We both sit down on my sofa and, before we start to talk, I notice she's a little tearful. I have built up a good rapport with Sam over the last year and especially over the past couple of months.

'Well chick, I've come to wish you well and want you to know that it's been great working with you. For sure your team and all the management staff will miss you. Your guy has given us permission to have a small leaving party for you, so Sunday, the day of your weekly sales meeting, will be your last. I will ensure that your entire team are present. Just come to your office as normal. Your leaving work will only be announced on Sunday morning for security reasons.'

I look deep into her eyes and I watch the excited expression on her face. She squeezes my hand as a sign of reassurance.

'Lindsay has been coordinating with Mojat and his security staff. It's all happening very quickly Janey. How are you?'

'Just listening to your words it all feels so final.' I open a box of tissues for her and have to wipe my eyes too. 'I suppose it's hard to get my head around the fact that I will not be working in real estate anymore, or even working again in my life. I am happy but I'm having to get used to the intense speed of all the planning. The word security keeps spinning around in my head.'

'That's because it's new to you chick. Soon it will be the norm.'

'Do you think so?'

'I'm guessing this has been your guy's way of life for most of his adult life. For us peasants it seems bonkers!'

I laugh. 'Yeah you're right, for us peasants we can go anywhere at any time. We're as free as birds.'

Sam agrees. 'Chick, listen to me.' Her calm accent is familiar and soothing to my ears. 'You have chosen this life now and you have to get a grip girl. I agree it has all happened at a quick pace, but it really has to. Once you'd accepted his proposal of marriage you cannot carry on with normal life. Remember Lady Diana in your country? Within just a couple of days she was moved to Clarence House in London for similar reasons.'

'Sam I know, I know.' I stop crying and smile. She gives me a big hug. 'I am not in Lady Diana's league.' I start to laugh again.

'Chick, you're not that far apart, you are still so naïve about the real Arab world! That will soon change. Please listen to me.'

I sense she wants to lift the energy.

'I want you to take a leaf out of Liz Taylor's book.'

'Liz Taylor?' I look at her amused.

'Yes — a great woman. I have just finished reading her memoirs.' Sam recounts one of her famous quotes: 'Pour yourself a drink, put on some lipstick, and pull yourself together. It's true, and who would bloody argue with that! Now let's have a quickie — pour us a small Bailey's and let's toast to Liz Taylor's very sensible advice and, of course, your future.'

The smooth Baileys cream slides into the small glasses.

'In the office on Sunday there will be no alcohol, just light refreshments. So come on, stop blubbing and we will both enjoy, as you say in England, a little tipple!'

The whisky liqueur goes down a treat!

I love Sam — she is a great woman. There is no beating about the bush; it's straight to the point with her. I walk her to the door and we stand out in the corridor saying our goodbyes.

'By the way Janey I forgot to say — love the ruby ring.'

Sam walks past the lift to take the stairs. The lift door opens and that woman emerges — the one on the phone last night. She smiles at me and walks right past my door, disappearing around the corner. James was right, that is a nasty scar — but a very attractive woman.

I walk back into my place and head straight for the bathroom to apply my bright red lipstick, taking a leaf out of Liz's book.

Simone arrives one hour later to tell me that David has had a phone call this morning from Mojat. 'He has invited us to dine with you both on Saturday evening at The Royal Palace Hotel,' she says. 'A great location, how nice of him.'

'That's a nice surprise Simone. By the way, did you see a woman with a scar on her face in the corridor?'

'A woman with a scar? There are women everywhere in this apartment block, mainly very attractive, but I can't say I have seen one with a scar.' She pulls a face at me and the subject quickly changes when she looks down at my left hand. 'Wow — that's what you call a statement piece!'

I glance at my ring finger again and smile. 'I have fallen on my feet and I know how lucky I am.'

Of course Simone wanted to know an up-to-date plan of where I was going to be living and what sort of place it might be?

'It might be old Arabic? It could be contemporary? I really have no idea. But, of course, it's a temporary arrangement at the end of the day.'

My time with Simone is precious. I know in my heart that this will not happen very often now, if ever again? I sense that she knows this too. Our friendship will always be there, but as Mojat and I begin our life together, gone are all those girly fun nights that frequented my little apartment.

Nothing stays the same forever. That is one thing you learn as you get older. Enjoy the moment, try not to dwell on the past and always look forward to tomorrow. I seem to recall these words of wisdom from someone.

'Your furniture Janey, what is happening to your apartment?'

I go on to explain that, for now, it will stay the same. 'I cannot possibly make a decision yet. Anyway, I still have a few months before my lease expires.'

The rest of the morning passes very quickly. Simone leaves and I finish packing the rest of my personal things. My stomach is now in knots, anticipating the next stage of my life. What if he's not the person I think he is? You do hear stories of women, and men, who get sucked into a life of debauchery and fornication or, even worse, get sold and become sex slaves for some fat slob of a sultan who smells of a gorilla's armpit and has crumbling brown teeth. I have seen films that make the hairs on your neck stand up!

I decide not to let my thoughts run away with me. My daydream comes to an abrupt end as my phone rings.

'Habibie, I am on my way now and will arrive at your apartment in five minutes. I have sent Amal; she is part of my security team. She will knock on your door very shortly to help you.'

'Amal?'

'Yes, dear Amal. I will explain soon.'

I quickly dash to the loo; my bladder always does this to me in times of excitement or stressful situations. Amal is a Lebanese name and my woman's intuition tells me that I won't be surprised if she has a scar on her face!

Amal presents herself in a military fashion at the door. She wears a tailored grey trouser suit with a white starched shirt tucked in neatly with just collar and cuffs showing. A slim but muscularly attractive lady, you could presume she was an ex-gymnast. Her dark shiny hair is tightly tied back exposing a deep inflamed scar glistening with sweat.

She introduces herself, shakes my hand firmly and walks into my apartment in a clinical way. The gaping scar consumes me, my inquisitive and enquiring mind wanting to ask how it happened?

Amal briskly walks through my apartment and out on to the balcony overlooking the road. She turns around and looks me straight in the eyes smiling, for the first time revealing lovely high cheekbones.

'Ma'am your car has arrived, have you got everything you need?' she asks in her Lebanese-Arabic accent.

Amal wheels my case through the apartment. I pick up my handbag and laptop case and lock the door. She makes a call to Mojat as we swiftly walk down the corridor.

'The stairs, ma'am, we take the stairs today.'

I don't question her. I suppose the lift could be a problem from a security point of view. Our exit from the apartment all seems to move with precision. There is no conversation between us and I get the impression it might interfere with her assignment to deliver me safely. We move swiftly with ease and yet I feel a tension between us. What is the Lebanese connection I keep thinking to myself?

Mojat stands outside the car waiting in anticipation. Kulpreet has the boot open ready and he turns and smiles at me as I walk towards him with Amal. He acknowledges Amal as she now steps to one side. Mojat's beaming smile says it all as he takes my hand and kisses it.

Kulpreet loads my case and, within a few seconds, the car pulls away in style from the expat life I had grown to enjoy and love. I sit and reflect. No more frolicking around the pool with the usual crowd until late at night, sneaking in the wine and beer in cool boxes, not letting the compound's security guards see us.

Time moves on, I have to let go. It's the end of a life-phase and an era has come to a close. As with any change it is better to embrace it than resist. For me it's easy as I am in love. We are two people uniting after long periods of uncertainty in both of our lives.

Chills run down my spine as I sit in the back of his car. I feel like a princess, but I'm under no illusions. My English middle class roots are firmly on the ground.

We head through the dense traffic and smog of Jubai. There is so much construction in this city that we seem to have more days of greyness than blue skies.

He holds me close not saying anything to me; he is intuitive as he senses my thoughts. To my surprise we head up the beach road passing my head office and, after a couple of miles at the end of the road, the car starts to slow down. This is the start of the older part of the city just prior to the main Jubai fishing port.

I look out of the window to see a large white government building behind a high white wall. I have driven past it many times. It has the UAK flag flying high with many old trees surrounding it. We turn in towards the large black heavy-duty gates where two security guards in military uniform check my passport and papers. There is a gold plaque on the turret style gateposts with the inscription: The White House, Official UAK Government Property. Underneath this there is Arabic writing.

'Janey this is where all the foreign dignitaries stay as a guest of the sheikhs. Politicians and their wives from many countries have enjoyed these apartments and the beautiful grounds here. It is very safe and secure and still in the heart of the city. There are views out to sea from the back gardens. I already have an apartment here and you will have the adjoining suite.'

I look around and take in all my new surroundings.

'I am relieved you are next to me!'

'Of course my dear, where else would I be staying?'

'How long have you had your apartment?'

'Twenty-five years at least. I have lost count. Neither Haya nor Gretal have ever been or stayed here, as this is where I do most of my business. It's like an office for me.'

The gates close with a clanging drone from their heaviness and we drive up to the house. It's impressive. I step out of the car and the first thing that strikes me is the lack of traffic noise. The trees obviously act as a buffer. In fact it's hard to believe we are in a busy city as the gardens look so tranquil and pretty.

'My dear, the staff are locals and have all worked here for over ten years. The gardeners have been here longer than me! Anyway they are prepared for you and are all looking forward to meeting my English fiancée.'

Three manservants and a woman all stand at the main entrance door. I am proudly introduced to them and they greet me with a warm smile. We exchange a few words then Samira, who looks slightly older than myself, steps forward to speak.

'Miss Janey, I will be your personal maid when you reside here.'

I thank her, I could not help but notice that her head was not covered in the usual Arabic way and her features are very different. She has a fine bone structure and her hair is long, neatly trimmed and just tied back with a small multicoloured scarf.

Mojat decides to show me the whole house and, as we wander around together, he takes great pleasure in explaining the background to this unusual, lovely building.

'Janey the architect that designed it was a Swiss/French gentleman called Le Corbusier.'

'Yes,' I say. 'That does not surprise me. The chairs in the morning room look like his design.'

Mojat seems amazed that I would know such a thing, as I have never trained in architecture or design. I explain to him that I am well read generally and, as I love the arts, I understand that Le Corbusier's designs are world-famous.

'The more I am with you, the more you turn me on. It's wonderful to meet such an intelligent woman, who is also very beautiful. I'm such a lucky man.'

He flatters me more than anyone I have ever known, he knows what a woman likes to hear. As an older man, I guess he should know by now.

We walk up the wide marble staircase. Oil paintings of the sheikh and his family, plus various pieces of art decorate the walls. An oversized Venetian glass vase, displaying a spectacular array of fresh flowers, sits on an old antique table at the top of the staircase.

He opens my apartment door. 'This will be your home for the next few months Janey.'

My apartment consists of four rooms, two of which have sea views with French doors out on to a balcony. There is a spacious bedroom with a separate, very large, bathroom. The dressing room has built-in cupboards and a lounge opens out on to a good-size balcony with a sea view. It is beautifully furnished with an old mahogany free-standing clock in the lounge which, on closer inspection, is a French antique. It's a mixture of contemporary furnishings with a few classic old pieces. Old Turkish rugs of deep reds line the floor areas. I like it straight away — it is so tasteful.

Mojat stands in front of me and points to the far wall in my bedroom. 'Look Janey, in the last week I have had a builder in your room to knock down part of this wall and to construct a concealed adjoining door into my apartment.'

I start to laugh — it's all too much. 'I love it!' I say. I realise by now that he obviously has a thing about secret doors!

'You are so naughty Mojat. Does the sheikh know that you've removed nearly a whole wall just so you can make love to me?'

I stand looking up at the wall that he's pointing to and cannot see what he is talking about. 'Where is this door?' I ask. The next second he presses a small tag device he is holding and, to my utter amazement, part of the wall moves back electronically to reveal his apartment.

'Now that is seriously clever Mojat. In this old ornate building a piece of space age has been created.'

I look more closely and wonder how on earth it had been done in a way that you would never know a door was there. So ultra-modern.

'I hired a German architect for this job. It was tight.'

'You mean the time?'

'Yes, I only had a week to turn this job around and, of course, in addition to the materials and workmanship, the men had to have a full security check.'

'So you don't just hire a couple of local builders here?'

'Janey, what planet are you on? There are no Arabic builders here. Jubai is built by the Indians and designed by the famous architects of Europe. I flew in a small team of Germans and, with them, they brought all the materials and equipment.'

'That will have cost you a few dirhams. It's impressive though — very!'

'You see Janey, in the Arab culture it has to look respectful — even at our age — that we do not sleep together until we're married. The secret door means we can live as we please and the outside world will never know. Other guests staying here will only see the two separate apartment doors from the corridor.'

'What about the servants?'

'They are long standing and have all signed secrecy oaths. They are well paid and have homes in the grounds. Why would they risk their jobs and homes? Anyway they are well treated and happy in their work.'

'Tell me about my personal maid?'

'Yes, of course my dear, she will become a big part in your life now. Samira's father was Arabic and her mother was half Swiss and she was brought up in a very liberal, mainly Arabic, family here. She has her mother's features and looks.'

We are then interrupted by a knock on the door. I walk from the bedroom into the lounge and open the door. Samira greets me with a smile.

'Ma'am, I just wanted to know if you are both dining in tonight as the chef is preparing for two other guests?'

I turn to Mojat who is sat on my sofa relaxing. He answers on my behalf. 'Yes, eight o'clock would be perfect, thank you.'

I close the door and notice on the inside a brand new type of Yale lock has recently been fitted and the key has been left in. I remove this after checking the door is locked. 'So it can only be opened from the inside or with a special key from the outside,' I whisper to myself.

I turn around thinking Mojat might have heard and, to my relief, he is not on the sofa. I place the key next to my handbag and then I walk back into my bedroom.

He is sitting on the edge of the bed, naked and physically ready for me. I walk up to him; his eyes have already undressed me. He takes my hands and pulls me on to the bed and starts to kiss my neck. Arousing needles of pleasure rush down my body and prickle into my pubic bone.

I am wearing a fitted dress to my knee with high heels. Before I can remove my shoes his hands are inside my dress grabbing and squeezing hard the thick cool flesh of my thighs. He pulls my panties to one side and his fingers are now massaging my lubricating vagina, the earthy fragrance of my secretions running all over his hands — which arouses him further.

He whispers in my ear. 'Baby, the scent of your juices is making me crazy. It's like nectar and is sending me wild.'

I like his talk, I like his craziness and, most of all, I like to feel his hardness pulsing in my palm.

I lay on my back as he pulls my dress up to my waist, he quickly removes my panties and then bends my knees up into my chest holding me there whilst his fingers arouse me further.

One shoe falls on to the floor, he does not seem to notice as he pulls and turns my body over like a rag doll. Only a few days away from me and he seems to have doubled in size!

I am now face down on my knees with my bottom being held

high in the air by his oversize hands. He tilts my bottom up towards him and my swollen lips are ready to welcome his hard penis.

He heaves and pushes himself forward, entering me, maintaining a good hard rhythm. I enjoy him and right now I am his bitch on heat again.

Mojat is eager, he talks loudly in Arabic, slapping my arse hard and making me squeal. My face is being pushed into the bed sheets. I feel like I'm suffocating as I try to move my head to one side, gasping for air. His talk is loud and I suspect it is dirty filthy, but I don't care. I tell him that I want more — the excitement is just too much as he bends and shapes me for his pleasure.

I am addicted to our sex, it is earthy, spontaneous and powerful but, unfortunately, this time it is short-lived. He finishes and leaves me in a high state. I make him pleasure me until I enter the waves of internal joy bringing me to the edge of pure ecstasy.

In the aftermath his heart beats fast and his body releases short hard shocks as we lay in stillness. We lie quietly looking out to the jealous sky. Dusk is upon us in the stillness and calm. Our breathing settles, he eventually speaks quite softly.

'Spontaneous sex is always the most exciting.'

I agree with him. I lie in his arms with a stinging tingling bottom. I know I have the power to keep this man forever hungry for me.

Ask any worldly woman who has loved and lost; spontaneity keeps the relationship healthy and the man on his toes. If you are an intelligent woman who enjoys sexual pleasure, you learn to let him feel like he is the one taking you, chasing you. It's a game we all play! Once the man loses the chase his interest fades!

CHAPTER TWENTY

The Shamal Season

We dress for dinner and go down to meet the other guests. I glance at the dining room table as we walk past. Khalid, the chef I was introduced to earlier, has prepared a dinner of Middle Eastern delights.

A couple are sat in the lounge relaxing on easy chairs. We walk over to them and immediately the guy jumps out of his seat and embraces Mojat. They begin talking very loudly in Arabic — a fun sounding type of banter.

Mojat then introduces me in English. They are a good-looking French-Lebanese couple. Antoine, a silver fox with grey-white hair, is a slim, petite man. His wife, Cyrine, is statuesque and voluptuous. They couldn't be more opposite.

He is an old establish friend here on an official visit. Cyrine informs me that she has spent the day shopping whilst her husband attended his meetings.

Mojat stands and looks at me holding a bottle of wine.

'Janey there is always wine for the guests if you would care for a glass?'

Of course, alcohol! It had slipped my mind that we are in a public room of an official Arabic government building. I decide to go with the flow and just have a soft drink.

The evening is enjoyable and the couple entertain us with many interesting stories. Antoine does not speak of his work or mention his meeting, though he was obviously involved in politics as he studied in the UK on the same course as Mojat. I try to bring the subject up a couple of times but the theme of the conversation moves quickly on.

Cyrine informs me that she is an ex-model, now hosting a TV show in Beirut. I connect with her straight away. She is eager to talk about the show, but I keep getting distracted by her enormous breasts. Mine are of good proportions but Cyrine's are just, well, bloody huge!

She catches a glimpse of me looking at them. 'I know luvvy, aren't they just the business? I paid a lot for these,' she says smoothing her hands over them.

I'm intrigued by her openness. 'How much are breasts nowadays?' I ask casually.

'I paid ten thousand euros in France. Mind you, that was three years ago now!'

'I take it you're pleased with the results then?'

'Pleased! I am delighted! I've had quite a few bits and pieces done over the years but these are the real prize!'

'They're the icing on the cake!' says Antoine chipping in.

Cyrine admires her perfect body sliding her hands over her waist. 'Yes, he got the surprise of his life when the surgeon removed the last of the bandages.'

'I bet he did,' I answer with a smile. I suddenly have this vision of Antoine at her bedside.

'Talking of icing on the cake,' she says. 'I am ravenous now and haven't eaten all day. The shopping seems to have taken over.'

Cyrine stands up and totters across the room in her six-inch gold mules to take a seat at the table. The rest of us follow suit.

Everything about Cyrine is almost too perfect. Her skin, bone structure, lips, teeth and a great figure for a woman in her forties. She studied fine art in Paris in her early twenties. For some reason that quite surprised me, as it doesn't quite fit with the image. You don't really put the two together, fine classical art with an ex-model and TV host. I am not sure what sort of ex-model she was, but I look forward to her next instalment. I just can't quite put my finger on her — something is not quite right.

Just before midnight, after an enjoyable evening, we all retire to our rooms. Mojat and I snuggle down into bed together and he wraps his arms around my naked body, immediately falling asleep. It has been a tense couple of days, what with Mojat in Iran and me sacrificing my apartment and work for our new life together.

The calling to prayer wakes us both up. I turn around and kiss him and in my playfulness I say. 'Hadn't you better get up my love — they are calling you?'

Of course there was no response. One thing about Mojat, he is not a hypocrite. He enjoys a pint of beer, a glass of wine, or a stiff gin and tonic. Although I have never seen him eat pork.

He had a strict upbringing until his eighteenth birthday. His parents then became far more liberal when he left to study in England. He was a young, highly intelligent man who his parents believed could then make his own decisions. Mojat never talks about his spiritual faith. I know he is not religious.

Regarding his culture, I would say there is a strong Arabic influence, but he is more westernised, more European. He has a London apartment in Knightsbridge where he resides during the year. He adores England, our history and, especially, the architecture.

It's Friday, the traditional start of the weekend and I'm feeling playful as we drink hot tea in bed. Mojat seems more concerned about the wind outside. He puts on a robe and walks over to the windows tutting loudly and shaking his head. Most Arabs I've met here always tut loudly. He comes back to bed muttering some Arabic words under his breath.

We drink our tea and in-between we kiss like a couple of teenagers. I find him very sensual being an older man with status. I think about the future for us and imagine, after spending entire days together, it's bound to get a lot more familiar. Then we'll have to rely on other qualities that stimulate and sparkle the senses. He has a great sense of humour. If he retains this, I imagine we will have no problems, as I like a man that can make me laugh.

After breakfast we take a stroll around the garden. He reminds me again that the shamal season is now upon us. The wind is much stronger than I envisaged, blowing from the direction of the sea. Trees are beginning to bend and the branches of the palms are creaking. Flower petals fly up in the air and the roses are now almost down to bare sticks. The tall fluorescent aqua sea grasses rustle and shake like a wild stallion's mane.

Mojat pulls a face. He is not a happy soul as he looks around the garden.

'Janey, this is not good — we will not be sailing this weekend. It's that time of year again and I think we have a shamal whipping up. I was anticipating that we might get a good sail on Sunday or Monday but this blasted shamal has arrived earlier than I anticipated.'

He picks up his phone and starts to speak to Herman about buttoning down and securing everything on board his yacht. He speaks in a tense manner, scowling, showing deep furrows across his forehead.

'Janey we will go to the sailing club now as I am needed to help do some checks. It seems the radar equipment is not working properly.'

We rush back into the house and I pick up my bag and jacket. I have deck shoes on his yacht, which he insists I wear when we are sailing.

I do remember a sand storm last May when all cars parked around the city were covered in a terracotta dust. The locals call this Al-Haffar. The fishermen stay in port and huge depressions appear in the desert during this time. *The Gulf News* reported last year that a ship had broken up in the Gulf Sea during a shamal. Thinking about this now, having experienced a small storm on his yacht, makes me feel very nervous.

We sit sheltering in the open stone porch of the house, waiting for Kulpreet to bring the car. Mojat turns to me. 'Habibie, you are daydreaming.'

'I was just thinking about the shamal.'

'This evening would you like to go dancing at the Lebanese Club with Antoine and Cyrine? They return to Beirut tomorrow and I know how much you love to dance.'

'I would thank you. It'll be fun, especially with Cyrine.'

He turns and smiles. 'So you enjoyed Cyrine's company last night?'

'Yes I did, she is interesting in a fun way. She has striking looks don't you think Mojat? You never comment about her.'

He shrugs his shoulders. Kulpreet arrives at The White House gates in one of his highly polished Bentleys. Mojat stands up having never answered me about Cyrine, walks forward and opens the car door for me.

On arrival at the club the car park is busy. Kulpreet parks in his usual place and, as he opens the car door, there is a loud eerie high-pitched screaming sort of noise. I have to raise my voice above it.

'Mojat what is that deafening noise? It seems to be coming from the boats, sorry yachts.'

'It's the rigging making that sound!'

We walk along the pontoon gangway that leads us to his yacht and we climb on board. The wind, which is now gale force, is blowing against us.

My long hair blows in all directions across my face as I try to tie it back with a band. I stand and look around the yacht whilst holding on to a rail. His crew are moving around at great speed on deck.

Mojat shouts above the wind. 'Janey, there are around thirty yachts here and when a high wind forces itself through and around the rigging it creates a ringing screaming sound.'

'I have never heard anything like it!'

'Habibie if you prefer to say boats that's fine. You are so natural, so endearing the way you speak. Don't ever change.'

I shout above the eerie screams. 'The rigging sounds like a hundred Tibetan singing bowls all chiming out of sync!'

He starts to laugh, dispelling some of his tenseness.

'I think Buddha is making an appearance, teaching everyone to be mindful.'

He surprisingly agrees and laughs again, whilst holding on to and pulling one of the heavier ropes. 'You might be right habibie. You've reminded me of when I was in Chiang Mai in Thailand. I entered a Tibetan monk's temple and it was something else! An amazing feeling came over me! One of those special moments, never to be forgotten.'

As he tugs at one of the ropes we strain to have a conversation above the intense noise. He then passes me a rope to hold as I stand next to him. I find I have to shout even more as the screaming rigging noise and the wind whipping around my ears is deafening.

'Maybe you should convert to Buddhism Mojat?'

'You're so playful Janey.'

'You know that Richard Gere, Sting, Leonard Cohen, Jeff Bridges, Tina Turner, Angelina Jolie and Brad Pitt are all Buddhists? And, oh yes, the CEO of Apple Corporation is too!'

His voice is raised and agitated. 'Okay, okay, okay Janey — maybe I will follow them all! Maybe I will become a monk! A celibate one at that!'

He is tying off the ropes, pulling hard and shouting instructions to one of his crew.

'Not celibate Mojat, no!' I say. 'Anyway you could never manage without sex, not now you have found me.'

'True yes, very true my dear. Janey, will you go downstairs and check that all the cabin porthole windows are tightly secure?'

I move through the bedroom suites quickly, knowing in my heart that Herman would have checked all of these. I walk into my room, shut the door behind me and stand for a few seconds, wanting to see behind that false door again. I open the wardrobe and my clothes are all still hanging neatly. I reach into the back and open the door. Just like before it's unlocked and all the guns and canvas bag remain inside. I close the door quickly and then go into his suite to check the windows and curiosity gets the better of me.

I open his wardrobe door and, just as I had suspected, he has a false door too. I turn the handle and it seems locked. I try again and, yes, it is securely locked. I lean back and shut his wardrobe door.

Before leaving his room I quickly check the windows, which are fine. Strange that his secret door is locked yet mine is still unlocked. I really do not know what to make of this. There must be a key somewhere in his room. Just when I thought I would go back and look again, Mojat suddenly appears and startles me.

'There you are?'

'All the windows are secure,' I say.

Today the sailing club is a hive of activity. I can hear raised voices from the members, as they're all busy rushing around helping each other to secure their vessels. A sense of urgency is in the air. I return on deck to see what's happening.

Mojat's dishdasha blows up like a tent. He attempts to hold his clothing in place whilst also trying hard to secure the yacht's equipment with his crew. It is now hard work for anyone to stand up straight.

The clubhouse is full of excitable, contagious conversations. I glance down at several children who've gathered around a table listening to the adults discussing the wind speed and the potential damage it might cause. Their faces are a picture of alarm for a few moments, then they're distracted and all resume playing their games.

I remember high winds as a ten-year-old when my parents had a house built on top of a hillside in Derbyshire. During our very first winter there we endured fierce gales and, one particular night, the howling wind kept us all awake. When we emerged downstairs early the following morning, to our amazement the garage roof had blown off and had landed, in one piece, on our back lawn. This was much to my father's dismay!

As a child it felt exciting as many of our neighbours visited to offer advice and support. It almost became a party in my child's eyes. Even the milkman stopped for a cup of tea that day and walked around examining the garage roof with my dad. Both wondered how on earth it managed to stay in one piece. Over the next few days the milkman and our neighbours were frequently in our kitchen, having cups of tea, whilst they all decided on the best strategy to repair our garage roof.

I went to school the following day and Mr. Thompson, our teacher, always had a morning slot talking about the news. I put my hand up and was given permission to speak. 'Sir, I have some news.' I stood up in front of my class for the first time ever to talk about our garage roof. Everyone applauded and Mr. Thompson praised me for my little talk. The children's faces in the club just reminded me of that excitement, mixed with fear and anticipation of what might happen next?

Local news is now being broadcast on the club's 60-inch television screen. The forecast wind speed of this shamal will reach thirty-three knots within the hour, decreasing later tonight.

'Thirty-three knots Mojat. What is that in miles per hour?'

'It's thirty-eight habibie but don't worry, it's strong but not too threatening. One year it was recorded at forty-three knots.'

I look around the clubhouse, which is now full to capacity. All the serious sailors, their wives and children are here. The camaraderie is great and the club staff also look after yachts for members currently out of the country. The chef has pulled in additional staff to deal with the extra meals being ordered. They are doing a roaring trade! The children play in a designated corner so that all the tables are freed up for food and drinks. More wooden stools have been brought out of storage to equip every member. The children are drafted in too to help position the tables.

Only the odd person ventures out through the main door leading on to the terrace. The outside tables and chairs are now chained and tied up and in the distance, looking out to sea, there are hundreds of white tails.

The club has a small private beach next door; I can see one umbrella rolling around on the sand that must have been overlooked. I stand looking out of the main clubhouse window down the beach. The sand is flicking and blowing upwards, hitting the side window facing the driveway where Kulpreet has parked the car.

A layer of fine dark red sand dust is now coating the Bentley. Mojat has not batted an eyelid. This is life in the desert town during the shamal season.

I feel an arm around me and I look up to see Simone and David with their girls.

'Have you all just arrived?'

'David insisted we come as usual,' replies Simone. 'You know he gets withdrawal symptoms if he's not down here on Fridays for lunch on the terrace. He calls it his wine down time, meaning his usual bottle of Italian Frascati.'

I laugh. Simone has a similar sense of humour to mine and it's so true what she's saying. He loves the club on his days off work.

'Mojat has his table tucked away in the corner, come and join us.'

David had just been to check on his boat, he has a small twenty-foot sailing yacht. He then looks around for a spare stool and draws it up to our table.

David begins a conversation. 'Jesus Janey, I flew in from Kuwait late last night after securing a business deal. I'm relieved to say I made it home just in time.'

'That was lucky David. I presume all flights are cancelled here and in the Arabic states around us?'

Mojat walks up to the table carrying the menu of today's specials. On hearing our conversation he says. 'For sure they are all cancelled and in Kuwait the shamal is worse than here this afternoon.'

David looks up and greets Mojat. 'Man ... I know. I left two hours earlier than normal as I had a tip off from my taxi driver on

Singing in Silence

my arrival.'

'That's good you took his advice,' replies Mojat.

The Second World War spirit is in the club today. It feels a humbling experience that everyone is working as a family, a team spirit that mum used to talk about from her experiences of living through the war.

The yachty lifestyle sounds and looks glamorous from the outside, but the work you have to put in once you own a yacht or boat is constant. The maintenance, mooring fees and general running costs are only for the dedicated sailors. At the club they are nicknamed The Diehards.

Mojat's super yacht is in another league, but what I love about him today is that he's just another sailor in the club with the same worries and concerns as any other member.

Buxom Brenda has just walked in. Simone has kindly pointed her out to me. I have to say she looks like she's been dragged through a hedge backwards. Still wearing her tiny, tight hot pants and her usual skimpy low cut top, Simone had described her to a T. But this time she's wearing a windproof nautical sailing jacket over the top of her hot pants.

Very sensible Brenda, I think to myself. Although her jacket is not fastened, her push up bra has hoisted her boobs so high they're almost up to her neck. I witness the men gawping at them as she makes her way through the crowded room.

Her gold bouffant hairstyle is now more like a bird's nest without the bird.

She spots Mojat in the corner and makes a beeline for him, just as Simone had described to me. By all accounts she is a very capable sailor and is always trying her luck with him. She breathes in and squeezes her body around the table. She rubs past David and another couple that had also joined us, just to sit next to Mojat.

I stand at a distance with Simone as she orders drinks for her girls. I am amused as I can tell Mojat looks uncomfortable. Brenda removes her professional sailing jacket to reveal her uplifted protruding thirty-eight double D cup breasts, squeezed into what looks like a size ten navy and white striped Bri-nylon tank top from the early seventies.

She gently touches her hair in different places to ease it back into place.

I walk back with two cappuccinos in my hands as the waiters are too overrun. I put the coffees on the table and ask Brenda if she would also like one. Mojat is now looking quite put out and extremely niggly. The thought of me waiting on Brenda whilst she sits at his side is all too much for him.

He waves furiously at the manager for him to take the order from our table and insists I sit down next to him on his other side — I think to relieve him from his fan club friend.

Buxom Brenda smiles as she swoons over Mojat's every word. Her deeply tanned and raised veiny hands are wrapped around her latte glass revealing several diamond rings and long orange chipped nails. How she manages to skipper her yacht with those nails, God only knows! She speaks with a plum as though she is aristocracy. I am fascinated — what an unusual character!

I start to make conversation with her. 'Simone tells me that you're advertising for crew on the club's noticeboard?'

She smiles. 'Yes, for my next adventure — I mean, sailing trip.'

'Where's that then?' asks David.

'To Barbados and the other islands of the West Indies of course. That's if I can get some strong fit men together on board with me for a couple of months.'

'We'd all like some strong fit men Brenda for an adventure,' says Simone.

All the guys start laughing around the table. She looks quite indignant until she relaxes and sees the funny side of Simone's comment.

Simone quietly whispers in my ear whilst everyone else is chatting. 'The story goes that's how she gets her nooky, after several weeks out at sea the guys are just dying for it by then. She is the only woman on board, so not much choice for them. She works this in her favour by only advertising for men as crew.'

'Simone, you never surprise me, you're a mine of information — or is it just gossip?'

'I'm just relaying what I hear from my sources! Remind me later to tell you about a party on-board Brenda's yacht when she sailed around the Greek Islands. She was with Mickey Most, the Irish guy who works down at Jubai's port.'

'Why don't you tell me now whilst everyone is talking?'

'He was a strong bruiser of a guy, used to lugging large crates of meat and fish for a living. Anyway he joined her crew two years ago.'

'When you say he was a strong guy, what happened to him?'

'Well, exactly, it's a long story, but not for now.'

My mind boggles. We all get distracted as Steve, a recent new member, joins our overcrowded and cosy table. He puts his pint of Stella down and sits opposite Brenda. Her eyes begin to sparkle as she eyes him up and down. We all say hi and he introduces himself in a very confident way. He looks like a sculptured bronze with a full six-pack.

Brenda's lights have just been turned on, it's as if she's been magnetised. Blackpool illuminations have nothing on her glistening irises.

Brenda's luck is in, I think to myself,

Steve has joined our table, as he's interested in her advertisement for crew. Well it's as if her birthday and Christmas have both arrived at once.

She now moves away from Mojat's side and manoeuvres her way around the table, brushing everyone with her uplifted boobs and sneaking in at the side of this fit looking athlete.

There are smiles at the table as they become engrossed in discussions on yachts, the Caribbean, maybe even in seafaring shanty stories. She orders another round of drinks.

Brenda sits crossed-legged, her raised varicose veins well

hidden under her dark tan. She is being entertained by Steve's enthusiasm to sail to exotic lands on the other side of the world. Brenda's white kitten heels are dangling off the end of her foot in anticipation.

Mojat sighs with relief as David gives me a wink. Our plans have changed, we forget the souks we were going to visit over the creek and now Kulpreet drives us both back down the beach road to The White House. We are windswept and tired after a full afternoon at the club.

The palm trees that line the road are all bent over and many branches are flying around in the air. Some are strewn across the road as Kulpreet swerves in various places to avoid hitting them. Mojat confirms that the evening plan with Antoine and Cyrine is still on. The forecast suggests that the winds will begin to die down by 10pm.

CHAPTER TWENTY-ONE

My Nurturing Personal Maid

Samira is waiting anxiously at the door and offers to run me a bath. I accept graciously. How wonderful and decadent this feels to have my own personal maid.

Mojat squeezes my hand as he always does when he is happy. 'Enjoy your bath and being pampered, this is your new life now.'

Feeling light-headed and dusty from the wind I walk into the large spacious steaming bathroom. Samira stands in front of me.

'Ma'am you have sand in your hair and around your eyes — be careful.'

She pulls over a small rattan chair for me to sit on. She then wrings out a hot damp flannel and begins to pat the facecloth all around my eyes and cheeks. It feels good as she fusses over me, lifting my hair up away from my neck.

'You have good skin ma'am. I can see you have looked after yourself.'

She begins to talk of the old folklore traditions connected to the shamal. My ears prick up as I find facts on this culture and their traditional ways fascinating.

'Ma'am, many locals come down with respiratory and eye infections. And, as it is a full moon tonight, we have to watch for …' She hesitates and does not finish her sentence. I am listening and, for some reason, I undress in front of her standing naked whilst she checks the temperature of the bath. She looks back to me and nods, as if to say, it's okay the temperature is fine.

I step into the deep bath and sit down. Before I sink further she settles on a small wooden stool next to the bath and starts to sponge warm water down my back and shoulder blades in gentle methodical strokes. I permit this without questioning. Maybe this is what personal maids do? I don't know, but what I do know is, I like it. It feels nurturing and comforting.

After she has soaped my back and neck for a few minutes she passes me the sponge to finish off the rest of my body. I lay in the hot water whilst she chats to me from her small wooden stool.

'Ma'am, the full moon and a shamal together is not good.'

'Really, why is this?' I ask.

She now positions herself next to my head, then takes my hairbrush and teases out any tangles, whilst holding the weight of my hair in her hands. In a calm tranquil voice she says. 'The wind has tangled your hair.'

She pours a little Arabic oil in her palm and begins to very gently massage my scalp. She does this as she continues with her story.

'It's wild ma'am, always wild when it arrives on that full moon. People dread it if the two coincide. Babies cry in the night, the local dogs howl and howl. Many things happen.'

'It sounds unnerving Samira. I suppose most people in the outside villages don't get much sleep with all that going on.'

'No ma'am, you can see lights on everywhere in the small houses around — it whips up and creates plenty of damage too. Freda, my close friend, and her family come into the village from the desert just for shelter. They are tribal Bedouins ma'am.'

'Where do they stay?'

'With cousins ma'am who live just on the outskirts. People come down with fevers and sickness and many of the old are taken.'

I sigh, presuming she means the old die. Samira stays with me through the whole process and I act as though this type of pampering is what I am used to.

'What does your friend Freda do?'

'Mr. Mojat knows Freda and her family; she works with the

tribal elders. They are traditional healers.'

'Gosh, how interesting.'

'She forages for plants, bushes, rare saps from desert trees and collects snake and spider venom. Then she distils them to make medicines.'

'Sounds like homeopathic medicine that I use.'

'People from all over the Gulf ma'am, including some professional doctors, buy from the Bedouins. Homeopaths and herbalists in Europe all come to buy, the tribes make their living this way. Only the true Bedouins know where to forage in the vastness of the desert. Traditions past down ma'am, from generation to generation.'

'It's truly fascinating.'

Samira then tries to impress me with her talents. 'Ma'am I have many skills as a personal maid.' She continues with my scalp massage.

'I am sure. I am enjoying being pampered.'

'No ma'am this is normal, not pampering. I will look after all your personal needs — this is my job.'

'Okay,' I say, loving every moment as my scalp tingles from her touch.

She finishes by teasing all the tangles out of my hair and then brings warm towels over to me. As I stand up in the bath she wraps them around me, at the same time looking down at my pubic hair. She gives a big tut, then another.

'Ma'am no hair! Arabs no hair here! Not clean to have any hair here.'

I look down and could not agree more. It's been a while since Frances waxed me a Brazilian at Beautiful Lady.

There is a chaise longue in the bathroom. Samira pulls it into the centre of the room and lays a large thick towel over it. She insists on waxing me, whilst still tutting away to herself.

'Its easy ma'am, the steam will have opened all your pores and they will come out easily. I am quick and good at this and will make you very fresh.'

I lie down on the chaise with a warm towel over me, recalling that Frances had said something similar. Meanwhile Samira proceeds to rip up pieces of white cloth into wide strips and mounts them at her side. She positions her little wooden stool closer to me and coats a spatula with warm melted wax. She lifts my breasts and tucks a towel securely underneath then draws my legs apart, plastering the warm honey liquid firmly on my cunny … still tutting and shaking her head at the disgusting sight of pubic hair.

I look down at myself, thinking, it's not that bad — only two or three week's growth!

I close my eyes and try to relax as I had done with Frances, so hopefully it won't be such a shock this time. Her nimble fingers move all around me as she pushes the cotton strips on to my skin over the wax. She presses hard on the strip and lifts one end ripping the hair out. Samira is right, the steam has made it far less painful than my experience with Francis. She does all my outer area quite quickly. I lay there enjoying the sensation of the warm wax.

Samira then changes her tactics and moves her fingers very gently around my clitoris. She lifts my outer lips open to one side and very carefully, in a methodical way, layers the warm wax. Then she repeats the cloth on the other outer lip and presses into my warm damp cunny several times. I sense from her that she has noticed that I am enjoying her touch.

'Ma'am you are comfortable?' she asks in her half broken Arabic.

I nod my head.

'Just you relax ma'am I will make you clean and fresh.'

I think to myself — fresh — I have heard this somewhere before.

'Yes Samira, you have a gentle touch.' I look at her plain lovely face then close my eyes again — her task is nearly complete.

She mutters to herself. 'Just a few stubborn little ones.' She reaches for her tweezers and holds my labia and outer lips, moving them from side to side for a couple of minutes, tweezing out the hairs that the wax cannot reach. As she rubs a final steaming hot cloth over and around my clitoris, she presses down firmly on my outer lips. It is the most wonderful sensation. I then feel a few drops of warm oil and, with the tips of her fingers, she massages the whole of my pubic area in circular movements.

'Ma'am this will prevent a rash.'

She lifts my right leg first and places it on her shoulder, manipulating my thigh area and then moving up to my groin. Then further up, again lifting and moving my outer vaginal lips. She repeats the whole process again with the left leg, massaging upwards from the thigh and around my pubic bone, spending extra time stimulating my clitoris.

It's a wonderful feeling. She has amazing precision in her nimble slim fingertips as though she has done this hundreds of times. I am pulsing and tingling throughout my body. She eases my leg down then turns me on to my side. She now lifts and separates my buttocks and adds a few more drops, the oil is now quite hot and makes me jump.

'Okay ma'am, it is meant to be hot around your anal gland.'

Anal gland, I think to myself. I thought only vets tamper with the anal gland!

She begins to massage again but this time pressing in and around my anal area, still holding my buttocks slightly apart. She then moves her nimble fingers up from my anus to my outer lips, again circulating firmly on my clitoris and up to the pubic bone. She repeats this process many times. Her therapeutic touch is provocative, stimulating and beautiful, creating waves of tingles throughout my body.

She finishes off by spraying rose water all around my pubes, then covers me with a towel.

'Ma'am, we might as well do these too,' she says looking at my legs.

By the time she has finished I am dozing, half asleep.

'Next time ma'am, I will give you a full Arabic body massage — a very beautiful experience. I have very special oils at home for this treatment that Freda gave me. I will bring them for you.'

'I look forward to this Samira. You're looking after me very well.'

'I am your personal maid,' she says again.

She helps me on with my bathrobe and notices a couple of hairs around my nipples. She sits me back down, gets her tweezers and very gently eases these hairs out. Then she puts a little oil on each nipple, massaging them between her fingertips. Tingles shoot down my body.

'You have to keep them well-oiled ma'am. Yours are very pink and delicate like Scandinavian ladies. You are so lucky to have such large pink nipples. They are beautiful.'

I look down at myself thinking, yes, I know one man who just wants to suck the life out of them!

'I will look after and care for your assets ma'am. Did you enjoy my touch — was it to your liking?'

I feel as though I am entering a trance, the way she touched my nipples was sublime.

'This is now your job Samira. You can look after my delicate body.'

'Very good ma'am.' She then scrutinises every part of me. 'Very well, I will take care of your body and keep it very good and fresh.'

'Yes very fresh,' I say in my transcendental, meditative state. The late Maharishi Mahesh Yogi would be impressed as I am now floating in the air, hovering around the ceiling.

She begins to clear away and tidy the bathroom. I rinse my hair with the showerhead and begin to blow dry it.

'Anything else ma'am before I depart for the day?'

I look at her face, smile and give her permission to leave.

I have never experienced this pleasure before. Is this normal here? Or is it just what's expected if you are fortunate enough to have your own personal maid. Is it part of their duty to care for their lady in such a gentle, erotic way? The culture differences are interesting. In that steamy large bathroom I felt she was nurturing me and my sexual assets. I remember Lola saying, as we drove away from the Beautiful Lady salon, that all local women go for a special fresh waxing every ten days — if you're not lucky enough to have your own personal maid.

I sit at the old-fashioned dressing table gazing at myself in the mirror. I think about what to wear for Samir's Lebanese Club.

Mojat walks in with a gin and tonic each with sliced limes hanging over the sides of the glasses.

'Ooh lovely, thank you.'

'Habibie, do you feel relaxed after bathing?'

'Yes, very much so.'

Quietly I say. 'Yes my love it was erotic encounters of the third kind.'

'Sorry my dear, did you say something?'

'I just said she massaged me too.'

I did not want to reveal to him which part of my body was massaged, and how amazing it is to have an Arabic personal maid that attends to me in such fine detail.

'Your maid Samira — she is looking after you well? Are you happy with her?'

'Yes she is very caring and attentive. I'm extremely happy with her.'

'Good habibie, she has never married.'

I'm not surprised, I think to myself.

'Of course, it was her choice, not sure why.'

I defend her and say. 'Well marriage is not for everyone.'

'I know her family' says Mojat. 'They tried to arrange it, but as a young woman she rebelled and her father, deep down, did not want to let her go. She looked after her parents until they died, which I am sure suited them in the long term.'

'I'm sure it did.'

There is a knock at the door.

'That will be our sandwiches.'

Mojat returns with a plate of pastrami and gherkin sandwiches, which I thought was a little unusual.

'Hope you like them,' he says.

I did and we polish the plate off in no time. It was rather cosy sitting together, looking out of my lounge window towards the sea, sharing a plate of sandwiches and sipping our drinks. Mojat then goes to his bedroom and brings back a bar of Swiss chocolate.

'Now that's what I call telepathy.'

'What do you mean?'

'I was only just thinking that I could finish off with a few squares of chocolate.'

'Habibie, I must have read your mind.'

'It's not the first time this has happened between us.'

CHAPTER TWENTY-TWO

Behind Closed Doors

We leave The White House at 9:30pm in order to meet Antoine and Cyrine at 10pm at the Lebanese Club. Our table was booked. Mojat looks sophisticated in his Italian dark grey silk suit. His pale pink shirt collar is open and he wears his usual stylish fine leather slip-on shoes. I am wearing a black cocktail dress, a classic with an elegant sash at the back, just below the knee. The Chanel shoes and handbag that he'd bought for me when I first stayed on his yacht, compliment it perfectly. I feel so lucky that I have walked into a lifestyle that most women would kill for.

I have secrets — we all have secrets. I've had times in my past when life was difficult and I've struggled. These are now behind me. Mojat grew up with a silver spoon so I don't think he would ever understand.

I don't want to talk about the past. Live for the moment, it's kinder and easier on the heart.

Our table is perfect; it is situated to the right-hand side of the stage and at the front. It takes us a few minutes to be seated, as Mojat seems to know so many people and they are all pleased to see him. As we walk around the many tables he introduces me as his fiancée to almost everyone. I can tell he is proud of me and I feel privileged to be at his side too. I feel his love and he shows it to me and the entire outside world.

Antoine and Cyrine arrive a little later. The club is busy and all the tables are now taken. The band starts to play and out strides a very handsome male Lebanese singer. The audience stands up to applaud, shouting and whistling as he takes a bow.

Mojat claims he is well known in the Arabic world. His name is Wael Kfoury, a handsome man around the age of fifty. His first two songs go down well but I have listened to so many Arabic artists in the past. When someone is talented they usually bring their own band, and his consists of six guys with two female backing singers. He is good and lively and most of the audience seem to know the words and sing along.

Antoine orders a bottle of whisky for the table, which duly arrives with five glasses and a bucket of ice. Why five glasses I wonder? Mojat did not seem to notice this as he was in deep conversation with Antoine.

Cyrine looks stunning in her long white evening dress, which has a slit up the side to her thighs. Her legs go on forever and she resembles a Hollywood film star. Her dress is strapless with a full diamanté bodice and her glossy auburn hair falls heavy down her back. Cyrine's whole look is way over the top for an evening out with us. Antoine looks typically French — stylish and understated.

Wael the singer departs after several songs and the resident club band arrives on stage to perform some good dance music. The lead female vocalist seems to have the gift of getting everyone up on the dance floor.

Cyrine and I are chatting and getting to know each other a little more when Wael the singer, all of a sudden, pulls up a chair to join us. Wow, this is a bit of a shock! He and Cyrine make a huge fuss of each other and Wael shakes the guys' hands. He then turns to me and kisses me on each side of my cheeks. And so the fifth glass is now half full. It seems that they have known each other for many years.

After just ten minutes Wael departs to go backstage, then Antoine takes Cyrine's hand to dance. And, yes, what would you expect — they are both great movers. So good that they end up with their own audience.

I glance over to the dance floor and Mojat takes my hand too. We join them and it is magical dancing with him. He leads the way with confidence and is a complete natural. His arms securely hold on to my waist, he swings me into a turn and then pulls me back in. It's a very sexual Latin move that turns many heads on the floor. We dance through several songs finishing our time with a ballad. He holds me close singing along in my ear and giving me a tender squeeze. Of course I don't know what he sings in Lebanese Arabic, but it's so romantic.

Antoine and Cyrine are still dancing and I look over to them several times. I cannot help but notice that Cyrine attracts a lot of male attention and Antoine seems to enjoy and thrive on it all.

Mojat notices that I am watching them both.

'I know what you are thinking Janey.'

As the song comes to a close I pull back and look into his eyes.

'Do you?'

'Yes I do,' he whispers. 'But I am the lucky one.'

'What makes you say this?'

'Antoine loves and enjoys the image of an ex-model and TV presenter in his arms, but his desires are far more down to earth.'

'Really, you know this do you?'

He nods his head and turns to Antoine and Cyrine dancing together. 'I have known Antoine since our university days and he hasn't changed a bit.'

I wonder what he is really talking about, such a strange statement to make.

Cyrine disappears and Antoine is now seated, enjoying his drink whilst talking to someone on the next table. There is a short interval in the entertainment.

I have a little walk around and then visit the ladies room. An old-fashioned, neon theatrical sign hangs over the doorway that reads in English 'Ladies Powder Room.' I smile, wondering where on earth they managed to find this old art deco sign in the Middle East.

I walk in and see Cyrine standing in front of a full-length mirror, positioning her boobs back into her tightly fitted dress.

'I have to do some adjustments, luvvy, as they expand at night. You know don't you?'

I stand watching her struggle. 'Not really, you mean water retention?'

'Don't be silly luvvy, it's the heat!'

I still don't understand how the heat from the club could expand her boobs, but I smile as if I know. She fascinates me as I watch her pushing them up and down, first one then the other in order to get the balance right.

She then takes a pale pink crystal lipstick out of her evening purse and pouts her lips to recoat. I watch as she slips on her long white lace evening gloves and notice, for the first time, that her hands are quite large. I stand next to her almost in awe of her statuesque body.

She presents herself in front of me looking directly into my eyes.

'How do I look? As I am off to do a turn now.'

I am still mesmerised by her presence, she is a glamorous Rita Hayworth lookalike.

'What? You mean sing?'

Cyrine laughs. 'What do you think a turn is? Don't look so shocked. I have many strings to my bow.'

'I don't doubt your talents Cyrine. If you were to tell me you are a Hollywood movie star I would believe you.'

The six foot one inch Barbie doll now leaves the powder room. I know her height, as Antoine seemed proud to announce it earlier after he'd polished off a few drinks. He is quite the opposite — a small petite man in comparison. There is still something niggling me about Cyrine.

I join the men back at the table and Mojat tops up my glass. Wael returns on stage to loud applause for his second set. He then introduces Cyrine and they perform a duet together in English. They sing the well-known hit by Frank and Nancy Sinatra — 'Something Stupid.' I have to say she sounds similar to Nancy, but with a sexier husk.

Singing in Silence

I look at the men whilst Cyrine is singing. Mojat seems completely distracted and Antoine is reading a text on his mobile. Strange, very strange. Either they have both heard this so many times before, or there is something else that's distracting them. As the song concludes everyone applauds and cheers. Antoine looks up from his mobile and, at the last second, stands up at the front applauding and shouting something in Lebanese — I guess something that translates similar to bravo!

Mojat is not at the table and nowhere to be seen. Could he not have waited until she had finished singing? Did he not want to applaud his close friend's partner? I would have thought common courtesy was in order. Unusual, as this is not like Mojat!

Mojat returns and the evening draws to a close. Kulpreet is waiting at the rear stage door to take us back to The White House. Wael says his goodbyes to Cyrine and we all sit in the back of the car chatting.

Back at The White House one of the male staff is there to welcome us at this late hour. As we step out of the car, the wind is still blowing hard. Mojat and I bid farewell to Antoine and Cyrine as their flights leave Jubai early in the morning for Beirut, weather permitting.

We return to our apartment, it is now nearly 3am. I cleanse my face and shower and we both sit in bed enjoying a picnic of freshly made omelette sandwiches.

'A great idea,' I say, complimenting Mojat.

'Umm, I like my English sandwiches. Anyway we never ordered dinner this evening. We were too busy dancing and I can't survive on nibbles.'

He is down to earth in so many ways. Right now there is a glint in his eyes, a twinkle from his English university days. As we sit munching in bed, I want to find out more about our friends tonight.

'Mojat, how long have you known Antoine?'

'I have known him since university — I thought I had told you this?'

'Yes, sorry, I think you did last night. And Cyrine?'

'Well my dear, Cyrine is a different story.'

'Is she?'

'Oh yes.' He then takes another bite of his sandwich and there is silence as he wipes his mouth with a serviette. 'Well Janey, she is complicated.'

'Complicated! In what way?'

'Well Cyrine is really Cyril.'

'You mean she's a man?'

'Was!'

'Oh my God! Really? A man?'

'Janey this is confidential, but when Antoine met Cyrine she was female. But later, much later in fact, Antoine found out that she'd had a sex change.'

'Good God! I knew there was something about her. Incredible looking man!'

Mojat switches his bedside lamp off. 'Come on my dear, let's sleep now as it's been a very long day and tomorrow who knows?' His voice goes softer as he shuts his eyes and puts his arms around me. He mutters to himself. 'That bloody shamal might be back.'

I lay very still in his arms — my thoughts are with Antoine. I can't get my breath about Cyrine being Cyril.

Imagine you start dating someone and … well, what about the sex? That's an interesting one, what with Antoine finding out much later. What did Mojat say to me earlier this evening; that Antoine's desires are far more down to earth? I wonder what? The mind boggles.

My man is falling asleep beside me but I am restless from his last statement. I nudge him. 'I want to know about Antoine's desires? And how come he didn't find out that Cyrine had undergone a sex change? Mojat … are you listening?'

He keeps his eyes shut and, still holding me tight, he speaks softly in my ear. 'Yes, yes I am not asleep yet. You see Janey; life is not what it seems on the surface. Antoine has been gay ever since I've known him. He hides behind Cyrine. She knows this and loves him for his kindness, and he loves her for her personality and TV model-like status. I'm tired, can we talk more tomorrow? Can I go to sleep now? Please!'

I lay next to him, intrigued.

'So they've never enjoyed sex?'

He is now getting very exasperated with me. 'Janey please go to sleep. No sex! They would never have sex! Never! Now can I go to sleep?'

'Yes, goodnight my love.' I lean over and kiss his head.

I want to say out loud, 'Well chuff me!' My mother used to say this. You never know what goes on behind closed doors in relationships. Cyrine's hands should have been a giveaway? I think of this as I drift off into slumberland.

CHAPTER TWENTY-THREE

Transformation and Change

It's Saturday and we awake to yet another fierce wind, but less so than yesterday.

Mojat peers out of the window whilst pushing his mop of hair back off his face. He sighs. 'It remains very strong my dear, the trees are still pulling inland. Well, let's hope the shamal moves on later today.'

We take breakfast together downstairs in the morning room. It faces east and reflects a hue tangerine colour through the large window. This room has a fresh energy; maybe that's why it's called the morning room.

Mojat is to attend an important business meeting today. I presume it's regarding the peace process.

'Habibie, I will try not to be all day.' He kisses me long and hard before he departs.

Kulpreet waits in the car outside and Mojat enters. I watch as they drive out through the gates. Mojat has his window down and one of the guards bends down to speak to him, then subsequently waves the car through out on to the busy road. Immediately the gates are closed again.

The male staff in the house are moving large old trunks upstairs to the landing. I am just finishing my coffee and toast and marmalade when Samira arrives at my side.

'Good morning ma'am. Today you need help as there are many trunks containing your clothes that have arrived this morning. I will help you organise your wardrobes.'

'Would you make a start now Samira — and good morning to

you too!'

A busy start to the day; it feels as though my life is passing by very quickly. I worked last Wednesday and I go in tomorrow for my leaving party. And that's it! Tonight it's dinner with Simone and David. I must ring her to check all is okay.

The morning passes by quite smoothly. Samira does a wonderful job, pressing everything and arranging my clothes, handbags and shoes. She displays my personal photographs and tidies up everything in her path. She strips the bed and takes freshly laundered bed linen from a huge cupboard.

'These are new ma'am. Mr. Mojat has ordered from Egypt especially for your moving in. They are beautiful cotton, for your beds.'

The crisp pure white cotton is edged with a gold silk thread and the same thread is piped around the extended Oxford pillowcases.

'How many sets Samira?'

'Four like this ma'am and four edged in silver. Mr. Mojat says it's for your rooms only — no other guests.'

'I see, well that's good.' I say feeling the quality.

'They have all been freshly laundered ma'am.'

I thank her for all her help.

My day passes with ease. I am organised with most of my things in place. Simone called me earlier to confirm all was good for tonight. The wind is still high so I don't venture out for a walk around the grounds. Instead I sit in bed with just a loose dress on and read a book. I nod off to sleep.

I wake up to a kiss on the lips and, as I open my eyes, Mojat is knelt by my side.

'Janey are you sick?'

'No, I was just relaxing reading when I must have dropped off.'

'I have a present for you habibie.'

I sit up and he positions himself on the edge of the bed and hands me a red package, the size of a shoebox. I look into his smiley heavy-lined eyes.

'Go on open it,' he beckons, as the red gift paper falls on to the bed.

I open the box to reveal a silver evening bag with my name inscribed on the clasp. Inside it's plain black silk with two deep zip pockets. The bag sparkles with crystals, all hand sewn, and has a long silver chain.

'It's lovely, beautiful Mojat.'

'I thought you could wear this tonight with one of your black dresses.'

I look closely at the bag and feel the edges. It's pure class.

'Janey we will fly to Lebanon together on Monday for a few weeks.'

'Is this what your meeting was about?'

'Yes habibie, we will attend a big dinner at the president's house just outside Beirut. They're also my personal friends.'

'Oh I thought you were going to arrange for me to meet Sheikh Saheed Ira on your return from Iran?'

'Yes my dear, I have spoken with Saheed and we will now meet for dinner on our return from Lebanon. The peace talks and president's party must take priority. I will be leading the talks and I wish for you to be present. Many delegates are flying in from other countries.'

'I am fine with this Mojat.'

'Samira will prepare your things, as I know tomorrow you have to be in the office to say farewell to your staff.'

'I do.' I sigh.

'Are you sad my dear?'

'No, not sad. For sure I will miss them, but now look forward excitedly to our future together.'

'I need to hear these words habibie, I always feel insecure with you.'

'Why are you saying this now? I have told you many times how much I love you.'

'I know, but it's always me talking about our future, our plans, always me. You understand don't you?'

'Maybe I do hold back a little, because of my past. I have a fear — a real fear — of being disappointed.'

'I will never disappoint you, NEVER!'

He said the word never with power and strength. Was his insecure mood related to his previous meeting?

'I am forever chasing you, chasing and chasing! Always chasing!'

What is wrong with him? I pull back from him. 'Maybe I like you chasing me.'

I laugh out loud at the way he says the word chasing. He sounds haughty and slightly superior! And how many times does he need to repeat it? I could not stop myself as, for some reason, I find it funny and laugh again.

He is clearly not happy with me laughing at him and seems to take it very personally. I feel strong and powerful. Very clearly I think, yes, he needs to chase me. He has power, money and security but, most importantly, he has royal status! He has everything — everything! He needs to chase me and keep chasing. I am the one thing in his life that does not come easy and he is lucky, so lucky, to have me!

'I am amused Mojat by your haughty precious attitude! Why shouldn't I laugh? You are acting spoilt!'

His pride is wounded and I can see there is unfamiliar hurt written all over his face. He pins me down on the bed and gets on his high horse, his royal stallion, displaying indignant feelings and anger!

'Don't you ridicule me young lady.' He holds my wrists firmly down on the bed.

I say loudly. 'Get off your high horse then!'

He holds me down harder. I sense the years of suppressed emotions are about to explode as he shouts. 'Me — on my high horse?'

'Yes your mighty Arabian stallion!'

He looks fiercely at me and I wonder if Gretal, or any other woman, has ever challenged him before? If I had to make a guess, I would say never!

I try and push him off me, he really likes this as it makes him stronger and turns him on. I try again harder, but his strength is overpowering. He then lets go of my wrists and grabs hold of a chunk of my hair, yanking my head back and pulling it to one side. He begins to kiss and eat my neck.

It does not take long, we are both as high as each other with sexual excitement, wrestling, shoving and pushing each other around on the bed. It's as if he has a fever — a mixture of sweat and saliva is now oozing from his mouth.

'I will show you what happens when you ridicule me young lady!'

My clothes are now being ripped from my body and this seems to be his big turn on. I am quite breathless in the tussle between us; it's a wrestling match of power and indignation.

He opens his trousers, his wide erect cock is pointing to the ceiling.

'I want your fanny now!'

He takes me straight away; his trousers slide down on his hips as he thrusts hard inside of me.

'Your fanny is mine; I will take it, whenever I feel or need it. Are you listening to me?'

'Yes,' I shout, 'yes.' I am listening to you.

His words excite me more than I would ever admit. He has claimed my fanny for his own and he's going to take me as and when he wants. Erotic turbulent waves throb from my throat down into my cunny and thighs.

He acts like a warrior, stimulating every nerve ending and my imagination flows … a warrior who wears a red cloak … the colour of passion and aggression as he fights for self-assertion in love's complexities. His pride and masculine strength attract me. I am Aphrodite, the goddess of erotic love.

Later:

Kulpreet drops us off at the hotel for 8pm. Simone and David are having a drink at the bar. David is tall, slender and very good-looking in his dark suit and white evening shirt. Simone has long mousy brown hair to her shoulder blades that's highlighted in a natural sun-streaked way. She is wearing a long aqua-blue evening dress with a cashmere pashmina in cream over her shoulders.

We join them for a drink at the bar and then all enjoy a wonderful dinner together. Champagne flows and Mojat and David seem to hit it off, whilst Simone and I have our usual fun conversations.

The hotel is one of the very finest, with its palatial gold decorative interior and huge crystal chandeliers. We finish off with coffee in the lounge area, where a pianist is playing classical music. The sofas are modern, low and squashy. Mojat puts his arm around me and it feels intimate and comfortable as we chat with my close friends.

On our way home in the car, he pulls me close to him and kisses the top of my head.

'Simone and David, they have been good to you and very supportive.'

'Yes they have, I couldn't have managed without them.'

'The first time I ever saw you in the sailing club, you were with your friends.'

I smile and kiss him.

'I could not take my eyes off you and, I have to say, I was relieved that I never saw a man at your side. I suppose I did not want any competition once my sights were set on you.'

As I am listening to him, my cunny is aching and sore from our hectic sex earlier. He has put his claim on me, which I find erotic and stimulating. I then cease daydreaming and say in a bit of playful fun. 'What about Brenda?'

He laughs a little. 'Brenda!'

'Yes Mojat, buxom Brenda. She is more your age, and from good stock — as we say in Yorkshire!'

'Yes, Brenda, umm ... well I am not sure what to say really. An independent woman of the sea, somewhat stuck in an era somewhere between the fifties and sixties.'

'You are very diplomatic.'

'That's my job Janey, a diplomat for foreign affairs.'

'She's right in your face Mojat!'

'I know habibie, it's somewhat embarrassing.'

'You are always kind to her, that's a quality I admire in you.'

Mojat's thoughts:
Today she has pushed me to the limits. No woman has ever challenged me like this before.

She says what she thinks, maybe I do act spoilt as she calls it? Perhaps I need to be challenged?

Her naturalness and strength of character take me to the edge of a precipice, an imposing cliff edge. I cannot see what lies beneath and, as I leap into uncharted terrain, I trust in the madness of ecstasy that she brings to me.

CHAPTER TWENTY-FOUR

Outpouring of Emotions

I wake up to the alarm at 7am. I sit bolt upright in bed gasping for breath. It's Sunday.

Mojat, in his comatose state, grabs my hand. 'Janey what's happening?'

I sit on the edge of the bed leaning over my knees and putting my head between my legs. 'I think I'm going to be sick!'

He picks up the phone and rings down to the kitchen for a glass of lemonade. 'My dear, you look as white as a sheet, like you've seen a ghost?'

This would normally be my first day back at work after the weekend. Saying goodbye to my team and the thought of seeing their faces, is churning me up.

Mojat has a confused look about him as he opens the window wide trying to capture a breeze. He positions a Lloyd Loom chair right in front. 'My dear, come and sit down.'

There is a knock at the door, my lemonade has arrived, with extra sugar on the side. I sit quietly and take a few deep breaths. The air is fresh and I can taste the salt on my tongue from the sea breeze.

As I inhale deep breaths through my nose and out through my mouth, I recall my one and only yoga lesson with the Guru Rany Chakrah, Jubai's first taste of Indian mysticism. Though a distant memory it's all coming back to me. Maybe If I'd continued with this I would not be in such a high state of anxiety right now?

Still confused as to what is the matter with me I say. 'Mojat please try and understand me.'

'I am trying my dear, believe me I am.'

'When I left Yorkshire it was such a wrench. The guilt of leaving my family behind nearly killed me and I cried myself to sleep most nights for months. Have you ever felt guilty Mojat?' I am upset and don't wait for him to answer. 'I love my children so much, but was driven away to see if I could find a better life — a life I could survive in.'

Mojat looks a little startled.

'It was my work team, Simone and David, that helped me find myself. They gave me back my sanity, stability and happiness.'

'I see, I do understand.'

'Do you Mojat? I don't think you do? You've never gone without? Having to watch every penny you spend, budgeting the housekeeping money to make sure it feeds everyone for a whole week. How can you possibly understand?'

There is silence for a few seconds.

'Habibie, you are such a sensitive woman and you no longer have to worry about the past or money.'

'No I don't Mojat, but I still carry guilt, terrible guilt! I am a mother who walked away — it's shocking! I have suffered deeply within and deserved to do so!'

Will I ever be able to make it up to my children? Will Geoffrey ever forgive me? Can I ever forgive him for driving me away? Whilst pondering these thoughts I start to sob from the pit of my stomach — deep hard uncontrollable sobs that send tremors throughout your body.

'You can't change the past habibie, but you can look forward to a future with me.'

I walk around the room and, for some reason, I ignore him again. He is concerned and tries his best to empathise with me, which is what I need from him right now.

'Saying goodbye today, it's another wrench for my soul. Once more I have to let go of everything that has given me stability since arriving here. Please don't take this in a bad way. I am looking forward to my new life with you.'

He positions a small bedroom chair very carefully next to mine at the open window. 'Come my beautiful woman. Sit with me and wipe away your tears.'

We sit together and he offers me his hand of comfort.

'You have been enduring such agony, I had no idea of just how much you've been suffering.'

'I am a mother and need you to understand, to really understand the woman you want to marry. I left my family behind and they will never get over it. I wonder if I can ever forgive myself, but I was driven away. There was no love — nobody cherished me. I felt alone, it was too hard and I think I had a breakdown!'

'Come on Janey, pull yourself together for your office party.'

'No I won't pull myself together, you have to know everything. I want you to know the truth about me.'

'I know already.'

'Yes, I suppose you do. Another fucking government security check I assume!'

I am a rattled bushmaster snake, loquacious and toxic. As the words roll off my tongue the venom rapidly emerges.

'I know about Wisteria House and the life you were living.'

'Do you Mojat? And what sort of life was that then?'

'Janey, let's just say, I understand why you were driven away and why your marriage broke down.'

He was now choosing his words carefully, having never before seen me this angry and upset.

'Yes and what Mojat? Tell me — what drove me away?'

I am waiting for him to answer, what could he possibly know about what goes on behind closed doors of any marriage? I suddenly feel enraged that he has intruded into my past life!

'Mojat, you can walk away now, go on — back to your silver-spoon lifestyle. How dare you look into my private life, just to see if I'm the perfect match. Well I'm sorry to disappoint you but I have flaws and I've made mistakes. This is what makes us human and I've certainly had to learn a hard lesson in life.'

'Geoffrey is now learning his hard lessons!'

'Is he Mojat? You know this do you?' I currently feel like a nest of snapping vipers!

'I know everything there is to know Janey. Of course, I wasn't aware of how much you'd suffered and your emotional struggles. No one could have told me these personal things.'

I sob whilst looking out of the window, trying to calm myself. There is a heavy mist outside and the morning dew has created little goblets of crystals on the windowpane, which reflect a rainbow in the first tangerine light.

I sip the tart lemonade and eventually smile at him. He gives me the familiar squeeze of my hands, which I find so reassuring.

'Everything will be fine, just fine. Habibie, never again will you have to walk alone or start a life again, or suffer disappointments like before. I promise.'

I catch my breath and begin to feel much calmer.

The hued red and orange tones of the flowers keep peeping through the mist as I look outside. I sip more of the homemade lemonade.

I leave the room to wash my face, brush my hair and return to Mojat.

'Do you feel okay now habibie?'

I nod my head.

'It's best to let everything out, I love you and what's past is past, we need to look forward.'

I lift my navy blue pinstripe trouser suit out of the wardrobe and lay it on the bed. Of course my team are oblivious to me leaving today.

'Janey that's too formal and businesslike. Why don't you dress up and bring a little glamour to your office party?'

'Yes, good idea, I think I will put on a dress. I like it when you talk to me like this.'

Singing in Silence

'Well it's your party, not a work day — and it will only last for a couple of hours.'

I return to the wardrobe. 'I think your right, let's see if I can find something suitable.'

Mojat is hovering around me cracking his fingers, a nervous gesture he does occasionally. I wonder if I have upset him?

He pulls out a red dress. 'This one?'

CHAPTER TWENTY-FIVE

Letting Go is Never Easy

Kulpreet drops me right outside the office. A few of my sales agents are loitering around the reception area conversing on their mobile phones. Some look at me through the large expanse of glass as I walk up the steps and through the door.

'The lady in red walks into the office,' says my California agent, looking at me in amazement.

'What's with the chauffeur-driven Bentley?' ask both Charles and Tom, the Iranian-Swedish brothers. They look absolutely stunned as they stand drinking coffee in reception. 'How do you do it Janey?'

'I don't know how I do it.' I reply, enjoying their surprised faces.

I proceed into my office and put my bag down. Prasitia brings me my usual cup of coffee accompanied by a homemade biscuit.

'Janey is something happening?'

Why? I ask.

'The fridge is full of soft drinks and there must be about thirty glasses laid out on clean muslin tea cloths. When I arrived an hour ago Sam called me on my mobile, not the office phone. She asked me to inform everyone that breakfast will be delivered at 10am, after the usual meeting.'

I look into her eyes, walk over to my office door and close it for a little privacy.

'I am leaving today. Mojat has asked me to marry him.'

'Is this the older man friend from the sailing club, who sent you the pearls and flowers?'

'Yes, well actually Prasitia, he is not that old.'

'Okay, big changes for you?'

'Sam will announce this in the meeting.'

Tears flow from her eyes. 'I knew it. I knew it was love, as you have looked so radiant recently. Why do you have to leave so suddenly?'

'Because of his job Prasitia. He wants me to travel with him.'

'His job?'

'Yes.' I explain to her that he travels for private business, as well as owning the sailing club.

Prasitia is a young thirty-year-old woman from Kerala in India. She has been my PA and confidante from day one in this office. I owe her an explanation as to why I am leaving so suddenly.

My team are present when Sam arrives. She walks through the office with an air of self-assurance. 'Good morning everyone,' she says in a feisty voice. 'Please take a seat so we can make a start.'

Lindsay then arrives greeting a few agents and myself. She walks towards Sam after saying a few kind words to the receptionist. Sam's straightforward approach begins our brief meeting.

'Now are we all present and correct?'

'Not sure about the correct bit!' quips Tom.

The team look towards Lindsay as she steps forward. The whole office, even the tea boy Kareem, look curious, intrigued and full of anticipation. The big boss has never set foot in this office since it was built two years ago.

Sam continues. 'We are all here today as Janey is leaving for a very happy reason. She is getting married! Lindsay and I would like to say a big thank you for your leadership and hard work.'

There is a rustle of whispering between the agents.

Sam goes on to do a touching speech and then announces the sales figures. She also advises that she'll be standing in personally until they find a suitable replacement for me. Everyone applauds as she sits down and picks up a glass of fruit juice.

Lindsay walks forward and presents me with an arrangement

of long stemmed pale pink lilies and white flowers. She also hands me a framed photograph of myself and the team, a smaller version of which hangs in the office.

Lindsay clears her throat and everyone falls silent.

'Of course we are losing a good manager, but it's not all bad news. The good news is that Janey will be getting married to an Emirati man, who happens to be an old friend of mine.'

There is rapturous applause as Lindsay concludes after a few minutes. Next, Tom, my top earner stands up and prepares to speak.

'I am saying these words on behalf of the entire team.' He looks around to see them all nodding. 'We all agree that we've really appreciated having Janey as our manager.' He speaks for a few more minutes, finishing off by saying how I will be greatly missed.

Then it's my turn. 'Having built up the agents from twelve to twenty-five, it has been challenging at times, but mostly enjoyable.'

I go on to speak about the importance of teamwork and follow up with the story that I'd told Mojat earlier this morning about how they have helped me too. A few tears are being shed as I gaze around the office.

A weight has been lifted from me and it's finally out in the open. The team encircle me, some of the female agents are in tears and the guys are being supportive, seemingly happy for me. I'm of course getting asked if I'm going to sell my recently bought BMW at mates rates? Typical guys! Always interested in cars and a good deal.

The breakfast arrives, Kareem organises the drinks and everyone circulates. The atmosphere is wonderful as we all chat and laugh. I am being asked so many questions, the most prominent one of course being, who on earth is Mojat? I tell them he is the businessman from the sailing club, who it turns out, actually owns the club! This seems to satisfy their curiosity.

Svetlana, my pretty Russian agent who is as hard as nails, can not take her eyes off my ring. She gently takes my arm and pulls me to one side. In her harsh soviet voice she asks. 'For sure he is filthy rich, how did you pull this one?'

Svetlana is a tall Russian beauty with very long jet-black hair that touches her waistline. She has a porcelain complexion with very large blue eyes.

'Well Janey, are you going to tell me how you bagged this man?'

I reply quite flippantly. 'Fate Svetlana, fate. That's what we say in England.'

'How do I get this fate thing?'

'You don't. It comes to you unexpectedly.'

She shrugs her shoulders. 'I don't know what you mean.'

'Ask anyone in the office. They will explain to you how fate operates.'

'Fate operates?' she says, repeating my words. She then pulls a disgruntled face and walks away.

Lindsay takes me to one side. 'Honey, let's slip into your office for a moment.' We do so even though the party is still happening. She picks up a package that is sat on the floor. 'This is for you Janey. Please never doubt you will have a good life with Mojat — a very good life.'

The gift is wrapped carefully in silver and mauve paper. I lay it on my desk and ease out a framed piece of modern art. I smile as I instantly recognise the vibrant watercolour. The artist being Abdul Quader Al Rais, a local man.

'I am touched Lindsay, it's great! It sounds corny, but I will treasure this.'

She gives me a hug and wanders back into the main office to announce to everyone she's departing.

The party eventually winds down and I sit with Sam in my office and order coffees. I take her through all the files, what deals are presently on the go and whose contracts we're exchanging this week.

It's nearly midday and the agents have now returned to work mode, some having already left the office to see their clients. It's relatively calm, just the background hum of phones ringing and agents chatting. Our tea boy, Kareem, has a clean cloth laid across his shoulders like a waiter. He is clearing away leftover food and glasses and wiping things down before any visitors arrive in the office reception area.

'Right chick, is that everything?'

'Yes, pretty much.'

'Come and have lunch occasionally with me when you're in town.'

'Of course I will. Sam, I know you had your doubts.'

'Listen Janey, you don't have to justify anything to me, if you can adapt to his way of life you will be fine. And, after speaking to Lindsay, I understand that he is more westernised than I anticipated. I wish you both happiness. I have said before chick, you are a born survivor in this life, like myself, and that's why we've always got on so well. We've both survived hell and high waters in the past.'

Together we laugh, as secretly we both know what this really means!

CHAPTER TWENTY-SIX

The Paris of the Middle East

Beautiful Lebanon. I peer out of the misty porthole as the plane begins its descent. I look down as we cut right through a mountain range, swerving into a U-turn that takes us along the most spectacular rugged coastline. As far as the eye can see there is pure white surf and a deep blue sea.

The mountain towns and the casino caves come into view. I had no idea how beautiful Lebanon is. Ever since the early sixties, Beirut, its capital, has been known as the Paris of the Middle East. It has a vibrant nightlife, glamorous people and a prominent French influence. Lebanon is seasonal with long summers that last until the end of October.

We are met off the plane by two military soldiers who lead us straight through the airport via a very small first-class lounge. We then enter an official office that has a crooked security sign on the door. The airport is modern and has a wide expanse of pale green marble floors that are crystal clean.

There is a feeling of tension as I can't help but notice that there are more airport security guards than travellers passing through. Thinking about it Beirut is hardly a holiday destination.

Mojat and I are finally greeted by an official. His name is Mr. Khalil and standing next to him is Edward, Mojat's English bodyguard and security advisor. I am introduced and we all shake hands whilst we wait for Mr. Khalil to check our documents. Not only is Edward Mojat's bodyguard, but also his travelling companion of many years. He is a solid, stocky, dark-haired man standing around five feet ten tall. He speaks fluent Arabic, French and Italian.

Edward is rarely needed in the UAK. However, everywhere else around the world he is always at his side, guarding and protecting him. After fondly greeting Mojat in Arabic, Edward then turns towards me and smiles. 'I am so pleased to finally meet you Janey.'

He wears a snug pale-grey suit with an open-necked sky-blue shirt. His shoes are well-polished, black leather with laces. I notice he is armed.

We all have to sign a large diplomatic book in order to enter the country, then our passports are returned to us. Mojat and Edward have to sign a green form, something related to Edward being an armed bodyguard.

We are now clear to enter Lebanon. I don't know what it is, but airports and security always make me feel tense.

Mojat leaves the room to remove his long white dishdasha and returns shortly afterwards wearing a classic suit. He then folds his Emirati dress and head cover, carefully packing it into his cabin case. Mr. Khalil informs us that our cases have now been transferred to a diplomatic car that is waiting outside.

There is a clear Mediterranean feel as we emerge from the airport to be greeted by sunshine, clear blue skies and a freshness that is gusting down from the mountains. Lush green trees are swaying in a gentle breeze and tropical colourful bushes line the airport car park leading out on to the main road.

I feel content as I breathe in the air. Edward looks at me with a smile. He moves us on quickly. 'Wait until we drive up into the mountains,' he says. 'The air is so pure it will make you dizzy.'

'Really, I look forward to that.'

Edward's movements are military, organised and precise. His eyes are on full alert, scanning everyone around us as we head towards our diplomatic vehicle. He opens the car door with a look of authority and we take our places on the back seats.

The airport car park is not busy but there are plenty of military personnel around giving us the once over.

Mojat has booked a suite at the Beirut Season's Hotel and an adjoining room for Edward. The hotel is situated in the centre of the city.

The president's party takes place this weekend and, after that, we're due to travel high up into the mountains to a remote villa in an area called Faraya.

I feel excited touring as a couple for the first time. Edward sits next to Samir, who is dressed in his driver's uniform. Samir is a smiley guy with black slick back hair who speaks broken English. He is just one of the drivers employed for the Lebanese president and his family.

Mojat makes polite conversation with him as Samir informs us that he knows Beirut like the back of his hand, having lived here all of his life.

'Cee sir, every back alley, every tiny road, every building, cee. I know so much and who is good man and who is bad, cee! And their family! I know everyone and everything sir.'

Mojat replies. 'Good Samir, this is good, very useful.'

We head north out of the airport following the signs for Beirut city. It is not long before we hit the busy traffic and our car slows right down. The buildings are mainly small off white apartment blocks and in-between there are townhouses. Trees, hedges and bushes surround each block giving the area a lush Mediterranean feel.

We are now on the outskirts of the city and the look of the place becomes more distressing. Buildings contain bullet holes and look worn from previous wars. The journey into the centre is fascinating, but the sight of so many war-damaged buildings makes me feel uneasy, especially when we pass a school splattered with deep holes.

'Janey, you looked shocked?'

'I am. How can they live like this? There is no war now so why don't they repair the buildings?'

'I knew you would say this habibie. The Lebanese people believe it keeps them on their guard, as they are never complacent with life for one moment.'

'It's so alien to an English woman like myself to live that kind of life.'

'They believe in always being prepared,' he says, shrugging and pulling one of his faces as if to say why not? 'When you understand the people and what they've been through for generations, it's actually okay. I understand them — the Lebanese are close to my heart.'

'Well, I will have to take your word on that one. I do think it's interesting, never to be complacent and it's good that you have such a strong affinity with the people.'

We are now entering the very upmarket French quarter of Beirut. This area has a more affluent feel to it with French brasseries, restaurants and shops. The women walking around are dressed in a chic classic way. The men look very businesslike in their smart suit trousers and crisp, well laundered shirts. The women's clothes shops resemble Parisian fashion houses, the elegant shop windows echoing sophistication.

The car turns into a narrow tree-lined road leading into a lovely square. In the centre is a very old and well preserved Roman Catholic Cathedral, its large double doors invitingly open. Many people are carrying baskets of flowers into this magnificent piece of architecture. I never expected such a spectacular sight here in the centre of Beirut. It is quite breathtaking!

'What is happening here today?' I ask.

'Ma'am, they are preparing for a wedding,' answers Samir. 'A big wedding for the daughter of a wealthy businessman.'

There is a calmness here and the people have preserved it well. I sit upright in the back of the car, enchanted by the architecture. It resembles the old beautiful streets in Paris. I warm to it straight away, as I love people watching.

After another half a mile we arrive at the hotel.

The concierge staff all head towards our car but, before they arrive, Edward is out and opening our door in a matter of seconds. I notice how he scans around to check our safety before allowing us to emerge from the vehicle, his eyes hovering over everyone with great suspicion and causation. He is ready for action.

Edward's suit jacket is open and inside I can see a gun in a holster. He gives the okay to the hotel staff for them to remove our luggage from the car.

Mojat takes my hand and looks seriously into my eyes. 'Please do not make any conversation with Edward now that we're out of the car.'

I acknowledge his words. Edward walks at our side, not talking, just remaining focused. He checks everything as we enter the foyer of the hotel. Having never had a bodyguard, I understand that I mustn't distract him.

The foyer has a general feeling of opulence and the staff seem friendly and efficient. Our suite is large and well-furnished and it's comforting to know that Edward is in an adjoining room to ours.

A light lunch of salad and chicken is brought to our room. It is an international hotel and Mojat assures me that we can eat European meals and drink English teas, so I will take advantage. I ask for a pot of Earl Grey.

After lunch I busy myself unpacking whilst Mojat converses on the phone. There is a knock on the door. Edward enters with a strange device in his hands.

'Janey it's a cat device,' he says, in a clear British accent. 'This little darling picks up bugs. It's very clever, the latest on the market and made by the Japanese.'

He takes a walk around our room pointing the small laser light in various places, under furniture and around lights.

I watch him surveying the scene whilst trying not to appear naïve. I don't comment but, I think to myself, I never gave it a thought that we might actually be bugged. After about five minutes he stops.

'Fine, all good. I'm satisfied.'

I decide to ring my family to inform them that I'm staying in Lebanon with Mojat. They are a little shocked to say the least. I try to reassure them by saying, 'We have a bodyguard it's fine.' But to them they wonder why on earth we need such protection, if Mojat just owns a sailing club?

'Yes I quite understand,' I say. 'Just to be safe.' I am digging myself deeper into a hole.

My daughters are now worried, the most sensitive of which is nearly freaking out. 'What the hell are you doing in Beirut mum?'

After fifteen minutes of trying to reassure her, I finally put the phone down, wishing now I hadn't bothered. Well I couldn't say, we've been invited to a party at the president's house could I? It was never my intention to alarm any of them. I should have said I was in Palma in Majorca and they would have been none the wiser.

'I am not good at lying, never have been,' I say to Mojat.

I have been so wrapped up in love and getting carried away with emotion that I'm not thinking clearly. I have to keep reminding myself that I've entered a new life that will take me to places right off the map for normal people. Lesson number one for me from now on is discretion! Lindsay's word — discretion!

I walk through into the lounge area of our suite.

'Good, your just in time, come here my dear.'

Mojat and Edward are discussing the arrangements for the first week of our trip.

Edward steps forward, lifts up a black case and positions it at the base of the bed. He clicks it open and inside there is a small chunky stainless steel case. Funny, I can't remember seeing this as we checked in at the airport. He lifts it out, opens the lid and, to my amazement, two revolvers sit side by side, one slightly smaller. My stomach gripes as I peer at their faces. I feel a sinking feeling.

'Expecting trouble?' I ask.

Edward's tone of voice is razor sharp. 'Just a precaution.'

'Okay, yes I understand.'

Singing in Silence

'Now, I need to sort you out Janey, there is always a chance that we may face a precarious situation.'

Mojat opens his cabin case and takes out a Gucci bag. He removes the cover, slides out a beautiful evening bag and hands it to me.

'A present,' he says smiling as he places it in my hands. Both Edward and Mojat look at each other with a curious grin.

'Yeah right!' I say, knowing there is a catch somewhere.

Edward speaks. 'This is not a normal Gucci bag though, of course, it looks exactly like one.'

I open the clasp. There is a padded secret pouch attached to the lining and, as Edward steps forward, he positions the smaller of the two guns within this pouch. You would never know there was a weapon inside.

'So, Janey, when you open this neat little bag, inside is a lipstick, a mobile and a compact,' says Edward. 'The compact is a device you can use to speak to me or Mojat. Open it and the mirror will connect you with five-seconds to speak.'

I nod my head whilst admiring the well designed padded pocket, just large enough to contain the lipstick and phone.

Edward takes the lipstick and twists the base. 'It releases a scent or gas which will choke anyone too near for comfort. Right now it's sealed so don't worry! It won't kill them, just make them pass out for ten minutes to give you a chance to get away.'

Edward then picks up the mobile. 'Don't worry Janey it's just a phone, a special one to be used in Lebanon only. All your calls will automatically come through to this new number, which only Mojat and I know. It cannot be tracked and will work in the mountains. We have a special connection set up at the highest point here for all three of our phones.'

I look at the Gucci bag containing the revolver. 'Wow, it's amazing how it all fits together.'

I begin to look in more detail and try not to get too carried away with my own personal Gucci gun bag.

Mojat sits at my side as if he's awaiting my reaction. I admire the lipstick and compact a while before placing them back in the bag.

'Next Janey, a small pen, but not to write with,' advises Edward. 'Remove the top and, if you press this button, a large hypodermic needle appears. If pushed into flesh it releases an endorphin, bringing on an artificial state of euphoria. This will make your attacker very drunk and happy within three-seconds.'

'How long will this last for?'

'One hour, giving you plenty of time to make your escape.'

'Okay.'

Now Edward lifts out the gun and runs his hand over it. 'Hold it and feel it Janey. Get used to it. It is not loaded right now.'

I take the gun and feel its smooth line.

'I am giving you a Walther PPK.'

'That means nothing to me I'm afraid.'

'Of course, I would not expect you to know anything. How does it feel? The weight? Does it sit well — the size?'

'I think so.'

Running my hands over it I familiarise myself to its smooth edges. It is compact and fairly light. I put it down and pick it up a few times to get used to its weight. Edward then goes through very carefully how I should use the pistol. How to load it; take it down, the safety switch and where the ammunition is kept within the Gucci bag.

'Very impressive,' I say.

Everything has been especially designed to fit into this evening bag. I notice my J. G. initials are even imprinted inside.

'When we reach a remote area in the mountains you will then get your chance to practice,' says Edward. 'I want you to feel confident so that you'll never be in a position of panic! You'll be with me all the time from now on, so don't worry. I have other weapons up my sleeve if ever we need them. It's all just a precaution for self-defence.'

Edward's pure English accent reminds me of Q in the James Bond films. He's the one that gives James all the weird and wonderful gadgets — deadly instruments for his protection against Blofeld and other bad villains of the world.

I stand up. 'Okay, what's next?'

They both look at me and laugh.

'Well habibie you have taken all this in good part.'

'What do you mean?'

Edward pats me on the shoulder as if to say well done!

Before he leaves the room, Mojat moves closer and puts his arm around me.

'My dear, most women would have got uptight and bloody hysterical at the thought of having to defend themselves with a gun. But you are taking it all in your stride. You're amazing!'

'Will that be all now Mojat?' says Edward, as he stands poised to leave at the door.

Mojat gets up and walks towards him. 'Just a second Edward. Habibie rest a while — read or relax. I will be about an hour.'

He leaves the room taking with him the remaining gun in the chunky steel case.

CHAPTER TWENTY-SEVEN

My Overactive Mind

I lay on the bed and position my pillow around my neck, trying to concentrate on my intake of oxygen. All this helps me to relax and get used to the fact that I'm now a woman not to be argued with. Especially now I have my Gucci bag!

I spend several minutes repeating the deep breathing techniques, learnt from that one and only yoga lesson with Ramy Chakrah. I then lay flat out on the bed stretching, whilst trying to remember what else I was taught to help me enter a meditative state.

It's a pity I did not continue with that yoga course, but I had a weak bladder at the time, which tended to let me down in certain upside down positions! Embarrassing to say the least and infuriating, as I could have become quite good at it given the chance to carry on. But hey — what does one do? Thank goodness I eventually found a wonderful surgeon.

I am relaxed but still finding it difficult to empty my mind. I think of Samira, such a gracious humble woman. How nice it would be to have her here next to me. She could be preparing a bath and I could be keeping fresh with one of her special Arabic massages.

I have concluded that we English are far too inhibited and reserved. I think back to the time with Samira in that steamy bathroom. I recall the multi-coloured headscarf she wore to hold her hair back from her petite olive-skinned face and the way she worked her nimble fingers on me. I felt like a totally rejuvenated woman.

I remove my clothes and pull the white cotton sheets over my body.

I am tired but at the same time my mind is working overtime. I still reflect on the secret supply of guns on board Mojat's yacht and the false door so conveniently locked in his bedroom suite. What was inside? I would imagine more guns. Then why was it locked, when my false door was open? There must be something else hidden away.

Now Edward is teaching me how to use a personal revolver. What the chuff am I doing? Have I gone insane? What the hell is a Walther fucking PPK anyway?

I talk quietly to myself. 'It is quite obvious Janey Green, the only reason you have been given and taught how to use weapon by a highly trained ex British Agent is … you might bloody need it!'

What am I really getting myself into? That's the question that's really worrying me!

I imagine my mum and dad turning in their graves. 'Well our Janey's always been a bit of an adventurer. She can be quite rebellious at times!'

'Not this sort of adventure mum,' I can hear myself saying!

At heart, I am just a country girl with my roots attached to the bleak moors of North Yorkshire. I lived in the sadness of Wisteria House, but at least it was civilised. The only gun I ever heard was from the local farmer shooting rabbits, usually when he was intoxicated from whisky on a Saturday evening. He used to shout at them, as he would aim his rifle. At the top of his voice he would go nuts, bloody nuts shouting … 'I will get you fuckers!' Then he would shoot and laugh out loud whilst shouting, 'Got the bastard!'

This was often his Saturday evening pastime, the rest of the week he was perfectly polite and friendly.

Mojat has all the right credentials. He is intelligent, funny, and overwhelms me with affection. But I sense there is another side. Not to his personality I mean, but another side to the life he lives — like a double agent. Another life I am about to discover here in

Lebanon, or any other country he frequents.

My eyes feel heavy as I begin to doze. I am drifting off, floating in a deep afternoon slumber.

I wake up to his moist lips on my neck and his hands massaging my breasts, lifting my nipples into his mouth. I am now semi awake and putty in his hands. For an older man he has a very high libido.

He moves closer to my ear and in a soft husky voice says, 'I need to fuck you.'

His erotic talk feels natural and stimulating as his torso glides over my body. Our foreplay is wild as we are now familiar with each other's needs.

In our unrestrained state there is a sense of urgency. He pulls my legs together then lifts them, at the same time bending my knees and pushing them into my chest, then over to one side. He heaves himself over me and drags me towards him and then presses down inside me at a totally different angle.

In his rasping euphoria he says. 'Prepare yourself, this will be deep.'

I look at his face and moist skin as he moves inside me, it's painfully deep but at the same time it pleasures me. His energetic body does not stop.

I physically jerk, his rhythm increases and my juices evaporate. He screams out a word in Arabic as he releases himself. Christ! A meteorite from the outer universe has shot into my vagina, stimulating every nerve ending.

One hour later:
He prepares me a gin and tonic as I sit in front of the mirror styling my hair for tonight.

'Mojat, I was thinking about Samira earlier.'

'What about her? Actually don't answer that as I know what you are going to say habibie. You need your personal maid with you.'

'What makes you think this?'

'Arabic women always travel with their personal maids.'

'Do they? And do Arabic women have an Arabic maid?'

'Yes habibie, always Arabic, but a general maid or housekeeper can be of any nationality. An Arab lady of status might have two personal maids.'

'Why would she need two?'

'This might be if she has more than one property, or a house in another country. Everyone needs to have weekends and time off each month and then the two maids could alternate, so the lady of the house would always have one with her.'

'That's interesting Mojat. What about a more middle-class Arabic lady?'

'Just the same.'

'And the poorer people?'

'I am not sure, but even a poor woman would have a close companion.'

'It's an interesting culture.

'Habibie, our culture dates back, like your Christian culture, to the time of Jesus and before. Are you missing being pampered then?'

'Well, I miss Samira's presence.' I watch his face for any reaction.

'Of course a familiar woman.' He picks up the phone and speaks to the Spa reception.

'If you go down now they will prepare a room for you. I know it's not like having your close companion.' He looks at me and smiles. 'But a massage will make you feel good.'

'Thank you, but you didn't have to arrange this right now.'

'Habibie, go and relax and enjoy a little decadence before you get ready for tonight.'

I quickly finish my gin, then walk over and kiss his forehead. He gives my hand the usual squeeze. I have noticed he does this when he's at his happiest.

'Enjoy your spa massage.'
I then pick up my handbag and head off to find the beauty floor.

CHAPTER TWENTY-EIGHT

The Cedar Shiatsu Treatment

When I arrive, a Lebanese beauty therapist is waiting for me. I am her final client of the day. She directs me to a room and leaves me there to undress and slip under a large heated white towel. When she returns she locks the door and places my hair in a large white band, replacing the towel with two warm ones — to cover my breasts and bottom half.

Compared to Beautiful Lady back in Jubai, this place is five-star luxury. A spacious room with background music, the fragrance from the oils is reminiscent of Neal's Yard Remedies in Kensington.

'Madam, what type of massage?'

I decide on a deep tissue. She organises her preparations around me whilst I lay comfortably on a luxurious couch massage bed. I'm aware that the stiff gin and tonic I shared with Mojat earlier has gone to my head.

On one side of her worktable are large-to-medium polished stones laid out in a row. On the other side lies a row of wooden balls placed in order of descending size. I know all about hot stone therapy, but I'm not sure about the balls?

She begins the massage. I lay on the deep sunken bed enjoying the tranquil spaced-out music of waves hitting the seashore and dolphins calling me to play. I'm very relaxed for the first ten minutes enjoying the whole process as she warms up my muscles.

My Lebanese lady is called Mona and she's dressed in a white shift dress edged in navy blue piping. She has a good firm touch as she begins to move into the deep tissue areas that need a little firming up, mainly my thighs.

She presses firmly to release all the knots and bubbles in my back and shoulders. I ask her about her clientele.

'Well ma'am, many are more affluent local ladies that visit the spa and, of course, tourists from all over the world.'

She continues to push into my back, making me moan and grunt a little. She stands up for a while to stretch herself out and I question the wooden balls.

'This is cedar treatment ma'am, for stimulation. Many ladies like this.'

She passes me a ball to hold. I know cedar is famous in Lebanon as the tree appears on the country's flag. People call Lebanon 'The Land of the Cedars' — mainly due to the huge cedar pine forests that frequent the country. I take in the aroma of the ball and return it to her.

'Would you like to try?'

'Why not? Yes I would, thank you.' I anticipate that these cedar balls will be rolled around on my skin.

She reaches into a cupboard and brings out a new sealed pack containing three different sizes. Each one has slightly raised points and she begins to roll the largest ball all over my body.

'Ma'am this is a little like Shiatsu massage.' She explains a little further. 'I roll then hold, roll then hold and, finally, a good press in. It has a stimulating Shiatsu therapy quality. Ma'am, have you laid on a Yantra Mat?'

'Yes I have. I bought one a year ago and I have to say it's been amazing for my aching back.'

'Well, this has a similar effect, but for massage.'

She has a good touch, just like Samira. She rolls the largest ball all over my body and, after a few minutes, exchanges it for a more compact one, about the size of a small apple. This has more points on it, giving my skin a more invigorating feel. I lay back fully enjoying the experience of the therapy as Mona moves the ball up and down the inside of my arms and legs, then the outer parts. She removes the towel from my pubic area and continues with the ball, rolling it over my stomach, abdomen and pubic bone area.

She looks at me and smiles. 'You like it ma'am here?'

I clear my throat. 'Yes it's very stimulating.'

'Are you happy for me to carry on?'

I nod. By this stage I am nearly falling asleep and floating off somewhere with the mermaids.

'Yes it feels very good.' I wanted to say it felt amazing, just like when Samira massages me with her fingertips, except Mona uses a cedar Shiatsu ball.

It's so good that I'm drifting off, almost fantasying. She opens my legs wide, leaning forward over the bed and dripping the ball in a little more oil. She then runs it up and down my thighs, which really tingles!

'Ma'am would you like deeper tissue pressure?'

'Yes that's fine,' I say, feeling so sexual and relaxed.

Now I've given her permission she begins working the ball harder on the inside of my thighs, still smiling at me and checking all is okay.

'Ma'am this will prevent varicose veins and is good for lymphatic drainage.'

The thought of anything varicose at forty something makes me grimace!

Mojat had taken me for his pleasure less than one hour ago and now, with Mona's special touch, I feel stimulated again to the point of igniting!

She moves up my inner thighs, easing off a little more gently around the outer lips of my cunny and up to my clitoris. I give a sigh.

'Ma'am, I can tell this is good for you.'

I nod with my eyes closed.

To my astonishment she then inserts her long fingers inside me, opening my vagina lips wide and neatly inserting the ball.

Oh Jesus! I did not expect this. Her left hand fingers squeeze and hold my outer vaginal lips together to secure the ball inside me, whilst her right hand begins a more confined massage on my lower cunny from the outside. My legs are wide open with bent knees as she pushes the ball up inside me.

'Ma'am I move you in closer, this way it gives you one of the best feelings you will ever experience.'

I do not answer and just let her continue giving the ball discreet little pushes further up inside me, whilst holding the stretched outer lips of my vagina together. It is a sensational feeling. My God! I can barely contain myself.

'Ma'am this internal massage, is it good for you?'

It is clear to me that this cedar technique works. My body pulses from my neck down to my knees. Those little pressure points on the ball are just so invigorating. My hands hold on to the sides of the massage couch as I groan in pleasure.

'You like ma'am, I am pleased. Many western ladies are discovering our Lebanese techniques.'

She now moves to my face and covers it with hot steamed cloths to cleanse me. I take a deep breath and reply softly to her. 'Yes, very good lymph drainage treatment, very good.'

'All women who discover our treatments here in Beirut want to come back, but this is very old Arabic technique.'

'I bet they want to come back!'

Mona proceeds with a facial, massaging my temples and down to my neck, cleansing and stimulating me with creams and oils. She removes the towels and replaces them; the heat again on my body is wonderful. She finishes my face by putting a mask over my eyes to help me relax. She then lifts the towel from my pubic area, inserting her hand to remove the ball from my vagina. I had quite forgotten it was still in there. She then wipes all over my outer vaginal lips with rose oil.

'Madam, are you happy for me to continue?'

I nod, thinking, is there more?

Lying quietly with this dark mask on, she could have done anything to me. She begins to gently massage on my fingers and hands, moving up my arms. She clicks and cracks on my shoulders. I have always had issues in this area. Then she lifts me and cups my breasts in her hands. I can feel the oil drops running down on to my nipples and, very methodically, her hands move around them.

I open my eyes again as she says. 'Pink nipples ma'am, wonderful large pink nipples.' She carries on giving each breast her close attention, parting and playing with them. She takes the smaller ball out of the package and massages each breast in turn.

'Ma'am each ball has a place you see?'

'Yes I am beginning to.'

Since my arrival in the Middle East, and now Lebanon, I feel I have stepped into an enchanting world of women who nurture other women. They sense your needs and stimulate every part of you.

I am relaxed, just taking in her every movement as she glides over my breasts. It's wonderful. My Brazilian friend, Lola, once said to me that if you're not sure where to go for your beauty treatments, always follow the local ladies and enjoy their old traditional methods. Lola's words now take on a different meaning. She was right.

Back at my suite, Mojat is dressed and ready.

'You look so handsome.'

'My dear I kept looking at my watch thinking, how long does a massage last for?'

'I had a facial too.'

'I suppose that explains how two hours can pass — you ladies like your treatments.'

'And you men appreciate having a relaxed beautiful woman on your arm.'

'We do indeed Janey, well that's that then.'

CHAPTER TWENTY-NINE

The President's Party

My initiation into the Arabic world has enlightened me to the unspoken culture. I'm now privy to the private lives of ladies with their personal maids and beauty therapists.

'Janey, I don't want to rush you but we need to leave in fifteen minutes.'

I assure Mojat that I will not be too long. I am excited as tonight, the party at the president's house, was always going to be special.

I sit at my dressing table looking into the mirror, putting the final touches to my make-up and hair. Mojat stands behind me in his dinner suit. I look up at him in the mirror — he looks dashing and elegant. His hair is swept back from his face, showing off his defined eyebrows and large eyes.

He lifts my hair in his hands, bends forward to kiss my lips and softly says, 'I love you habibie.' Then he places a small box in front of me. 'For you my beauty.'

I open it and inside is a platinum band Arabic ring with a cluster of pink diamonds. He then reaches into his suit pocket and pulls out a rectangular box with the hallmark, Tiffany. Inside is a matching choker — it's so beautiful. I turn to him and we kiss with such passion.

'Tonight my dear, I want you dazzling next to me.'

I sit in my bra and panties admiring my gifts, before reaching for my dress. I step into a gown that's three-quarter length, dark blue with material that's a mixture of silk with a faint silver thread running through. It's a figure-hugging dress with a low back, in the style of Audrey Hepburn. Mojat chose it for me and it's, well, very sixties. I am midnight blue with sparkling pink diamonds and, of course, my Gucci bag.

We arrive at the president's villa in style. Samir, our driver, pulls up outside and Edward escorts us in. The house is more akin to a palace than a villa and is spectacularly set on the side of a mountain, with a full view of Beirut city and the coastline beyond. The grounds lead down to a rocky beach and are beautifully illuminated. Each rock also displays several lights.

As we enter the house the party is already in full swing. There's a live band playing fifties big band swing-style music. Many couples are dancing and a local Lebanese man sings old hits from the likes of Frank Sinatra and Dean Martin.

After being introduced to many people, and paying our respects to the president and his family, we finally sit at a table.

Before I manage to finish my first glass of champagne, Mojat whisks me up on the dance floor. We dance and dance and, at the appropriate moments, he twirls me around causing my dress to rise and reveal my knees.

A compère arrives at the microphone to announce several happy events regarding the president's family life, including an announcement of his youngest daughter's engagement to a local businessman. Cheers and toasts occur, then the evening continues.

In the dining area is a large buffet table containing local food. Seemingly endless champagne is flowing. I am constantly meeting new people, most of whom seem to know of our engagement.

Edward stays within a reasonable distance of us, always surveying who enters and exits the room. Mojat ventures outside for a cigar and Edward follows.

With the men temporarily out of sight, many thoughts begin to enter my mind. If anything bad is going to happen, I feel it will be tonight. Perhaps I'll need to use the gun after all?

Mojat returns and we manage to spend some time with Faoud and his lovely wife Katalina. They've been married for over twenty-five years and still seem very much in love.

Edward is one of the many bodyguards dressed in dinner suits — all wired of course. He speaks briefly to some of the others, but I observe how seriously he takes his duties and never gets too involved with any of them.

For a brief moment I sit alone at a small table, watching couples dancing and the band playing. The Gucci bag sits firmly on my knee. It's now 1am and the music turns to ballads.

The president's house and surrounding grounds is teeming with security guards. I am conscious that Mojat has a gun attached to his calf under his suit trousers, as I had felt this in the car when his right leg brushed against mine.

I focus on this huge room and can honestly say that this is the best party I have ever attended. The women all look glamorous and everyone seems very friendly. Mojat is well known here, his life in Jubai is more like a hermit's in comparison. It seems to me that most of his friendships have been formed here in Lebanon.

Mojat appears at my side and takes my hand to dance. I of course accept and he proceeds to hold me extremely close on the dance floor. As we both embrace the wonderful music I look up at him and smile. He is quiet and seemingly deep in thought.

Mojat's thoughts:
I look at Janey in her beautiful gown and her blonde waves falling over her shoulders. She is stunning and I am totally besotted. The pink diamonds, that I presented her with earlier, sparkle and reflect in her bright green eyes. The way she dances tantalises and turns me on!

'Mojat you're dreaming, are you okay?'
'I was just thinking that I am the luckiest man alive to have you in my arms tonight.'
'You certainly know how to woo a woman.'
'It's true habibie, this is how I feel.'
'I'm happy to be on such a pedestal.'
The evening draws to a close. We say goodbye to our host and

his extended family and step outside into a clear starry night. The air is chilled and I glance up to the sky and notice the moon is full. I put on a short jacket that matches my dress as Mojat lights up a cigar. We walk to the edge of the grounds whilst Edward ventures off to collect our car.

We chat to some of the guests, many of whom have taken the opportunity to light up a cigarette. Mojat enjoys mingling with this small social gathering of smokers. The sea lashes against the rocks below us and many couples chat as they leave the house. Laughter is in the air, creating a warm ambience.

'It's been a great evening Mojat. I have met so many lovely people.'

'I noticed my dear that you were circulating well.'

I wrap my wool pashmina around my neck and watch him take a few more puffs on his cigar.

'Janey, you don't mind me having the occasional one do you?'

'Why should I, as long as you don't expect me to join you!'

'We all have our vices,' he says, as he grins and turns away to puff once more.

'I suppose we do.'

'What's yours Janey?'

I am silent, trying to think.

'Come on, everyone has vices?'

I shrug my shoulders. I've been put on the spot and, luckily for me, I am saved by our car's arrival. Edward sits in the front passenger seat alongside Samir. Mojat pulls me close to him in the back and puts his arm around me. I am thinking of what vices I might have, then I'm suddenly sidetracked as we kiss. I'm dizzy in love and dizzy thinking about my new found pleasures of women. The erotic encounters of the third kind!

Faoud's security men are busy keeping the flow of cars moving as we all exit the estate. I cling tightly to my Gucci bag, anticipating that something might happen once we leave the grounds. Samir joins the traffic queue on the long sweeping drive. Finally he is able to accelerate from the president's gates out onto the main road.

If we are to be a target surely it will be now, I think nervously to myself. Thankfully there are police and guards lining much of the main road back into Beirut city centre.

I feel expressly relieved as we reach our hotel safely and park up outside the reception entrance. It's late and there is a wedding celebration on the ground floor. Drinks are still flowing and the ballroom floor heaves with guests dancing into the early hours. The Lebanese can party!

We stand at the doorway watching the band for a while before making our way up the stairs to the third floor and, thankfully, our suites are on a quiet corner. We say goodnight to Edward on the landing area. I feel reassured when I recall the adjoining door. My palms are sweaty from gripping my Gucci bag too tightly — I am obviously tense!

My first night out in Lebanon was a success. I don't know why I felt so strongly that we would be a target. I must relax — all will be okay. The journey back to our hotel felt as if I'd completed my first hurdle as an armed woman.

I put the kettle on, then remove my make-up and hang up my dress. I make us both a cup of tea.

'This is lovely my dear, sitting in bed drinking tea in the early hours. It's homely and comforting being with you.'

I acknowledge him and smile. 'Edward never looks tired. Have you noticed?'

'No, I can't say I have.'

'Is this something to do with his military training?' I ask, as I am curious to know of Edward's background. 'I've watched him throughout the evening and he seems so focused.'

'Habibie he should be, he is SAS! Edward was part of an elite unit working with the British Special Forces. You now know he is always armed?'

'Yes of course,' I say in an extra intelligent voice.

We drink our tea in silence. I like the fact that we have many small things in common, just like the English. We drink tea in bed and enjoy sandwiches late at night. And around six in the evening Mojat always prepares us both a gin and tonic with slices of lime — a ritual we enjoy.'

I start to think about my pistol, as Edward calls it.

'If Edward is working for me too I'd like to hear more about him.'

Mojat puts his cup down and his head falls back onto the pillow. He then nervously cracks his knuckles and fingers. 'Well he is one of the best. Edward is highly trained to use HK MP 5K sub machine guns. They are for low-key overt protection. It has a shorter barrel and smaller sights and, when fitted with a fifteen-round magazine, it's comfortably concealed beneath his bodyguard's jacket. Ideal for covert close protection duties, like protecting you and me.'

'Bloody hell Mojat, I didn't expect the full security lowdown!'

'Well you asked! Here my dear, in the Middle East the British Special Forces are in demand. The officer that trained Edward was assigned to one of your retired prime ministers.'

Impressed I ask. 'Who was that?'

'Sir John Major, when he was in Bosnia.'

'How do you know all this?'

'Janey it's my work, I have to ensure I have the best as there are people out there who will stop at nothing to halt the peace process in the Middle East.'

'You mean fundamentalist organisations?'

'Yes, they are supplied by fractious groups in Iran and other countries too. Their arms are often bought from Russia and so it goes on!'

I finish my tea and move down the bed turning towards him, still tuned in to his every word.

'I have to personally insure Edward and all the weapons that he travels with. That's how I know every minute detail, as it's a huge insurance bill each year just to keep me safe. And now you too of course!'

I listen to him whilst I finish my tea.

'Did you notice the green document at the airport that we signed?' asks Mojat.

'I did, what was that all about?'

'It is for his sub HK.'

'No sleep for me tonight. All this talk has given me the willies.'

Mojat laughs uncontrollably and hugs me close. 'I have never heard of that saying before? Willies … yes — I like it!'

As I reach to switch off the light at our bedside, I can feel his hard penis pushing into my back. He is aroused — a night of dancing has turned him into a frisky energetic thirty-year-old. But, sadly, it is short lived, as he soon drifts into a deep sleep.

I lay next to him listening to his breathing, my mind still active from reflecting on the events of the day. The sex is thrilling with him. He is a highly sexed Scorpio — the glossy magazines always say that they make good lovers. They're intense and bring a variety to the bedroom. One thing's for sure, he certainly does!

I start to think about my cedar ball massage with Mona. That was a whole new experience, very different and highly sensual. How many women must experience that each week? Maybe their partners or husbands don't, or can't, make love to them for whatever reason? Or maybe they find themselves alone, widowed, divorced or just single? Whatever a woman's situation she must surely see this as a good substitute!

As I become more drowsy my thoughts turn to Samira. From that first moment when she ran my bath and I stood naked in front of her, I felt a natural bond between us. I imagine her brightly-coloured scarf exposing her petite, angelic face. Her dark eyes fill with grace when she smiles. She has enlightened me to the unspoken Arabic culture.

I sing when I feel happy. It uplifts, energises and soothes the soul. The vivid memory of singing in silence will stay imprinted in my DNA forever.

CHAPTER THIRTY

The Lure of the Mountains

The following day — Saturday:
I stare out from the hotel window on to the stark white buildings of Beirut. I am pleasantly surprised at just how many of the houses possess colourful rooftop gardens.

The sun is trying to break through and I have a sudden urge to get up into the mountains, as this will be such a contrast to the desert-locked Jubai.

A quick decision is made and we shall leave our hotel to drive to Faraya, a village at high altitude.

Mojat makes a call to ensure our villa will be ready for us. It belongs to one of his Lebanese friends, who uses it as a summer retreat for his family. He speaks to the housekeeper in French.

After the phone call he seems very excitable. In fact I have not seen him quite as giddy since the night he proposed to me.

'Janey, the air will be so clean and pure. The villa is set high in the cedar woodlands and, at this time of year, we might even see the snow-capped mountains.'

'Sounds great Mojat. I am looking forward to a new experience.'

'The mountain roads are a real treat as the views are magnificent, not just en route but also where Ralph's villa is situated.'

I am delighted to be leaving the city centre. It's silly I know, but with Edward's lecture about how to use my gun, amongst other security issues, I feel it will be safer up in the hills. I have no reason to think anything bad about the city, but looking at the plethora of bullet holes that reflect Beirut's history, I can't help but feel a little nervous.

With haste and enthusiasm I begin to pack.

'Habibie, only take your more casual things and maybe one dress for the evening. Leave the rest here.'

'Why here?'

'These suites are booked out to us.'

'Are they, for how long?'

'Indefinitely! So we'll return at the end of our trip, then I can show you the real Beirut nightlife.'

'Okay!' Wow! Booked out indefinitely! This seems a little extravagant to me but, hey, I'm not the one paying the bill!

Mojat goes off to inform Edward of our plans, whilst I continue to put a few of my things together. It suddenly feels like an escape rather than a holiday.

CHAPTER THIRTY-ONE

The Healing Power of St. Charbel

Within the hour Edward is driving our car, a Toyota Land Cruiser, out of the city and heading north towards the mountains. We climb continually whilst following the signs to Aajaltoun, a thirty-minute drive.

On arrival we stop for a late breakfast at the French patisserie, Moulin d'Or and sit outside taking in the views of the surrounding mountain villages. Mojat orders warm za'atar flatbreads and chicken shawarmas for us all, which arrive with the traditional olives, a small side salad and three coffees.

After we've eaten, we return to the patisserie to pick up a box containing fresh bread, olives, four types of cheese, jambon and a freshly made selection of flatbreads. Also a separate box of salad and fruit for when we arrive at the villa.

We take a stroll around the village square. Situated here is an impressive church and, behind it, a view to the sea in the far distance. There are just a few other shops in the village: a butchers, grocers and linen store. But Moulin d'Or is a fine centrepiece. A real French patisserie displaying an array of pastries, bread, biscuits and jams.

We drive up the mountain road passing many small communities with rows of shops. Local people sell fruit and olives at the roadside. Mojat informs me that many of the mountain villages have monasteries, some dating back to Roman times. St. Charbel's Monastery in Mairouba, is to be our next stop.

We cruise at a steady pace, climbing higher and higher. Edward glances frequently in his rear-view mirror, watching and checking for potential trouble. The road is narrow and winding with just a few pull-in places. There are no central white lines or lights now as we are a good one-and-a-half hour's drive out of Beirut. The car goes down a gear, then another, as the road becomes much steeper.

'Janey, you will enjoy St. Charbel's Monastery,' says Edward. 'It is an extraordinary place set high in the mountains with amazing countryside all around. St. Charbel was a Maronite monk with special healing powers.'

'Ah yes, I have read about this monk.'

After another twenty minutes we reach Mairouba, located at a very high altitude.

Edward suddenly takes a sharp left turn and Mojat and I are thrown to the other side of the car. He drives down a steep, almost rubble track for another half a mile, frequently checking his mirror. What for I wonder? There isn't a soul around and we've only seen half a dozen vehicles at most in the last fifteen minutes. We grind to a halt and step out of the car to take in the views down the valley. It's breathtaking!

Edward pulls out his binoculars and scans the whole area, including the road we have just driven along. When he is satisfied that all is well he begins to connect with us once more.

The locals farm the land on many levels; we can see olive and lemon groves. Figs are in abundance. It's just incredible looking at these mountain ranges, they're just as Mojat had described.

We leave our car and wander down a narrow pathway, which eventually leads us to the Monastery of St. Charbel. There is a special Arabic plaque on the side of the door. Mojat informs me that visitors from all over Lebanon and the rest of the world come here, as there is a special story attached.

'You go in and enjoy your time and I will tell you all about St. Charbel later,' says Mojat. 'As you will see Janey, it is still a fully working monastery. Take your time my dear as Edward needs a break from driving. We will wait for you outside.'

I quietly walk through the old monastery taking great care as I descend large, craggy, worn flagstone steps into an area called The Tomb Church. I look up to admire a beautiful arched construction that holds St. Charbel's tomb, which rests on a cedar wood pedestal. I am mesmerised by its age and wonderful condition. The energy is soothing and tranquil.

I walk into the prayer area, which is intimate. In front of me is a huge cross. I stand in awe of this for a few moments as the immense size of it takes me by surprise. I am feeling moved and emotional. Just a handful of people are gathered at the front, all of them kneeling on the floor deep in prayer and facing this cross. I do not want to disturb them. There are only four rows of seats so I quietly take a seat on the front row behind them. I look up at the old cross and close my eyes — I meditate and spiritually give myself. My breathing becomes deeper as I relax into my prayers, feeling light and warm. Time passes as I pray for my parents and children and ask forgiveness for leaving them behind. I also pray for strength for Geoffrey, at the same time visualising him at the rambling old Wisteria House.

I am now in a place of light and peace. For a few seconds I experience a sensation of spinning and then it stops. I spin once more and then it stops again. Next I see a colourful vision of Mary Magdalene cleansing Jesus' feet. I smile at such a tender image.

Then the picture changes as my breathing becomes deeper. With my eyes still closed, I see an image of a monk walking towards me. He holds out his hand and touches my right shoulder. Immediately I feel a heat sensation here that runs down my arm into my fingers on the right side. I feel overwhelmed and tears begin to flow down my cheeks. I can't hold back and burst out crying. I knew it was St. Charbel — it was so intense.

I then open my eyes, still sobbing. The people kneeling in prayer have all gone. I turn to look behind me to see if anyone is still present. A very frail old lady heads towards me with a warm smile across her face. She has seen me crying.

She sits alongside me. No words pass her lips but her face is a picture of kindness. She takes my right hand, squeezing it reassuringly. Then she presses a handkerchief into my palm and beckons me to wipe my tears away. She then stands up and kisses the top of my head before walking back past me out of the archway.

I close my eyes and sit for another minute or so, whilst I try to compose myself. Eventually I open them again and, yes, I am alone. I take in the special feelings I have. I feel light, so light …

I wander back through the monastery in the hope of seeing the old lady to return her handkerchief. I depart through the main door to find Mojat and Edward chatting on a wall. I walk over to join them.

'Janey, are you okay?' asks Mojat. 'You look upset.'

'I have shed a few tears whilst praying that's all. I was overwhelmed in there and felt a presence, a real presence. It was wonderful.' I begin to tell them about the monk touching my right shoulder and the sensation it gave me down my arm and into my fingers … 'What happened in there was incredible. A very old lady walked up to me and pressed this handkerchief into my palm.' I hold out the fine delicate piece of cotton in front of them both. 'She left a few minutes before me and I'd like to give it back to her.'

Mojat and Edward glance at each other with surprised looks.

'Habibie, no old lady has come out of this doorway and, in fact, you've been the only person to emerge! '

'What about the other people?'

'What other people? No one has left or gone in since you.'

'There were a few people kneeling in prayer. Ordinary people, not monks in robes. And the old lady and this.' I hold up the cotton handkerchief again. Mojat takes it and looks at it closely — it has my tear stains on. The cotton cloth is delicate, old and fraying at the edges.

Edward looks at me. 'I think, you've had a healing experience. It's not unusual for travellers to enter this monastery and emerge healed in tears. St. Charbel, after his death, still gives healing experiences to people to this day. You will have to look it up when we return. That's amazing, truly amazing!'

Mojat begins to explain the story. He informs me that St. Charbel's coffin, which lies inside, still has seeping fluid that heals. This is how this lowly monk became a saint. Miracles have happened to so many over the years. It's a long story my dear but when you read the books and the information on the internet, you will then fully understand.

Edward then recounts some of the amazing healing experiences people have had here, the most famous one being the story of St. Charbel healing a sister nun.

Mojat puts his arm around me and we walk back up the pathway, towards the Land Cruiser. I hold my healing handkerchief in my hand and kiss it.

'Janey, we can come back here and visit as often as you like when we are in Lebanon.'

'Yes, I would really like that. I need to explore a little more about my experience.' I still hold a clear picture of the monk in my mind, but who was the kind old lady?

Edward is now several paces in front of us, back on duty again. He stops and takes his binoculars out of his case and spends a good five minutes or more scanning the whole area, while Mojat and I continue to chat.

'Janey, you said the monk touched your right shoulder and the old woman took your right hand.'

'That's correct.'

'Well isn't that where you often have pain, in that arm and shoulder?'

'Yes it is, that hadn't occurred to me.'

We continue walking up the long pathway to the car. Edward has started the engine and we're ready for the next part of the journey.

I sit in the car holding this fine frayed cloth feeling blessed — so blessed.

CHAPTER THIRTY-TWO

Faraya in the Mountains

I am dazed holding on to my spiritual healing experience. Every now and then Mojat squeezes my arm and smiles at me. The healing handkerchief remains scrunched up in my hand.

For an hour we bounce around in the back of the car while Edward negotiates every twist and turn, still regularly checking in his rear view mirror. On these roads not only do you have to avoid potholes, but also the odd rock that has precariously fallen down from the mountains. Surprising pale heaps of grey rubble stones line the middle of the road as a primitive central reservation for cars travelling up and down.

The purer air is now starting to touch my lungs as we reach a very high altitude. The Faraya Mzaaar Cedars ski resort is signposted straight ahead with the village of Faraya off to the right. The temperature has dropped rapidly as the sun sinks slowly down the sky.

I open my car window, the powerful scent of pine and cedar feels so cleansing. Dusk is approaching and behind a glory of cedar trees I catch my first glimpse of a snow-capped mountain. It's breathtaking!

We pull into a side space off the road and all step outside the car to take in the views. I cannot believe the beauty of this area. Edward removes his gun and walks around checking. Why would he do this now?

'Is everything okay Edward?' I ask.

He takes his binoculars out again scanning for a few minutes before finally replying. 'Just being cautious.'

Mojat pulls me to one side. 'Leave him alone to do his job habibie. It's not for us to interfere or even discuss with him. You will have to stop fretting and trust in him my dear. Come on Janey, let's take in the magnificent view.'

'Okay Mojat, the snow-capped mountains are so beautiful!'

My mind seems to be on continual overdrive. Does Edward think for one moment that we are about to be jumped on up here? It's in my nature to watch everything but we've only seen a handful of cars coming up the mountain, most of which had overtaken us. There has been more traffic driving down on the other side. I can accept that this is his job, but as we're so far away from Beirut in this tranquil part of the world, it just seems a little over the top to me. Maybe it gives you a false sense of security, or am I just too trusting?

For the first time since our arrival in Lebanon I feel safe in this peaceful place. The pure sharp air makes my eyes smart and water and cleanses my sinuses.

CHAPTER THIRTY-THREE

Our Humble Abode

Edward turns off the main road in Faraya on to an unmade track. We now approach two small cottages, smoke bellowing from their chimneys. They both resemble something out of *Goldilocks and the Three Bears*.

We come to a halt just outside the doorway of the first cottage. Two German shepherds begin to bark, alerting their owners of our arrival as they run across the narrow lane in front of us. Mojat exits the car to make a fuss of the dogs and, as he kneels down, their tails immediately begin to wag. Of all the Arabs I have met in Jubai not one single person has ever liked dogs as they are considered a dirty animal, whereas here most homes have one. Mojat's reaction is so European.

An older couple simply dressed in country clothes, with ruddy complexions, emerge to greet us all. They hand Mojat the keys, as they are the keepers of the cottage for Ralph. A French conversation ensues.

They walk across to me and warmly say. 'Hello, Kyfak and Bonjour Madam.'

Kyfak means hello and welcome in Christian Lebanese Arabic, which is used all the time here. The Lebanese are devout Roman Catholics and in every village there is at least one church, if not several.

The couple, Fadia and Elias, have left supplies of food, wine and logs for the fire. There is no central heating — just extra blankets! I'm grateful that the fire has been made up for us as there's a distinct autumn chill in the air.

Singing in Silence

Fadia and Elias look as if they're in their late sixties, early seventies. Both have a healthy glow to their complexions. You can tell immediately that they live off their land, as there is an abundance of fig and olive trees and vegetable plots all around us. A small Renault van is parked alongside the cottage. I assume they live a simple life here with their two German shepherd dogs, but who really knows?

They inform Mojat about La Grillade, the local restaurant that has live entertainment tomorrow evening.

Edward drives the car very cautiously for another hundred yards as the unmade lane falls away quite steeply. There is a turning point just before our small cottage, which is tucked away next to an intensely planted fruit orchard.

A state of the art outside light shimmers as though it's about to go out at any moment. We enter the tiny villa to a warm glow, flickering shadows running up the walls from an open fire.

The water from the local spring feeds through the taps here and there is electricity for the lights, cooker and shower.

Despite a chill in the air the warm homely feel has taken the edge off the unlived atmosphere. I am grateful to Fadia for her hospitality. It's a cosy living room but upstairs still feels quite chilly and unlived in. Mojat can see I'm cold by the look on my face as I enter our bedroom.

'Don't worry Janey, the heat will rise during the evening.'

Edward has a bedroom downstairs at the other end of the cottage. It doesn't take us long to establish ourselves.

I enter the kitchen to unload our shopping and, on the small table, there is a large clay pot with a note written in French. Mojat translates. 'Chicken and vegetable hotpot to cook in the oven for one hour.'

I follow Fadia's instructions. As I reach for a bottle of wine Mojat notices a terracotta jug of the local Arak on the side. It is a clear liquid made here in the mountains and tastes of aniseed. It's of very high alcohol content and once you add iced water it turns white.

It feels safe and secure here. Edward has walked around and completed his usual checks inside and out and seems content.

Before it gets dark we decide to take in some fresh air in Fadia and Elias' orchard, which is laden with fruits.

All around the cottages are huge trees, bushes and flowers and, as far as the eye can see, spectacular scenery. There are villas in the distance with smoking chimneys and fields of various colours.

I have to remind myself that the villages are all located on the sides of mountains. Lemon groves, fig and olive trees are planted on terraces. Abundant flat parsley grows all around us. We follow a small stone intricate pathway that separates a variety of produce.

At the bottom of the orchard, over a wall, is a neatly planted vegetable plot and, further in view, is another lower level terrace of yet more planting.

On returning to the house the heat and flames give off an orange glow. We all settle down to eat in front of the fire enjoying the peace and tranquillity. It's the end to a perfect day. We break apart our French bread and dip it into our dishes of stew. Whilst taking the local drink we sit quietly staring into the fire, enjoying the flickering flames and the crackling, glowing embers.

CHAPTER THIRTY-FOUR

Danger on our Doorstep

The next day I wake up much later than normal. The pure mountain air has obviously knocked me out, as I feel rather comatose.

Mojat brings me tea and proceeds to sit on the edge of the bed kissing me. He then informs me that Edward left the cottage at 7am to enjoy the ski resort for a couple of days and will stay in the Intercontinental. By all accounts it's a lovely chalet-style hotel.

I am relieved at hearing this news but say nothing. Edward is now an important part of our lives and I have to accept that he will always travel with us.

The tea begins to bring me round from my unusually deep sleep. To be honest I can barely remember going to bed! I then announce to Mojat how good I am feeling and he comments on how well I look.

'Something has changed about you my dear.' He looks me up and down scrutinising. 'I really believe that you've been healed by the monk.'

'Something does feel different,' I reply.

'I thought we might go for a walk this morning to take in the stillness and beauty of the countryside,' suggests Mojat. 'Unfortunately the forecast is for rain later.'

Suddenly this appeals to me as it only rains for two or three days a year in Jubai if we are lucky. It will refresh us.

I finish my tea, have a quick shower and get dressed. I wander outside to find Mojat sat on the terrace drinking coffee in his gilet, jeans and a jumper, gazing over the countryside and snow-capped mountains.'

He turns to me. 'I am just taking in the views, it's so peaceful up here and the air is so pure. I have some good news Janey.'

'Oh, what is it?'

'I have just rung The White House in Jubai and have spoken to Samira.'

'Have you?'

'Yes, I have organised your personal maid to fly out to be with you. I have also arranged a room for her at The Seasons Hotel, where we will meet her in a few days' time.'

I give him a hug of appreciation.

'Well that has put a smile on your face habibie. She has a friend, Freda, who might be available in the future. She is from a Bedouin tribe and has been a personal temporary maid to some of my political friends' wives in the past.'

'She's mentioned Freda to me.'

'I might hire her, if this suits you my dear?'

'Yes it would, she sounds interesting.'

'We will see on our return journey to Jubai.'

Mojat finishes his coffee. 'Do you mind if I smoke a small cigar, as I feel so relaxed sat here.'

'Of course, enjoy — you're on holiday.'

'Quite Janey, quite!'

I absorb his every word as I enjoy his interesting stories.

'Freda is from a desert tribe of healers and they have been close friends for years. I've been thinking, the women can travel together with us and can be company for each other. If we're away for weeks at a time it can be quite lonely for a maid.'

'Yes I suppose it can. You are very considerate.'

'It would work in our favour for when we stay in Lebanon, which could be up to six months every year. Maybe we'll move here eventually. Anyway, nothing will be decided yet.'

'Yes, it all sounds a possibility, especially as Samira has known her for years.'

'I need to keep you happy my dear.'

'I am, don't worry Mojat. She sounds perfect.'

'When we return to Jubai, I will ask Samira to bring her to the house for a chat with us both. If she is happy and you are, I will offer her a six-month position.'

We are both dressed very casually as we walk down the road to check out the local restaurant for tonight.

The owner has an inquisitive look about him. Trying to appear polite and friendly he asks us where we are staying, as there are no hotels for miles.

Mojat is always on his guard; he speaks in Arabic whilst the owner continually gives me the once over. It's not every day up in this remote mountain area that you see a blonde English woman with an Arabic man. And an Arab man with a difference, whose accent is so educated! It's torturous not understanding the language but I'm beginning to learn a few words. I keep trying, but languages have never been my forte.

Mojat tells the owner a tale to throw him off and I hear Ralph's name mentioned a few times. Then suddenly all is good with the restaurant proprietor. 'Ah, cee Ralph okay, cee okay.'

Just before departing I receive a cautious smile from him. He shakes Mojat's hand and all seems more relaxed.

'Everything is good thanks to Ralph. We have a table,' says Mojat.

We head off the main road down a small lane to commence our walk. The countryside is wonderful. We see small dwellings and locals that farm the land. It is so different to anything I've ever seen before. The agricultural land is split into terraces and falls away down the mountainside. After an hour we sit on a wall and share a bottle of water whilst taking in the beauty and sounds of the area. The birds sing, a cockerel crows and the branches creak as they sway in the breeze.

'This is the first time habibie that I have roamed freely in the countryside. It's a real pleasure to be here with you as, when I'm out of Jubai, I usually have Edward or an entourage of people at my side.'

'You are free Mojat. Free for the next two days.'

We begin to share memories and speak of our parents and his older brother, the latter having caused considerable pain in his life. I tell him of my upbringing and then, our most recent memory, our chance meeting — or so I thought! We giggle like love-struck teenagers.

The intenseness of living in a busy desert city seems a distant memory at this moment. We hold hands as we walk.

'I love the tranquillity here in the mountains and our time together is so precious Mojat.'

I replay the scenario to him about the old woman in the monastery and the old frayed handkerchief. And the people kneeling and praying that subsequently vanished into thin air.

'For sure habibie, all I know is you're younger today, positively glowing! I should have entered the monastery and maybe I would have regained my youth too! It was all very mysterious you receiving that handkerchief.'

We laugh together and enjoy each other's company as we head back in the direction of Ralph's place. The villa is now in sight, the final two hundred yards being up a steep bank.

We arrive a little breathless and hungry. I enter the kitchen and begin to arrange lunch, a little bit of everything from what we collected yesterday including the local cheese, Laban, which is white and salty. I prepare warm flatbreads, a small dish of olives and some chopped up lettuce, flat parsley and home-grown large ripe tomatoes.

We sit on the terrace in the centre of the orchard enjoying our simple lunch. A light shower of rain begins to fall but this does not interrupt us eating under the shelter. It's liberating to walk freely and eat outside with no one around us, other than Fadia and Elias just up the lane.

We return to the villa and I decide to light a fire before it gets

Singing in Silence

dark. Mojat stands over me watching in amazement as I carry out such a practical job.

'Are you really going to make the fire?' he asks, looking down at me as I kneel on the floor.

'Do you think I'm going to get Fadia to do a job that I did every day at Wisteria House?'

I gather plenty of sticks and paper from the outside store area. There are firelighters and matches under the sink and Mojat collects a large basket of logs, which he finds stacked up inside the terrace undercover.

'All straightforward Mojat, not a problem!'

'This is really servants' work habibie and not something for your fine hands.'

'Oh Mojat, for two nights does it really matter?'

I tidy around the fireplace, light the fire and the flames begin to roar up the chimney.

We decide to have a siesta — our bed is still unmade from this morning. As we pull the sheets and blankets over us he very quickly grabs my breasts and starts to suckle and kiss my nipples. He wants me again!

Enjoying my nakedness he moves down my body kissing me tenderly. He touches every part of me smoothing his hands over my curves, feeling my flesh and every muscle. His hard penis pushes into my stomach; he then pulls the sheets back and examines my naked body by running his hands up and down me.

'I am hungry for you. I am yours, take me!' I say excitably.

He pushes my thighs apart and grabs my inner flesh, squeezing me. He then looks down at my body.

'Your beautiful fanny — it's the most exquisite fanny.'

His words turn me on. Fanny is an old English word.

He moves down and starts to kiss my female mounds of flesh, sinking his teeth in to me. I am in heaven enjoying his succulent lips on my gentle parts. He bends my knees and lifts my legs up and over my head. I am bent double, my vagina full to capacity from his wide manhood. I am a contortionist, a sexual trapeze artist who is supple and pliable ensuring his erotic needs are met.

  I notice his breathing accelerates as he maintains a good rhythm and begins to talk dirty, slapping my bottom several times. He commands me. 'Lie still and let me take your fanny!'

  I do as he says as he thrusts deeper and squeezes my nipples. He slaps me once again, this time a little harder causing me to flinch. Now his voice is more demanding. 'Keep your fanny still, I want to fuck you hard!'

  I stay motionless — he is turned on by my submission. My body is a fission of tingles radiating upwards from my thighs to my throat. I throb intensely, enjoying his all-conquering power. I let him act out his earthy sexual ways as he takes me and my fanny for his pleasure. Part of me feels embarrassed that his methods turn me on so much.

  Two hours later we awake in dark and peaceful stillness. I can hear the crackles of the wood burning on the fire. Mojat leaves our love bed to go and check on it. He turns on the lamps, draws the curtains and replenishes the logs.

  We dress casually for the evening and Mojat collects the champagne from the fridge and enters the bedroom with it. I finish applying my make-up and then we polish off two glasses of fizz each. Before walking down to the restaurant I pick up my special Gucci bag.

  'Interesting move!' says Mojat.

  'Just being prepared, especially with Edward away.'

  I am now hesitant. Am I doing the right thing? Of course I am, but I don't want to spoil the freedom we've been enjoying.

  'It's fine habibie.' He proceeds to lift up his trouser leg, revealing a special leather holster strap housing a revolver against his inner calf muscle. 'Just be careful where you put the bag as we are surrounded by strangers and don't want to appear too affluent. It's not Beirut city!'

  'I know we're out in the sticks here! Farmers' country now,' I say whilst laughing.

You can never underestimate a good restaurant with entertainment in Lebanon. We notice just how many cars there are parked outside and along the main road. We enter and it's extremely busy. There are local people that work the land, dressed in their very best clothes. Other couples and families have travelled many miles just for tonight.

'Well I did not expect this,' says Mojat. 'This place must attract people from all over the mountain villages and towns.'

The waiters rush from table to table and traditional Lebanese music is playing. Most of the customers have ordered their meals already and we are amongst the last to take our seats. I thought 8:30pm was early — obviously not in these mountain villages!

Our table is on the far side of the room. The wooden chairs have arms and boast decorative French lattice. They are very comfortable. Every table has a freshly laundered red gingham check tablecloth, a nice French influence. Also on each table sits a small case holding a piece of cedar and some wild yellow primroses. We have a good view of the huge open fire and the band area.

Our waiter takes our order and Mojat chooses a bottle of local red, a Cinsault from the Bekaa Valley. It subsequently arrives accompanied by two large goblets.

Mojat tells me about the Jesuits and how they were great winemakers of the area until 1972, when the civil war destroyed everything. I'm intrigued and enjoy his little history lesson.

'That's the sad thing about wars, they are syphilitic, destructive and evil,' he says.

'Mojat, you are a mine of information.'

'I love Lebanon Janey. When I retire I would like us to make it our home.'

'It certainly looks very appealing right now!'

Of course it's so easy to get carried away. At present we sit enjoying the wonderful ambience of this local restaurant, feeling liberated with our newly found freedom. Our love is new and intriguing — as fresh as a daisy, as my mother used to say.

The restaurant building resembles a large ski chalet from the outside. Inside there is a wide log fire at one end and around twenty-five to thirty tables. There is also a small stage. The lighting is generally low, except for the stage and bar area.

There is a festive feel as the nights draw in and the wine flows from table to table. We enjoy the atmosphere and the locals chat openly to us. Tonight we feel like one of them, as though we've been dining here for years.

The local band are good musicians and play upbeat songs, creating a party atmosphere. Then, all of a sudden, the music stops and a very attractive woman takes to the microphone. Everyone stands up and applauds, whistles and cheers as she begins to sing in Lebanese Arabic. The entire restaurant comes alive with men and women taking to the dance floor.

I glance at Mojat surprised at the sudden energy in this place.

'Habibie she is very well known. Her name is Myriam Fares and the Lebanese adore her.'

It is ten o'clock and the dance floor is heaving. Myriam has the most beautiful voice. People on surrounding tables tell us that they've travelled all the way from Beirut just to hear her sing tonight.

I realise now just how lucky we were to have secured this table yesterday. The evening is turning out to be wonderful. In this small mountain village we are being entertained by a performer of the very highest standard.

We dance, drink and frolic like lovers do. I pinch myself as I have done so regularly since meeting Mojat. I want this precious time to last for always.

After an hour, the band and singer take a refreshment break. The people take to their seats again. Further drinks and bottles of wine are now being ordered and the waiters, once again, are being rushed off their feet.

The outer door opens wide and all is pitch darkness beyond. Three men enter the restaurant and are shown to the last available table located next to the door. They order a bottle of Johnnie Walker Red Label Whisky. Then they sit down and immediately light up, whilst checking out the place.

All three of them look rather dubious and cagey characters to me. The waiter fills each of their glasses almost to the rim, as they take long drawn out drags of their cigarettes. They don't seem happy like everyone else in here, more suspicious and leery. They have a look of serious intent as they survey all around them. One, with a goatee beard, looks treacherous and slippery with evil piercing eyes. I find myself staring at him and thinking, he looks a nasty piece of shit!

I notice a few other people also looking towards them. Only glances, as staring for too long might intimidate and cause a conflict. Something tells me that they're not part of the normal crowd.

Mojat leans forward and pretends to kiss me, but instead whispers in my ear. 'Habibie, those greasy slickers have sat by the door for a reason. I must call Edward. Please act naturally whilst I am on the mobile — maybe lean over me and kiss me like you have had a little too much to drink. I do not want these men to know that we are on to them.'

How can Mojat be so sure that there is a problem here?

'Janey, trust me!'

I whisper back. 'Please don't go outside to make your call, I am terrified you will not return!'

Mojat tuts at me and takes my hand firmly. 'I'm not going anywhere habibie.'

He phones Edward from our table and gives me an over the top smile, as though he's talking to a close friend. The moment Mojat is on his mobile the greasy slickers all glance in his direction. At this point Mojat laughs quite loudly in a rather false way. I stand and begin kissing and embracing his neck, leaning all over him.

He then puts his arm around my waist making us both seem as if we've had too much to drink. I fall on to his knees, as we pretend to be oblivious to anything that is happening around us.

Mojat finishes the call and whispers in my ear.

'You're quite good at this.'

'I'm a good actress.'

The shifty characters begin to relax a little and continue with their bottle of whisky, which is now three quarters empty. They are ugly brutes, overweight and unshaven — old city slickers with greased back hair on badly receding hairlines.

The tallest of the men stands up, stubs out his cigarette and walks towards the loo. He tries to utch up his trousers but his huge pregnant stomach hinders any progress. The trousers resign themselves, slipping back down on to his lower hips.

Another Johnnie Walker bottle appears on their table and the smallest of the three, with sharp features and a goatee beard, checks his mobile and mumbles something with a restless agitation.

Mojat and I sit listening to the band and singer as they return on stage for the second half. The clapping and whistling whips up again from the excitable audience. For our own safety thank heavens the restaurant is full and all the customers are noisily enjoying themselves.

We continue to pretend we haven't noticed the slickers, as we kiss and jostle for space on the heaving dance floor. After five minutes we return to the table. Edward walks in and joins us. The old city slickers all look up and mumble something to each other, looking even more agitated. The atmosphere from their table changes and the goatee one makes a phone call.

Mojat says to me how relieved he is that Edward looks the part of an armed bodyguard tonight. For sure they were not anticipating this. Edward seems to think that the goatee guy is in charge.

My gut is now telling me that there's a real problem here. These shady characters are not here for the entertainment or the food!

Mojat turns to his bodyguard in a relieved manner. 'Well done Edward, only thirty minutes to reach us. I hope we have not inconvenienced you too much?'

Emotionless and cold he acknowledges what has been said, but now he is back on duty, protecting us both with military Special Forces precision.

Coffee arrives at our table. I am aware that all three of us have weapons and I can guarantee that the greasy slickers will be armed too. I look over to the owner of the club as he talks to one of the waiters. I get the impression that he too suspects all is not well at the table by the door.

Edward scans the room with his telescopically trained eye. In the meantime some of the customers are departing. The singer has completed her final song and the waiters are busy organising the end of evening cheques.

I wait until other women are heading to the ladies room before I pick up my Gucci bag, tuck it under my arm and vacate my seat. On my return Mojat and Edward are at the bar waiting for me.

The slickers have just left. Edward took a note of their number plate and has made a phone call to Beirut security to get the car checked out.

It is now midnight and we leave the restaurant alongside other customers. We climb into the Cruiser — Edward and Mojat have their guns at the ready. We drive back amongst many cars also leaving the restaurant. Edward continues to check all around us, holding his gun whilst at the wheel. He now makes another phone call to Beirut to glean more details on the slickers. He is informed that their vehicle has been traced to a south Beirut address, a very unsavoury area.

We arrive back at our warm cottage. Edward advises Mojat to leave and leave right now!

I feel disgruntled and angry and blurt out. 'Why now? Is our life really under threat? What's the real problem?'

Mojat raises his voice at me for the very first time. 'Listen Janey, I have told you before about the work I am involved in. Many people do not want this Peace Treaty.'

I stare at them both, the warm glow of the fires waning embers somehow seems less comforting than before. I feel incensed that our little bit of idyllic heaven is now coming to an abrupt end. My brain is working overtime, the champagne's effect turning to ice in my veins. Again I challenge this situation.

'Who really knows we are in Faraya? Surely, we were not followed up here or Edward would have noticed?'

Edward glances sideways to look at Mojat. I stand before them both, looking directly into their eyes.

I didn't mean to be confrontational, which has never been my nature. Before either of them have a chance to answer, I burst into tears, rush upstairs to the bedroom and begin to gather a few things together. I am seething and acting like a spoilt brat that is used to having her own way. I do not want this precious intimate period interrupted, the only time we have been truly alone. Our little love nest is being taken apart by some ugly old slickers.

Mojat appears in front of me, my eyes are full of tears. I wipe one then the other with a blackened tissue from my now smudged mascara.

'You're upset, but we have to leave right now!'

'Okay, I will be packed soon.'

'Pack! Are you kidding me? Come on.' He grabs my hand. 'Habibie, quickly, no time, come on!'

Edward is on the phone speaking in fluent Arabic to someone. I hear Beirut mentioned twice and Mojat is also straining to listen. I feel suddenly naïve and vulnerable, realising that I truly have no idea of the bigger picture.

'I am sorry as I don't really know what is happening, but I trust what you say. It's just a disruption I was not prepared for.'

Mojat only half listens to me as he is too busy concentrating on Edward's call. I don't really know why I was trying to justify my feelings or behaviour to them. Right now these two men are on a totally different planet to me.

I notice a handwritten note to Fadia and Elias has been placed under a salt pot in the kitchen. Edward is now off the phone and briefly utters something to Mojat. He then immediately walks out of the villa, runs past the sitting room window on to the terrace and sprints up to the car. He turns on the ignition.

I grab my Gucci bag and my real handbag as we swiftly exit the back door, slamming it shut behind us. My hand is now gripped firmly by Mojat to the point of pain. We dart to the car and jump on to the back seats. Before Mojat has closed his door Edward accelerates away, his foot down to the floor. We speed up the unmade lane like bank robbers making off with a few million in the boot.

Only a vague dim light shining from our neighbour's cottage window can be seen amongst the pitch-black countryside. Elias flicks his curtains back to look out.

Edward accelerates harder and the tyres, trying to grip loose stones on the uneven surface, emit loud cracking noises. There is deadly silence in the car, but outside it must sound like a motocross racetrack on a Saturday afternoon. We reach the top of the lane and I smell scorching rubber as Edward steers the car skilfully out on to the road without stopping. I sense this drive is not going to be for the faint-hearted!

Never before have I had to shift my body with such urgency. What on earth is happening? I can sense the concentration between the two men and don't dare to say a word. Despite being nervous and tense I'm trying to grasp the reality of the situation. Who were those cut-throat guys? What is all this about? How did they know we were even in the restaurant? I was certainly not aware of anyone acting suspiciously around the villa in the past 24 hours.

'Will someone please tell me what is happening — are we in real danger?' I ask, clutching nervously to my Gucci bag.

Before Mojat can open his mouth, Edward speaks in a clear

precise voice, whilst he grips the wheel with both hands and holds his back straight. 'The three men in the restaurant have been tailing us, we managed to lose them at St. Charbel's monastery.'

I swallow hard, my throat aches at the back. 'So you knew that we were being followed back then?'

'Yes, I had an idea. I knew by going to the monastery that it might throw them off our scent! And, as it turns out, I was correct. They took another route.'

There is a pause in our conversation as he drops down a gear to take a difficult bend. He then accelerates hard out, building up a fast speed as we head down the mountain. There are no street lights, only the moon and stars to guide him. I look out of the window and can visualise the sheer drop through the darkness on my side of the road. I want to say move over, but nerves prevent me from doing so.

We are being tossed about in the back as we approach bend after bend. I look behind us, there is nothing! Edward spots me in the rear-view mirror.

'Looking behind you Janey means nothing, these guys will have landmarks everywhere in the mountains.'

I look at my man, sitting in silence. His energy has a strange calmness as if nothing fazes him. Either he's put total trust in Edward or has been in this situation many times before.

We drive for another four or five miles in total silence. I am gripping on to the leather straps dangling from the roof as we bob up and down over rocks that have fallen down from the mountain, swerving to miss the bigger ones. Jesus, my mind is now working overtime.

'Who are these people?' I ask demandingly.

Edward, again, without a flinch announces. 'Hezbollah.'

Adrenaline is now pumping through my veins. On hearing this, my frame of mind changes. This is real! This is the real thing! Of course this makes sense. The address in south Beirut I overheard earlier.

Edward shows no consideration for us in the back of the car as he takes the next bend, swerving and throwing us to the other side. I am now kneeling on the floor attempting to get my balance back. Mojat shines the light from his mobile down to my feet so that I can see. I remove my revolver from the bag, which is now on the floor, and load more ammunition. At this point Mojat also takes his gun and adds further bullets.

I clamber back up on to the seat and position myself sideways in a comfortable fashion to be able to look forwards and backwards. Edward is now accelerating at a ridiculous speed down the mountain road, negotiating the bends on two wheels. It is hairy to say the least, yet still Mojat is silent.

There is a sudden flash of light coming from the left. Out of nowhere, there in front of us, is an old clapped out 5-series BMW driving like crazy.

'Where the hell did that come from?' I shout.

Mojat just tuts and mutters something in Arabic to Edward, who doesn't respond as he's concentrating on this mindless journey back to Beirut. Undoubtedly he's swearing like a trooper, but does not want me to hear.

I smile inappropriately to myself as my nervous erratic thoughts are taking over. This is it! Survival time! It's now or never! Kill or be killed! Mojat was right when he said never underestimate the evil powers that will do anything to stop the Peace Treaty.

Edward has the full beam on trying to dazzle the clapped-out car in front. Suddenly more headlights are behind us, also on full beam. Shit! It's like driving through the blackness of Colditz with an interrogation light in your face! Edward accelerates harder, attempting to overtake. It's blood-curdling stuff being sandwiched as we are and the BMW has no intention of letting us pass.

As we swerve from one side of the road to the other I begin to feel nauseous. The mountain road is narrow and I'm acutely aware that we are sailing very close to the edge. As we negotiate the bends, the headlights shine brightly over a dark space of nothingness — it's the edge of a precipice! This is it, I say to myself.

A beat up old Mercedes Benz sits on our tail and suddenly smashes into us.

'For fucks sake,' I howl, as it crunches us again for the second time and then a third. It jolts us forward to the point of whiplash! I am stunned and cannot believe what's just happened. To be smashed into like this at high speed is just crazy suicidal driving.

Mojat's eyes are now fixed on my next move; his facial expression is a picture! I lean out of the car window and aim and shoot several times at the car behind. 'They want action. I will give them fucking action!'

Suddenly I feel totally fearless and look down at my revolver. Now I wish it was a sub-machine gun. Any trepidation I had previously about using a weapon has dissolved rapidly. A huge adrenaline surge has kicked in and I am ready ... ready to kill! In fact I want to kill all these greasy fucking bastards.

'Bonnie and Clyde have nothing on us,' I scream, as high as a kite. Those 1930s American outlaws really lived life on the edge. This is me now — on the fucking edge!

Mojat is still as calm as a cucumber. 'No, I can see that my dear. I didn't know you had it in you?' He holds his shiny revolver looking absolutely staggered at my behaviour.

I lean back into the car after taking a second round of shots and glance at Edward. He is not losing face and drives incessantly at high speed as we enter the final section of mountain road. We are fast approaching a built-up area. All through this tense drive he has kept both hands clasped firmly on the wheel, shifting it from side to side akin to an experienced formula one driver.

Edward shouts. 'Keep low and hold on tight. I'm gonna try and shake them off.' Abruptly swerving he undertakes a high-speed handbrake turn down a side street, leaving the other cars on the main road.

'Jesus Edward,' I say. 'I don't know how you pulled off that manoeuvre! I've never experienced anything like it!'

'It will give us a little more time,' says Edward. 'But they will be back.'

We're now located on the outskirts of Beirut and this area contains small apartment blocks and rows of houses, with the odd shop in between. Edward turns off the car's headlights and begins to weave around the streets in total darkness. Okay the old city slickers have less of a chance of spotting us, but it seems madness to be driving a car with no headlights. Especially as we have to negotiate parked cars, rubbish bins and the occasional cat and dog.

On Edward's orders we are crouching in the rear of the car. My back is killing me as I try to hold this position, squashed as I am behind the driver's seat.

I try for a few seconds to analyse the situation from Mojat's point of view. These slimeballs want his blood and they're prepared to stop at nothing to kill him, whilst also putting their own lives in danger. And yet this man remains quiet and composed, putting all his trust in Edward. I can now understand how their relationship has a special bond and imagine they might have experienced similar situations in the past.

I look at my man and there is no expression of tiredness, fear or anger. He's just holding himself together.

I peer out into the darkness and say nervously, 'There must be a shortage of electricity here, as the street lights are not working.'

This amuses Edward as I catch him sniggering in his driver's mirror. 'Beirut has been on a grid for years,' he says, as if I'm meant to understand this.

Mojat has finished a call to the Beirut police and now speaks to the US embassy, as this is our nearest location for safety.

'I don't understand Mojat, why have you waited this long to call the police?'

'Janey, only the Beirut city police can handle a situation like this. We informed them before we left the villa that we might run into problems. The police are on high alert, I can assure you — they are!'

'We might run into problems? Mojat they're trying to kill us and almost ran us off the side of a frigging mountain! Only Hezbollah! Don't worry, just a minor problem.' I say sarcastically.

Neither of them answer me.

Edward almost comes to a standstill, our car's engine barely ticking over. He scans around to see if he recognises where we are. Then suddenly we're off again at high speed, negotiating the back streets in near pitch darkness.

I look up as Edward stops the car again. Not for too long this time I hope, as this neighbourhood looks dodgy, really dodgy! Much worse than The Bronx in New York or Chapeltown in Leeds!

Edward edges a little further along as if he's trying to find his bearings. 'I know where we are,' he announces. 'The US embassy is less than half a mile away.'

'Can't we just get back on the main road? Wouldn't it be safer?' I reply, in my naïvety.

'Certainly not Janey. One of their cars will be parked up waiting for us to pull out again. These guys are shrewd. It's much safer on foot, they will not expect this.'

Is Edward serious I think to myself? On foot — really? Yeah right, for sure we will be dead meat!

Mojat and I look around us. There is nothing! As the US embassy is not too far away, Edward agrees that Mojat should call them. I think pessimistically to myself — surely this is not going to help us?

'Where is the British embassy Edward?'

He ignores me at first, then, as a delayed reaction. 'Five minutes drive away, but too far right now.'

Mojat calls the US embassy and speaks to someone he knows. The security guard has been given clearance to let us in. A small side gate will be open for us, but not the large double gates at the front. It seems that we will have to enter as pedestrians as the front gates are automatic and take thirty-seconds to close. This poses too much of a security threat as, if our pursuers are nearby, they could potentially drive in behind us.

Edward pulls in close to the curb and switches off the engine. He removes himself quietly from the car and stands outside surveying the scene.

We are parked a few streets away from the embassy building, behind an old apartment block tucked down a dark and dismal street. Edward signals for us to exit the car. Mojat holds a finger to his lips, a gesture for me not to close the door or make a sound!

We emerge from the car slowly and carefully in order to avoid being heard or noticed. Edward whispers to me that the embassy is just a short run from here, then across a main road. He feels it's safer to abandon the car. My Gucci bag is over my shoulder and I'm holding my gun firmly. The men also have their firearms at the ready.

The three of us move quickly and quietly down a very long street, which seems to be everlasting. The only illumination is from the moonlight. Mojat and I are both breathless and we're relieved when we come to a temporary halt at the end of the road.

All three of us move stealthily along the wall of the end house. Edward holds his semi-automatic close to his body and is just about to check around the corner on to the next street when, suddenly, there is a huge explosion! We turn and look back — it's our hire car! We watch in horror as fragments of metal fly up in the air and bright orange flames rip out at all angles.

'Oh my God what is happening here?' I say, in an understandable state of panic. I turn to the men for reassurance as I've just witnessed our car being completely destroyed. It seems to me that our situation seems to be getting progressively worse the closer we get to the embassy.

There is no time for counselling as Edward implores us both to pull back quickly into the nearest side alleyway, which resembles a dark tunnel. Part of it is covered over and the end section is open to the sky. It leads us to a row of backyards where we can still see flames from the explosion reflecting into the moonlight. We then begin to hear people shouting at the scene of the explosion. It sounds chaotic.

Our eyes meet as we all huddle together like wild alley cats, waiting for Edward's next strategic decision.

He whispers. 'We need to move as I'm sure the other guys are nearby and ...' Edward suddenly falls silent. We find ourselves shadowing his every move as he quickly and quietly runs deeper into the dark alleyway. The main road is now in sight.

We can hear rustling, scraping and scratching noises. Hezbollah's men are on our tail close by.

Suddenly a shot is fired from behind us, echoing down the alley. Edward pushes me hard into someone's backyard and I go flying, hitting a wall and grazing my head slightly. Two of the slickers are moving quickly towards us. Edward fires again.

I am sweating, adrenaline pumping through my veins. Mojat is leaning against me crushing my tits against the wall. Although he tries valiantly to protect me, I gently push him away as I'm beginning to feel suffocated. I am trembling, exhausted and on the edge of collapse but have to suppress any thoughts of weakness. Anger always keeps the adrenaline high and, yes, I am furious, bloody furious! I want to explode inside from all this crap! I position my gun ready for the greasy bastards.

There is a scratching noise above us; we look up to the stars scanning the rooftops all around, hardly daring to breathe. Edward peers around the wall of the backyard looking along the alleyway. Again there are shots fired in our direction and Edward returns fire in retaliation. Then there is silence — deathly silence.

Questions are buzzing round in my head. How are we going to get across the road into the side gate of the US embassy? Where is our backup? Where is our fucking backup?

Suddenly, Mojat and I are engulfed in a heavy dark shadow. We look up and on the wall behind us, breathing down our necks, squatting and hovering, is the goatee-bearded slicker. This dark entity's bent body is the devil himself, his evil piercing eyes have a hypnotic effect. In a flash I raise my arm, fire and take him out. He falls off the wall backwards yelling, 'Sharamutah, fucking Sharamutah!'

Mojat gives me a confident look. 'Well done, I am impressed habibie! I have underestimated you — you're a damn fine shot!'

Under my breath I say, 'Bastard! One down, two to go.'

Edward gives us the all clear, pointing his gun up the alley towards the main road. It's a signal for us to follow him and we run for our lives. My chest burns with adrenaline, my heart muscle beats fast and my head pounds from the graze earlier. Additionally I notice my right hand has developed the shakes, probably due to the shock of shooting that goatee slicker!

The main road facing the US embassy is now in sight. There is a glimmer of light at the end of the tunnel.

Edward sees movement across a parallel alleyway and further shots are now being fired. Mojat groans and falls to the ground holding his shoulder. I scream out, worried sick for my man and petrified that I will be next! Edward responds with a round of firing.

I bend down at Mojat's side as he lies on the ground. Feeling flustered I realise I need to do the right thing and I'm frightened to put my gun down. With my gun firmly in the one hand I lift his head and hold him in the other.

'I wasn't trained to do this!' I scream out. 'Fucking bastards!'

'The road ahead is too risky to run across right now, as we'll be sitting ducks!' says Edward.

Mojat attempts to speak. I hold out my arm for him and try to pull him up. Edward is still firing and manoeuvres back down the alleyway in an attempt to protect us. Through my lack of strength and his weakness Mojat falls to the ground, hits his head and knocks himself senseless.

'Christ Mojat!' I can't believe it. Of all the times for this to happen he is out for the count.

Edward returns and looks down at him. 'Janey, we just need to get to the security gate across the road.'

I question again in desperation. 'Where are the Americans? Or someone! The police — why aren't they coming to our rescue?'

Edward whispers. 'Good question,' he says. 'Where are those bloody Yanks?'

There is now an eerie silence around us. I kneel down on the ground next to my love and cradle his head. His breathing is shallow. In this pitch of darkness I can only see the whites of his eyes as they roll to the back of his sockets. I press my lips hard on to his forehead and start to sob uncontrollably from the pit of my stomach. It is a knee-jerk reaction and a realisation of just how deep my love is for this man.

I whisper tenderly to him. 'I love you — please don't die on me. Our life has only just begun.'

Tears stream from me and fall over his bloodied head. I can sense his pain from his breathing, as though he is gasping for air. My right eye starts to pull and twitch, a stress thing. I look up to Edward who is cut off from all emotion, doing what he is trained to do — combat!

'Janey, this does not help, stay focused! Are you listening to me?' He grabs me. 'I just want you to stay focused.'

'I am trying to.'

Blood is now pouring from Mojat's chest and my hands are saturated. The smell makes me nauseous and I begin to gag! I press down hard on his wound trying to stop the flow.

Edward speaks again. 'I just need a sign and we will make a run for it.'

'Okay a sign,' I say, trying to pull myself together. 'Just a sign.'

'This ghetto is no place to hang around with these bandits on the loose.'

'Yes, you're right Edward,' I reply. His voice is incredibly calm given the situation.

Finally I can hear police sirens getting closer.

Mojat's phone begins to ring. I answer and am greeted by an

American accent at the embassy.

'Where are you?'

I pass the phone to Edward.

'We're in an alleyway diagonally opposite and to the right of the main gates. Please organise a doctor urgently as Mojat has been shot and his breathing has accelerated. I am bringing him in.'

Edward puts the phone in his pocket, stands up and says. 'That was my sign, now we move.'

I am still on the ground holding Mojat's head in my arms, pressing hard on his heart area.

A noise echoes loudly down the alleyway, we both look at each other. We can now see the fat greasy slicker lurking in the distance, and there is a scuffle as he loses his grip on the rubble and rubbish.

Edward hammers out a few more shots. The goatee slicker's voice is echoing from the alley behind us, he must be regaining consciousness. His strained tones sound as if he's smoked fifty woodbines a day for twenty years.

We can hear footsteps.

Edward whispers. 'I think the fat guy is trying to rescue his mate. Sorry Janey, this is not a good introduction to Beirut and is grim for you.'

'It's an experience I won't forget!'

Down this long tunnel there is silence. Blood oozes from Mojat's wounded shoulder all over me. I think he is losing too much of it and the smell is putrid. He now begins to regain consciousness and I reassure him that help is on its way. The police sirens are more audible, but still no sign of assistance.

There is shouting and yelling in the distance, dogs bark and flames from our burnt out car are flying high, still illuminating the night sky.

Edward decides to get Mojat up on his feet. He is more conscious now and we might stand a chance of getting to the side gate. He feels confident that Hezbollah's men have disappeared for now, as we are too close for comfort for the greasy slickers to be on foot. The police must be patrolling the area and the embassy is just over the road.

Edward signals to me. 'Janey, help me.'

It's a struggle to get Mojat to his feet, as he is a dead weight. He moans and groans as Edward heaves him awkwardly over his shoulder, getting him in to a fireman's lift. I am then handed the machine gun.

'Janey you will have to use this. There is a full round of ammunition and all you have to do is cover us whilst I run to the security gate. Are you listening to me Janey?'

'Yes, yes I am.'

'Well answer me then,' snaps Edward.

Edward takes my revolver and I am now left holding a sub-machine gun! He positions Mojat into a better place as he is still groaning in pain.

'Don't worry Janey he'll be okay, it's just his shoulder.'

I was not exactly sure where he was wounded but one thing's for sure, the smell is dank!

What I have learnt from observing Edward is that it's best to keep watch all around you whilst positioning the gun at every angle during movement. I ensure we are not being tailed and, despite being tense, I am ready for action. Fear and adrenaline surge throughout my body as we begin to move forward. We build up speed then Edward halts. He raises his arm gesturing for me to keep still and quiet in the darkness. I stand right behind him holding my weapon firmly, praying that I don't get the shakes again! Edward is taking the full weight of my man and the security gate is now in view, just across the main road.

'Are you ready Janey? We will make a run for it now, NOW...'

I am behind them trying to keep up, at the same time being acutely aware that I have to constantly scan the scene for potential trouble. Edward shifts at a remarkable pace considering Mojat is over his shoulder. Our destination is close and, as we approach, two guards release the security gate, which opens quickly. Edward carries Mojat through and continues purposefully towards the entrance.

All seems fine until, suddenly, at high speed, hurtling up from behind me is the screeching, battered, clapped out BMW.

I glance forward to check that Edward and Mojat are safe and, to my relief, they have almost reached the embassy entrance. Edward is a man on a mission.

The screeching car takes a handbrake turn, swerving right towards me as I stand in the embassy gateway. A security guard takes a shot at them, where it went I am not sure — into oblivion. One of the slickers leans out of the car window, cigarette in mouth, pointing and firing his gun at me.

'Greasy bastards,' I shout.

My compulsive instincts take over and I position the submachine gun, adrenaline pumping through my veins. I turn myself towards them and fire a round of ammunition, aiming at the tyres and the car. I feel like a wild banshee as the sub ricochets, pulling and jolting my whole body.

The BMW screeches and screams as it swerves right off the road on to its side, crashing through a nearby shopfront. The bullets had penetrated and burst its tyres.

The US guards look shocked, and then one of them says in a strong American accent. 'Impressive lady!' I drop the machine gun at his side and enter swiftly through the gate into the security of the embassy grounds, heading for the sanctuary of the entrance doors.

In the background I can hear sirens and men shouting as, finally, the police arrive. Just before entering the building, I stand in the brightly lit porch-way and glance back to the shopfront. Several police cars have pulled up and the greasy slickers are being dragged out of their smoke-filled vehicle, steam puthering from the car bonnet.

The fat slicker, with the dog-end still in his mouth, is the first to emerge. He waves his arms towards the embassy and shouts at me in Arabic, 'Sharamutah, bitch!'

I turn around quite calmly to find Edward at my side. 'What does that mean?' I ask.

'Trust me Janey, you don't want to know!' Did you enjoy your few moments of combat?'

I give him a grin. 'I appreciated the power and the satisfaction it gave me!'

'You did well to hit the tyres and bring them down. Well done!'

Edward walks me into the embassy hallway, relieved that I am unhurt and in one piece. We then proceed to a small gathering of Americans, one being a doctor who is attending to Mojat.

I turn towards my wounded man, my love, who is now semi-conscious and in agonising pain. He has an oxygen mask over his face. I hold his hand and kiss him.

Bending over Mojat I whisper. 'I love you. Keep strong for me — please keep strong.'

His eyes acknowledge me before they roll back, showing his bloodstained whites.

The American doctor holds a syringe ready to sedate him.

CHAPTER THIRTY-FIVE

State of Emergency on High Alert

Edward is talking to a handful of US embassy officials whilst I remain alongside Mojat and the doctor. He glances over and, on seeing my visible distress, breaks off from the conversation and wanders over towards me.

'Edward, I have many questions. What happened to our backup? Where were the Beirut police and the US embassy guards? Why were there only two security guards stationed at the side gate?'

He shrugs his shoulders and pulls a bewildered face.

'That's what I am trying to find out from these men.'

Edward gazes at the four Americans who look stressed, anxious and tired from having been disturbed from their beds at this ungodly hour.

The Beirut police enter the embassy building. They confirm that the two men arrested are both well-known terrorists belonging to Hezbollah.

'What about the other one?' I ask.

I am met by surprised looks. 'What other one?'

'The one with the goatee beard? He was driving a beat-up Mercedes.'

They are obviously not aware of a third man and, following a few phone calls, a search is soon organised in the area.

It is now 4am and the doctor has sedated Mojat. He informs Edward and I that it's too dangerous to move him. The bullet is in his left shoulder area and could easily move down to his heart.

A surgeon, with nurses and equipment, is being flown in by

helicopter from a private Beirut hospital. A makeshift operating theatre will have to be organised.

All the embassy staff have now been called in as a state of emergency has been registered with all the authorities, including the British embassy. In view of the third man still on the loose there is a real possibility of a further attack. The US officials are also concerned that additional Hezbollah terrorists could enter the area in an attempt to rescue him.

Edward and I both inform and listen to the officials and police. A full statement is given. Edward looks exhausted for the first time.

I go and wash myself in the rest rooms in order to remove as much blood from my hands, arms and face as possible. My clothes are heavily stained, but right now I cannot do anything about this.

Upon my return one of the embassy housekeepers brings me a tray of tea and biscuits. My hands shake and my body shivers. Edward sits with me and pours out the tea from a large teapot for us both. I can barely hold my cup still.

'It's delayed shock Janey!'

The staff have been given instructions to use the dining room as the temporary operating theatre. We sit in silence exhausted, watching everyone rushing around on a high state of alert. The dining room doors are wide open and I can clearly see the table that's being prepared for the operation. The doctor monitors Mojat, taking his pulse and blood pressure regularly. Sheets, blankets and equipment are now being wheeled in by the security staff. I think the helicopter must be here as a nurse soon appears pushing a trolley containing a set of temporary high-powered surgery lights.

The surgeon, Mr. Martin Laval, arrives at the scene and, at his side, is a small hunched-over elderly man. They are both French Lebanese and approach us in an unassuming manor. Mr. Laval introduces himself. I say how grateful we are for his services. He then introduces the older man.

'This is my anaesthetist Dr. Bertrand Breton, who has worked with me for many years.'

We shake their hands and briefly explain to them how Mojat came to be shot and then subsequently injured his head in a fall. We then introduce them to the American doctor, who is currently monitoring Mojat on a large couch. He announces to us that the patient is only just stable. He breathes a sigh of relief and is clearly pleased to see both Mr. Laval and Dr. Breton.

The doctor and surgeon exchange a verbal diagnosis and very tentatively, with the help of the two nurses, proceed to lift Mojat on to a stretcher. This is then extended and pumped up in order to manoeuvre him on to the padded out, temporary operating table in the dining room.

Mojat lies covered with sheets and blankets to keep his body temperature balanced. It is 5:30am and the heated dining room is now sealed off. Two nurses, an anaesthetist and the surgeon begin the procedure to remove the bullet that is lodged in Mojat's shoulder.

Whilst on high alert US embassy protocol is to bring in all employees immediately, including those on current leave. Individual tasks are now being given to the various members of staff.

The main room is a hive of activity as the media and TV stations have been informed and are on the scene. The police return and another handful of government officials have materialised for a meeting, two being from the British embassy.

Edward and I watch all the goings on from our comfortable seats. There is a high sense of urgency that's being created by the high-ranking officials that have now taken charge of the situation.

We find ourselves being questioned again about what happened, where and when. Around and around we go explaining ourselves, justifying our movements and detailing who was holding which firearm at the critical times.

Following the questioning I am tired and exhausted. The housekeeper, Dorian, now shows me to a small room adjoining the dining room. She gives me two heavily checked woollen blankets and I lay down on a sofa. Edward walks in and I tell him I'm feeling cold and shaky. In fact I am shivering uncontrollably from head to toe.

'Please Edward,' I say in a weak voice. 'Will you let me know when the surgery has finished?'

'Of course I will, of course Janey. You just rest for an hour or so and try and sleep a little.'

I smile in acknowledgement at his thoughtfulness. Right now everything is a strain it seems, all too painful to bear. I am so tired and emotionally drained with worry for my love.

Edward is also covered in blood and his drawn expression looks like a man carrying too much responsibility.

'One thing Edward; the goatee slicker — have you mentioned to anyone that I shot him?'

His honest expression reassures me. 'Of course Janey, in self-defence!'

Relieved at this, I lie back down on the couch and pull the heavy blankets over and around my neck.

'Janey I need to shower. I will see you later.'

As Edward leaves the room the American doctor walks in to examine me. He can see that I've lost my entire facial colour and am shaking with the chills.

'Hmm,' he mutters. 'Delayed shock, that's what this is, delayed shock. I am not surprised after your experience of the last few hours.' Then there is silence as he sticks a glass file in my mouth. 'What you and your friends have been through is like something from an action movie.'

I am nodding as the thermometer is removed. He takes my pulse and screws his face up as he reads the see-through file. 'Can't be right!' He gives it another shake, and sticks it back in my mouth. He then takes a reading of my blood pressure, closely inspecting the dial and screws his face up yet again.

Not losing my sense of humour I say, 'Do you want to borrow my glasses?'

He frowns at me and curtly says. 'I don't need them thank you.' He relieves me from the foreign body under my tongue and looks again, this time without any facial expression. He scribbles something down on his writing pad, then opens his eyes wider and also his mouth slightly, at the same time looking down his nose and straining his eyes!

'I see.'

'What do you see Doc?'

Surprised I have questioned him, he sits next to me touching my hand with confidence. 'Like I have just said, you are suffering from shock. Your blood pressure is raised but that is understandable. So keep warm, finish your tea and try and sleep for an hour or so. I will check on you again very soon.'

He returns his medical instruments to his doctor's bag, organising them in a precise and tidy way. He looks at me again and shrugs. 'So pale so very pale. By the way, are you in pain anywhere? Headache?' he asks, almost as an afterthought.

'No, only my heart is in pain from worrying.'

He clears his throat and in a dictatorial voice announces. 'Mr. Laval is one of the top surgeons and I can personally assure you that Mr. Mojat is in excellent hands.' His smile is brief as he abruptly leaves the room.

I am still shivering and when the housekeeper returns to collect the tea tray, she offers me a hot-water bottle and more blankets. I am very grateful to her and ask, 'Where is Edward?'

'It's his turn Miss Janey. He is now being examined and checked by Dr. Sullivan in the main lounge.'

'Thank you. Dr. Sullivan, so that's his name is it? I should have asked.'

I am now fading with exhaustion, chills are running up and down my spine and I cannot get warm. In the distant background I can hear all the commotion as this state of emergency continues to be investigated. An American voice keeps repeating, 'We are now on high alert!'

I drift and fade into a semi sleep, not letting myself fully go until I know how my love is.

CHAPTER THIRTY-SIX

Between Two Worlds

US embassy, Beirut, 3 days later.
I sit at Mojat's bedside cupping his hand to my lips. I press his fingers firmly and kiss him, hoping for a reaction. I feel anxious and desperate and just want him to open his eyes. It's been three days since the bullet was located and removed from his heart region, yet still not a flicker of an eyelid. I have cried and sobbed until I am parched dry. My nerves are completely frazzled.

This man walks into my life and sweeps me off my feet — my knight in shining armour. He has shown me so much kindness and love and has showered me with beautiful presents. I've been offered a life that most women can only dream of.

I stare at him lying in between the starched white sheets looking almost corpse-like. I lean forward, kiss his cheek and begin to whisper to him. 'So much, so much my love. We have laughed and danced together and spent many hours discussing our future. The excitement we have for each other is heartfelt, especially when you make love to me. Our brief journey together has felt like days spent in heaven. Please come back to me, please. I beg you, please ...'

I gently pull back from his face, wiping the saltwater tears of love from my cheeks. I am weak, pathetic, dazed and still confused as to how all this has really happened.

As I sit looking down at his face, I find myself willing him to live. It's as though I can hear his voice inside my head. I imagine him awake again and giving me that look. The type of look a man will give you when he's truly in love and besotted.

You read about it in psychology magazines, when you

experience similar thoughts at the same time. There is a telepathic communication as you work in harmony together. It's synchronicity on a cellular level and that's when you really know that you're in tune with each other. Your thoughts are his thoughts … God that's spooky!

Life can be crazy and scary. One minute all is well and you're happy, the next you're being chased down a mountain by some bastard gun-slinging terrorists, only inches away from teetering over the edge. What was that all about? Yeah, what the fuck was that all about? I want some answers — some straight fucking answers, especially if my man dies!

I am angry as I relive the whole bloody scenario again, especially the moment my love was shot and I witnessed his blood puthering and spewing out all over. At the time he was knocked to the ground, of course, I just had to deal with it. I was controlled and coped with the situation like the caring woman I am. I simply had to keep it all together, it was survival time and we were on the edge. The adrenaline pumping through my body kept me strong. I can barely believe that that was me only three days ago.

Back on those grimy backstreets in downtown Beirut I was encapsulated in flight or fight mode, thinking only of our survival and protecting my man who was lying helpless on the ground. I look at him now, reclined in this stark white room and fighting for his life.

My brain is like cotton wool since it all happened, woolly and fuzzy. I take a few deep breaths, in through my nose and holding for six-seconds before very slowly breathing out through my mouth. I repeat this several times, trying to bring myself back to a calmer place.

The embassy doctors and nurses are doing their level best. There is a constant stream of highly qualified consultants in and out of his room. I say highly qualified, as two arrived today who were professors, a man and woman from the Department of Neurology at Beirut Hospital.

I look again at Mojat's grey wax sunken face. The furrowed lines across his brow seem more prominent and his expression looks strained.

'Come my love, come back to me.'

I sense he is probably between two worlds right now making a decision. Shall I stay with Janey, or head off to question God? Did I get my life right this time, or should I return and finish off things not yet completed? Mojat is not religious at all so he would laugh at my erratic thoughts right now.

Two of the terrorists are safely behind bars but one, the man with piercing evil eyes, is still out there on the loose. This is a little worrying for me as I am the one who shot him! He is bound to want to come after me.

There is a light knock at the door. Samira enters the room and her presence immediately removes my dark and angry thoughts. She looks at me, walks over and puts her arms around my shoulders. I burst into tears and speak in a low voice. 'I know Samira, I have panda eyes and I look like s ...' I was going to swear, but thought better of it.

I go and kiss Mojat's forehead and whisper in his ear. 'I am waiting, please my love, come back.'

'I think you should return to your suite ma'am and take a bath and sleep. You look exhausted.'

'I *am* exhausted Samira.'

CHAPTER THIRTY-SEVEN

Wild Horses

I lay in a deep bath telling Samira the whole story of what seems, at the present time, to have been a surreal experience. I recount the entire car chase and how we finished up in the backstreets of Beirut. I let it all out from beginning to end. She tops up my bath with hot water as she listens and sponges my back. I need to free myself of the hysteria and the deluge of blood pumping images that remain hauntingly in my mind, especially of Mojat suffering at the hands of those evil men.

She massages my scalp for a few minutes. 'Don't worry ma'am, Mr. Mojat is strong.'

'Is he?' I ask. 'Is he really Samira?' Tears run down my cheeks into the bathwater.

'I believe he is ma'am. I'm sure in his job he has had scraps before, but perhaps he has never told you?'

'Maybe Samira, but if he dies I don't know what I will do.' More tears roll down my cheekbones.

'Ma'am he is not going to die, you must be positive.'

'You are right, I must be stronger.'

I stand up and she wraps warm towels around my body and I dry myself off. Then I slip on the newly laundered dress that she has laid out on the bed for me. Samira's olive petite face is full of compassion and I'm so pleased that she's staying in the next room to mine at the embassy.

'Ma'am can I get you something to eat?'

I sigh. 'Just soup and a little bread please, then I feel I must get back to Mojat.'

She looks over to me and nods her head, as if to say she would do the same. Samira understands me.

It is now 9pm and the embassy is relatively quiet. The political workstation here is to the far left of the building, whilst Mojat's temporary hospital room is on the quieter side facing the gardens. When I am not with Mojat, two nurses stay with him, alternating on two-hour shifts.

Security is extremely high around the grounds. As I stare out of the window I can see guards placed everywhere. This makes me think that the situation is more dangerous than I originally thought.

I turn to my love and watch the nurse change his drip. She also straightens the pristine cotton sheets. Edward enters the room for a short while, during which time we have a brief conversation about the lack of progress Mojat is making. Edward visits every few hours.

I pick up Mojat's clip chart from the bottom of his bed. All blood tests are negative, which is good. However all his blood pressure and pulse readings seem low.

Dr. Samir enters.

'What can I do doc?' I ask, looking anxious.

'Just talk to him as if he's sitting next to you, maybe something that is personal to you both — a special time. Keep talking as he needs to hear your strong voice.'

Before departing, Dr. Samir tests Mojat's reflexes and lifts his eyelids to shine a light at his pupils.

I dim the lights in the room, draw my chair up to his side and bend over to pick up his hand, firmly gripping it. I squeeze his fingertips and sigh, as my heart lies heavy. I know with each day that passes he is increasingly less likely to wake up. Do I resign myself to this — his death?

I clear my throat as it's dry, pour some water from the jug at his bedside and take a few gulps. 'Please God — don't let him die. Our life together has just begun.' I raise my voice a little, still clutching his hand. 'Mojat, remember when you proposed to me how giddy and deliriously happy you felt? Remember that moment?'

I begin to sing. The words flow naturally and the strength in my voice returns. I sing my heart out as though his life depends upon it.

Carefree living is easy to do
The things you desired I gave them to you
Graceless lady you know who I am
You know I can't let you just fade from my arms

I watch you suffer distress and pain
Now you decided to show me the same
I have my freedom but we have little time
For me to show you how I can shine

I shed tears in my hour of need
I want us to do some living before we die
Angelic angels couldn't drag me away
Angelic angels will take us both one day

I finish the song and look down at his face. He is smiling at me.

'My dear, you sing like a nightingale … you never told me you could sing? You have such a beautiful voice!'

His ebony eyes are open and the deep furrows on his brow have disappeared.

Happiness and elation light up my heart. We kiss and hold one another and the twinkle is back in his bewitching ebony eyes.

The next hour passes very quickly. To the relief of everyone he is talking, smiling and laughing again.

Dr. Samir breaks the news to Mojat that he's just emerged from a three-day coma. He also informs him of the successful operation.

Edward enters the room and joy is restored to us all.

*To follow — the sequel to Singing in Silence is coming ...
An explosion of incredible encounters and
experiences with Janey Green.
The answers to the shoot out?
The goatee slicker. Still on the loose!
Mojat's brother, Omani. A nasty piece of shit!
Freda brings a new energy.
The political tip of the iceberg.*